"On the left!" Jonarel called out.

As Aurora registered the command and responded by activating her energy shield, a low wail filled the air like the beginnings of a siren, followed by the patter of falling water as an enormous triangle-shaped head rose into view.

The greewtaith's skin was grayish-blue, but the spines on three sides of its body that were latched onto the bark of the nearby trees were dark brown and hooked like cactus thorns. The creature's forehead had a crest that flared upward as it opened its jaws, revealing thousands of jagged teeth.

However, it clearly wasn't going after them. They were at least thirty meters away from the aquatic nightmare and viewing it in profile. A flash of bright red and iridescence appeared just before the greewtaith's mouth snapped shut on its victim. The creature shrieked in pain, its head sticking out from the row of teeth.

"A relquir." The air punched in and out of Aurora's lungs. "It just caught a relquir."

The greewtaith's torso plummeted, the struggling relquir clasped firmly in its jaws. When it hit the water, the resulting splash sounded like cannon fire. The rest of the creature's long body followed as the barbs disengaged from the tree trunk and the greewtaith slid below the surface of the water.

THE CHAINS OF FREEDOM

Starhawke Rising Book Two

Audrey Sharpe

Ocean Dance Press

THE CHAINS OF FREEDOM
© 2017 Audrey Sharpe

ISBN: 978-1-946759-03-0

Ocean Dance Press, LLC
PO Box 69901
Oro Valley AZ 85737

Cover art by B&J

Visit the author's website at:
AudreySharpe.com

To D.C, P.H. and E.K.,
who taught me the meaning of friendship.
The Starhawke never would have flown without you.

One

"Kire, run!"

Captain Aurora Hawke grabbed Kire Emoto's upper arm and yanked him forward as her boots dug into the loose sand of the wide beach.

The thunder of a lake's worth of water hitting the ground fifty meters behind them kept her first officer from offering any resistance. Together, they sprinted toward the grove of trees that swayed gently in the balmy tropical breeze.

Aurora smacked her comband, praying her navigator hadn't taken the rest of the team too far into the island's interior. "Kelly, get back here. Now!"

"On our way." Bronwyn Kelly's complete lack of emotional inflection didn't indicate a sense of urgency, but Aurora had no doubt she'd have the shuttle at their location in record time.

Aurora snuck a quick glance over her shoulder as the sand trembled beneath her feet. What she and everyone else onboard the *Starhawke* had mistaken for giant lava rocks at the edge of the coast had just been revealed as something altogether different. The creature that was making its way up the beach with enormous strides resembled a moving rock formation, but with limbs the width of redwoods and a hinged mouth rimmed with saw blades.

She grabbed her pistol from her utility belt and whirled around, striking the creature's leg with a sizzling pop. It was like hitting the broad side of a barn. As a deterrent, however, the blow failed completely. The monster charged toward her with a roar of rage.

The beast's bellow and the fishy stench that came with it triggered her gag reflex and she stumbled backward.

Several answering roars reverberated through the air as more of the creatures lifted out of the ocean and turned in her direction. Great. The lava rock had friends.

She took off after Kire as the creature's shadow chased them across the sand. And to think only a few minutes ago she'd been walking along the shore enjoying a moment of peaceful tranquility.

Until she'd realized she was being watched.

"Any great ideas?" Kire yelled as she drew even with him.

"I'm open to suggestions." They were getting closer to the trees, although the fragile trunks wouldn't slow down the rampaging behemoth intent on making the visiting Earthlings a mid-morning snack. But they might provide some cover until the shuttle arrived.

She spotted movement to her right a split-second before a pinkish-green tongue whipped around them like a lasso, yanking their bodies together and halting their forward momentum. The noose tightened, dragging them backward toward the creature's gaping maw.

Enough of this! Being assaulted by an oversized boulder was not how she'd planned to spend her morning. Time to let this walking nightmare know it had chosen its victims poorly.

Pressing her left hand against Kire's back, Aurora shifted her focus inward, summoning her energy field. Its pearlescent glow coalesced around her and pushed outward, counteracting the pressure on her torso that was making breathing a real challenge. She spread the shield to include

Kire, then channeled an electrical charge into the soft, wet flesh that encircled them.

The acrid smell of charred tissue filled the air. The beast made a horrible mewling sound and released them instantly, its tongue flopping around like a dying fish in the sand.

Aurora hated inflicting pain, but then again, the creature *was* trying to eat them.

Flashes lit up the sky overhead as the *Starhawke*'s shuttle swooped into view. A volley of blasts streaked in the direction of the rock monster's companions, who resembled a mobile mountain range trudging up the beach. The shots found their marks in rapid succession and generated more ground-shaking roars of anger.

The beast in front of Aurora snarled at the new threat. Its scorched tongue slid rapidly back into its mouth as it swung one of its tree trunk legs in a slow arc. But it never came close to touching the agile craft.

The shuttle's weapons fired, successfully striking the tender underbelly the creature had revealed. The monster screeched, stumbling as it lost its balance and crashed to the sand. The resulting impact tremor knocked Aurora and Kire to their knees.

The shuttle dove toward them, leveling out a few meters from where they crouched. The hatchway slid open and they leapt inside in a tumble of arms and legs.

As the shuttle shot forward, Aurora snagged the collar of Kire's tunic and engaged her shield to protect him as their bodies smacked into the row of seats behind them. She felt a gentle but firm hand on her arm and looked up into the warm brown eyes of Dr. Mya Forrest.

"Welcome aboard." Mya's gaze swept over them, checking for signs of injury that her Lumian heritage enabled her to see without the aid of a medical scanner.

Aurora didn't feel worse for wear, but she wasn't sure about Kire. He gave her a nod of reassurance that he was in one piece, and she released the energy shield as they both pushed to their feet

"You two okay?" Celia Cardiff, the *Starhawke's* security officer, glanced back from the co-pilot's chair.

Aurora's legs wobbled from the after effects of the adrenaline rush. "We're fine." She dropped into the nearest seat and fastened her safety harness. "Nice shooting."

A frown marred Celia's smooth complexion. "I hate bullies."

"I second that." Aurora tilted her head toward the window and gazed at the coastline in the distance. She could still make out the shapes of the lava rock creatures as they trudged back to the water. She shook her head. At this height, they really did look just like...well...rocks.

"Destination, Captain?" Kelly asked.

"To the *Starhawke*." Tapping her comband, she opened a channel to Jonarel Clarek, her chief engineer. "Hawke to Clarek."

Jonarel's deep baritone boomed out. "Yes, Captain?"

"We're on our way back." Several hours early, which explained his next question, and the tone of concern that went with it.

"What happened?"

She glanced at her filthy tunic. She'd save the full explanation until they were safely onboard. For now, the less Jonarel knew the better. No reason to trigger his Kraed overprotective streak any sooner than necessary. "We encountered a native lifeform that wasn't very happy to see us."

His low growl indicated he wasn't fooled. "Are you

okay?"

She sighed. He wasn't asking about the team. He meant her, specifically. They'd been through some challenging moments recently during their mission to Earth's sister planet, Gaia, culminating in their current assignment. But she wished he'd stop worrying about her safety. "We're fine. I'll give you the full details when we arrive. Hawke out."

She closed the connection before he could reply and settled into her seat. Kire sat next to her, his straight brown hair sticking up in a couple places where the creature's tongue had slimed him, and his leggings and boots coated in grit. He resembled a child's discarded sandbox toy. She probably looked much the same.

But a sparkle of mischief lit his eyes. "So, not a good choice for the new Lumian homeworld?"

Aurora snorted at the gross understatement. As the absurdity of their encounter sank in, her chuckle rapidly escalated into a full body experience. Her meltdown triggering his, and they both doubled over in hysterics while Mya watched them with amusement.

Kelly and Celia glanced back from the cockpit, apparently uncertain why she and Kire found the situation so hilarious.

Aurora wiped the tears from her eyes as she grinned at Kire. "No." She shook her head. "I would say this is definitely *not* a good choice for the new Lumian homeworld."

Two

In the vast sea of space beyond the outer edge of the Gaian system, a lone transport ship chugged across the velvet black, its running lights flashing in the darkness.

The craft wasn't much to look at. In fact, the most remarkable thing about it was its complete lack of distinction. The dull expanse of grey that comprised its hull was devoid of emblems or designations that would signify where it came from or what purpose it served. Even the muted glow that fought to escape through the small portals at the bow and stern failed to add any definition to the shapeless hulk.

Inside, deep shadows ruled, creating lurking monsters around every corner. The air was sharp and cold, like an arctic tundra. The only sign of life was the steady hum of the engine as it propelled the ship to nowhere in particular.

And on the bridge, the captain's chair sat empty. Three long days had passed since anyone had occupied that chair.

The communication console pinged as it transmitted an automated message to an unknown recipient. A moment later a proximity alarm blared to life, the shrill sound cutting through the silence like a knife. The lights on the bridge shifted to a red glow of warning as the ship's automated systems altered the vessel's course to avoid a collision. A second alarm went off a few seconds later, indicating a new threat, and the system adjusted course again in an attempt to find a clear path.

Something connected with the hull and the ship shuddered like it had been snatched into the cupped hands of a giant toddler. The engines whined in protest as they fought to push through the unexpected resistance.

But it was a losing battle. The floor vibrated from the effort, alerts flashing on every console as the engines labored and finally overloaded, threatening to rip the ship apart. The internal system followed the only protocol available to preserve the ship's structural integrity. It shut down the engines.

The alarms cut off in mid-screech and silence dropped like a blanket, broken only by the groans of the hull. The communication console lit up briefly as the automated controls attempted to send a message, but this time the soft ping was replaced by the hiss of static.

The ship jerked to a halt. Loud clanging echoed through the corridors, followed by the scrape of metal on metal and a muffled bang. Heavy footsteps tromped along the passageways, growing louder as they approached the bridge. When they reached the entrance, the doors blew apart in a shower of metal and wiring that rained down on the instrument panels and empty chairs.

Muscled figures flowed onto the bridge, weapons at the ready. But the ship offered no resistance to the invaders. It sat quietly, accepting its fate.

Snarls of anger and frustration reverberated in the room. Several of the figures lifted their weapons, blasting the consoles into oblivion. The communication console exploded in a rainbow of sparks, forced to give up its quest to send the final message through the wall of static.

Smoke filled the air, creating a dense cloud that drove the invaders back through the doorway, their footsteps fading in the distance. A boom sounded from the depths of the engine room and the bridge fell into darkness.

Overhead, a lone emergency light glowed, fighting for life as the ship bled out. It pulsed...flickered...and died.

Three

Cade Ellis gazed at the display on the *Nightingale*'s navigation console. Another hour until they'd reach their destination.

He'd been in a lot of strange situations during his ten years with Admiral Schreiber's Elite Unit, but he'd never envisioned becoming the caretaker for three hundred displaced humanoids rescued from a life of imprisonment and coercion. And yet, here he was, piloting a borrowed medical freighter and heading for a remote planet where he planned to hide the three hundred Lumians while Aurora Hawke and her crew located a suitable homeworld.

Officially, the Lumians had been placed on a personnel ship, which had set off from Gaia shortly after the *Starhawke* left orbit. But the ship was a decoy. The Lumians had remained on a remote island on Gaia with Cade's team. The Admiral had monitored the decoy's progress to see if it attracted any attention. Apparently it had. Five days ago, the ship had disappeared without a trace. Cade had taken that as his cue to get the hell out of Dodge.

It was unlikely anyone on Gaia had noted the *Nightingale*'s departure. He'd planned their flight path using the planet as a visual shield, keeping the Rescue Corps Headquarters and the orbiting Fleet starship *Argo* on the opposite side. Gaia didn't have the elaborate satellite systems that surrounded Earth, which made it easier to slip away unnoticed.

Besides, the Admiral was keeping everyone on the *Argo* and at the RC busy with the continuing investigation into the attack by the Etah Setarips, the alien race responsible for bringing the Lumians into Cade's life.

The Admiral had been crystal clear that Cade needed to keep the Lumians away from any location where word could get back to the Galactic Council. Unfortunately, that left him with limited options. He'd suggested taking the Lumians to Drakar, the Kraed homeworld, since Siginal Clarek, the leader of the Clarek clan and father of Jonarel Clarek, had agreed to help build the Lumian settlement when a suitable planet was found. Hiding the Lumians on Drakar seemed logical. No one visited Kraed space without an invitation.

The Admiral's pained expression had spoken volumes. "Don't take the Lumians to Drakar, Cade. That's the first place I'd look. And I *cannot* know where they are."

He hadn't elaborated, but his comment had left a nagging sense of unease in Cade's stomach.

Despite the dire warnings, the journey from Gaia had been blissfully uneventful. Burrow, the planet he'd finally selected as their hiding place, wasn't ideal by any stretch, but it was the best he could do under the circumstances. He didn't know which direction Aurora had gone in her search for a homeworld, but since the Kraed were going to be part of the solution, it seemed logical she'd start her search in the quadrants near Drakar.

The smart move was to follow. Even if he guessed wrong, bringing the Lumians closer to the Kraed seemed like the best plan, as long as he didn't ignore the Admiral's warning.

That had left him with the question of where to land. Docking at one of the independent outposts wasn't an option because the *Nightingale* didn't have any valid credentials. While the dedication plaque was still affixed to the wall of the bridge, the ship's exterior Fleet designations had been scrubbed clean. From a distance, the freighter could be mistaken for a privately owned vessel. Maybe. But the subterfuge wouldn't hold up under scrutiny. Even if it could, requesting provisions for three hundred visitors, a third of which were children, was guaranteed to draw attention. It would be like holding up a neon sign that said *Lumians here*.

But even more critical was the issue of time.

The *Nightingale* had been designed for a standard crew of five and a maximum of twenty-five short-term passengers. Primarily, it was a cargo ship, hauling medical supplies and personnel to locations that had suffered an epidemic or natural disaster. It could also serve as a mobile medical unit.

It had never been intended to house three hundred individuals during a prolonged interstellar flight. Since leaving Gaia, the situation had deteriorated rapidly. They had plenty of food provisions, but their water and air supplies were reaching critical levels.

That's why he'd finally settled on Burrow, a habitable planet orbiting a yellow-white dwarf star. Until four years ago, the system had been the site of an ambitious biological research project that focused on the planet's dominant species, the Meer. While the race bore a remarkable resemblance in body shape and coloring to their namesake, the meerkat, they stood at shoulder height to an average human and had developed a mostly upright posture and opposable thumbs. They lived in tribal groups, moving among several semi-permanent underground locations as they followed the herds of cow-like animals that provided them with much of what they needed to survive.

The scientists had hoped to gain insight into how the Meer's development paralleled human evolution, and the reports for the first few years had been promising. But all that ended the day one of the Setarip factions had decided to raid the research station.

No one in the Council had ever considered the research facility as a possible target for Setarips because it didn't house the militaristic hardware and weapons that the Setarips needed for their civil war. It was also located near the Kraed border, which should have made it untouchable. The Setarip factions rarely ventured through any of the systems that bordered Kraed space. Not since they'd learned how deadly the race could be when angered.

Unfortunately, the misconception that Burrow was safe from Setarips had cost many lives. The orbiting space station had been hit first. Several members of the team had escaped to the planet's surface in a shuttle while the Setarips had slaughtered the rest. After the Setarips had stripped the station clean, they'd headed for the planet's surface. They'd captured the escaped shuttle and dispatching the crews of two of the three mobile research pods before the Fleet ship *Armstrong* had arrived on the scene in response to the distress call.

The Setarips had beaten a hasty retreat, leaving behind the bodies of sixty-three researchers and an unknown number of Meer who had been caught in the crossfire. The Meer had made a valiant stand against the monsters from the sky, but the Setarips hadn't hesitated to destroy the entire settlement and every Meer they'd encountered.

It was a dark chapter in the Council's recent history, one they'd vowed never to repeat. The *Armstrong's* crew had been put in charge of dismantling the space station while Cade's team had been sent in to clean up the mess on the planet's surface. They'd had strict orders to avoid all contact with the Meer, which had been easy considering the devastation to the local tribe. But the scene had hit Cade hard. Not being able to offer the Meer any assistance had been even harder.

By Council orders, Burrow had been placed in a rare category of one—a planet in Fleet territory that was strictly off limits. Cade was breaking at least a dozen Galactic laws by going there, but he didn't see any other options. The Lumians needed a temporary hiding place, and Burrow was his best bet. He'd just have to make sure their presence went unnoticed.

And then there was the other complication in his current situation—Aurora Hawke. He'd only heard from her once since the *Starhawke* had left Gaia the previous week. They'd each sent a message to test their relay system, which routed everything through Drakar to insure the messages couldn't be traced to the location of either ship. Admiral Schreiber had placed his faith in the Clarek clan, so Cade had as well, even though he had personal reasons for disliking Jonarel Clarek, Aurora's chief engineer.

"We must be getting close." Justin Byrnes, his first officer, stepped onto the bridge.

Cade glanced at the chronometer on the console. "About fifteen minutes until we reach the system."

Justin settled into the chair to his right. "Good." He stifled a yawn with his hand. His curly blond hair was flattened on the left side of his head and his clothes were rumpled, indicating he'd just woken up.

Cade grinned. "Looks like you've been hanging out with the Sandman."

Justin nodded. "Those bunks aren't half bad. I passed Williams on the way up here. He was heading down to the med bay to check on the Lumians."

Tam Williams, the team's medic, had spent most of

the trip to Burrow in the large med bay, which doubled as a cargo hold. Currently, that cargo consisted of the three hundred refugees. Like the rest of the team, Williams found the Lumians fascinating.

Justin ran his fingers through his hair, restoring a modicum of order to the tousled locks. "The Lumians are still sleeping on the floor."

"I know." The last time he'd checked on them, they'd been curled up together like kittens on top of a mountain of blankets at the center of the room, rather than sleeping on the convertible med platforms his team had set up. "After all the time they spent in their cells, it's what they're used to." Even med blankets would feel like a cloud compared to the atrocious conditions the Lumians had endured in their rows of tiny cages on the Setarip ship. "Besides, I think they need the feeling of connection right now."

"Yeah. That makes sense. Reynolds is down in the bay, too. She plans to stay with them until we land."

"Good. That should help." Tracy Reynolds, his security specialist, had been responsible for getting the Lumian children safely off the Setarip ship. She and Justin had taken care of the kids until the rest of the team had defeated the Setarips and rescued the children's parents. Most of the kids looked at Justin and Reynolds with hero worship. "They really respond to her. And to you, too. You're good with them."

Justin shrugged off the compliment. "They're easy to like. I've never seen a group that's so well behaved. And they've been doing a great job teaching me their language." As a communications specialist, Justin had been eager to bridge the language barrier. "I've been inputting the data into the translator, and I think with another week or so of fine tuning, I'll have it up and running to the point that we'll be able to have real conversations. That will help."

"Definitely." Communicating with the Lumians had been a challenge. His few interactions had involved a lot of nodding and gestures, which was frustrating. He wanted to know more about them, in particular how they'd ended up as prisoners of the Setarips.

They shouldn't have existed at all. According to what Aurora had told him when they were at the Academy together, the Lumian race had been exterminated during an alien invasion of their homeworld more than forty years ago. Aurora's mother had been part of a small contingent that had escaped and sought refuge on Earth. They'd successfully passed themselves off as humans since biologically, the two races were virtually indistinguishable.

However, the Lumians had an ability that humans did not—they could generate energy fields that affected the cellular structures of living things. They'd developed the skill in order to grow food and to promote healing and protection for each other. Unfortunately, at some point the Setarips had figured out they could weaponize the ability by reversing the process, leading to destruction and death rather than growth and life. For a while, they'd turned the Lumians into killing Necri slaves.

That was why Cade needed to keep the Lumians hidden. Recent events, including the disappearance of the decoy ship, indicated that whoever had imprisoned them was still on the hunt, intent on reclaiming their prize.

"We should be entering the system in a few minutes," Cade said. "Why don't you join Reynolds and Williams for the trip down, and send Drew and Gonzo to the bridge."

"You've got it." Justin headed for the doorway.

Bella Drew and Christoph Gonzalez appeared a few moments later. Cade relinquished the navigation console to

Drew, who slid onto the seat and tucked her short dark hair behind her ears.

"Any issues?" she asked.

Cade settled into the captain's chair. "Nothing so far, but we need to keep our eyes open when we enter the system."

Gonzo brought up the tactical display as Drew took them out of their interstellar jump.

The bridgescreen filled with the image of the large debris field that formed a near-perfect disk encircling the interior planets of the system. The mystery of the disk had been another selling point for constructing the Burrow research station. The total mass of the debris in the disk equaled twice that of Earth, as if two planets had been broken apart and the remnants sprinkled to create the disk. By comparison, the total mass of the asteroid belt in Sol's system was only one one-thousandth the mass of Earth.

The scientists had hoped to figure out how or why the disk existed, especially since Burrow didn't appear to be negatively affected. The presence of the disk, however, acted as a barrier for interstellar jumps. Any ship that approached Burrow had to arrive and depart through the debris to access a jump window.

"Anything on scanners?" Cade leaned forward, his body poised for action. After so many surprises on Gaia, he couldn't help feeling cautious.

Gonzo's fingers moved over the console. "Scanners are clear. No indication of ships in the outer regions of the system. We'll need to get to the other side of the disk to check the interior." He gave Cade an encouraging nod. "But it looks good so far."

Cade's shoulders relaxed. At least it was a start. "Then let's head into the disk. Take it slow. Shields at maximum."

Avoiding the large objects wasn't difficult. They floated along like boulders tossed by a giant. But the smaller pieces filled the gaps like a thin mesh screen. The shields flared as they made contact, creating a light show as the ship made its way to the other side.

The frequency of the flashes decreased as they reached the interior edge of the disk. Burrow appeared in the distance, the light from the star bathing one side in its glow, revealing shades of blue, brown, and subtle green.

Water covered less than fifty percent of Burrow's surface, compared to seventy-one percent on Earth, giving it a distinctly arid visage from space. However, vast channels of water flowed beneath the soil and rock, far more than expected. Despite appearances, water on Burrow was plentiful. You just had to scratch the surface to find it.

Drew guided the ship into their approach, the planet steadily filling the bridgescreen.

"Take us to the northwest region," Cade said. "Head for the canyon we used last time. But go easy. We don't want to wake up the locals."

Drew made the adjustment to their course. "We can stay on the night side. If any of the Meer are still in the area, they shouldn't see us. I've switched over to near-infrared illumination."

"Noise reduction settings are on full," Gonzo said. "That'll cut down the engine noise as much as possible."

The ship dropped through the planet's upper atmosphere before leveling off when they reached the cloud layer.

Cade gazed at the bridgescreen as the darkness outside wrapped the ship in its embrace.

"We're in range of the canyon," Gonzo said.

"Scanning for habitation."

Cade gave him a few seconds to check the results. "Any sign of the Meer near our landing site?"

Gonzo shook his head. "No. Not surprising, considering the destruction the Setarips caused." He held Cade's gaze, his expression uncharacteristically somber. "It looks like they've abandoned the area."

Cade nodded. It made sense. Why would they stay in a place where their tribe had nearly been wiped out?

Drew guided the *Nightingale* toward the canyon, skimming the tops of the rugged trees that grew in the crags and crevices of the rocks. The roar of the engines cranked up as she brought the ship into a hover over the southwest end of the box canyon and extended the landing gear. The ship touched down on the rocky surface with a small bounce as the supports took the ship's full weight, then settled down with the mechanical equivalent of a sigh.

"Well done." Cade left his chair to join Drew as she powered down the ship's flight systems.

He was the most experienced pilot onboard, but his unit had learned long ago that smart strategy required having more than one person who could perform each of the team's essential tasks. As an engineer, Drew had a natural interest in all things mechanical, so she'd been a logical choice to train as a back-up navigator. Gonzo wasn't half bad in the pilot's chair, either.

"Thanks." Drew gave the console an affectionate pat. "She's a good ship. Very responsive."

He agreed, although nothing would ever compare to flying the *Starhawke*. Talk about responsive. It was like the ship could read his mind.

"Anything we should know before we venture outside?" he asked Gonzo.

Gonzo shook his head. "I've set the ship's perimeter alarms and calibrated them to recognize the Lumians and our team. If anything larger than a rabbit approaches the canyon, we'll know in plenty of time to make a move."

Cade slapped his hand on Gonzo's shoulder. "Then let's get some fresh air."

They walked single file down the short set of stairs to the crew deck and continued to the spiral stairway that led to the lower deck.

Justin was waiting for them next to the main hatch, but the wide doors to the med bay were closed.

"We'll take a look around," Cade said. "After I give the all clear, you can see if any of the Lumians want to join us."

Drew touched the panel to the right of the hatch and the two sections opened along the midline, creating an overhang above and a ramp below that settled onto the ground with a soft thump. Outside, the hush of night lay like a sheet over the scattered trees and massive boulders that surrounded them. Light from the crescent moon near the horizon combined with the halo effect of the disk in the distance to provide soft illumination to the scene.

"Hasn't changed much since last time we were here." Gonzo gazed at the readings on his comband. The glow from the device cast his angular features and goatee in sharp relief. "The underground river is still accessible from the side canyon. We'll have plenty of fresh water." He glanced at Cade. "Since we're going to be here a while, we should consider building a well."

"Good idea." Their water needs would be substantial. At least they'd have plenty of hands to help with the work. The Lumians weren't shy about pitching in.

He nodded at Drew and Gonzo. "Let's get started."

Four

The soft fronds of low-lying ferns brushed against Aurora's boots as she pushed toward the distant sound of rushing water. Behind her, the heavier footfalls of her companion kept in perfect sync. After the incident with the rock monsters, Jonarel had insisted on partnering with her for all planetary visits.

If anyone else had acted that way, Aurora would have objected, but Jonarel's overprotectiveness was part of his Kraed DNA, and his special bond with her intensified that instinct. Resisting would have just gotten in the way of the job they had to do.

She didn't need that, or any other new challenges. This was the fourth planet they'd visited since encountering the rock creatures two weeks ago, and her hopes were fading with each one they crossed off the list.

The first planet hadn't made it past the orbital survey. It had suffered a recent meteor strike that had filled the atmosphere with a thick ash cloud, dropping the surface temperature into arctic ranges and killing off most of the flora and fauna.

The second had seemed promising until it revealed its predilection for sudden violent electrical storms. She could channel electrical energy, but she'd had zero interest in testing whether her energy shield could deflect lightning. The barrage had rocked the planet's surface for half a day without a break while she, Jonarel and Mya had taken refuge in a nearby cave until they could safely return to the ship.

The third planet had been nixed because it sat a

little too close to its parent star. Jonarel hadn't seemed to notice, but the glare and the sweltering heat had taken a toll on the rest of the crew during the few hours they'd spent exploring potential sites.

Which brought them to their current location. The tropical island in the mid-latitudes looked promising, but Aurora was keeping a tight rein on her emotional investment. Too many things could go wrong. But the list of potential planets was dwindling. If they didn't find something soon, they might have to seriously reconsider the possibility of co-existence with the rock monsters.

Mya had helped Aurora select this particular island from the loose grouping that pushed up through the azure water and stretched beyond the horizon. At the moment, Mya and Celia were exploring the landscape to the north. They'd acted like a couple of kids at Christmas as they'd set off to begin testing the local flora for safety and food viability. Hopefully the lush vegetation would prove to be edible as well as beautiful.

Kelly had remained with the shuttle at the landing site, and Kire was in command of the *Starhawke*, conducting planetary climate and environmental studies with the help of Star, the ship's Nirunoc. She was the *Star* part of the *Starhawke*, a sentient non-biological intelligence who inhabited the ship and managed its functions.

Like Jonarel, she was from Drakar. Her race had been created by the Kraed long ago, in much the same way that humans had created AI, but without the negative consequences. While the AI beings from Earth had eventually chosen to abandon their human creators and form a new society in a distant system, the Nirunoc lived in harmony with the Kraed, managing the functions of their advanced technology and living as equal members of the clan to which they were born. The Nirunocs were a carefully guarded secret in the Kraed culture, one the Kraed had chosen not to share with the human race. To her knowledge, Aurora and her crew were the only ones who knew of their existence.

As Aurora continued walking through the dense foliage, the roar and burble of falling water grew louder. She ducked under an overhanging branch and navigated through a small maze of waist-high boulders before finally reaching the river's edge. Sunlight glinted off the clear water, the deep browns and purples of the surrounding rocks providing the perfect balance to the lush greenery.

Jonarel stopped beside her, his tall form casting her in shadow. The light filtering through the trees made his deep green skin and mahogany hair glow. His coloring was so different from her blond hair and pale skin. Moments like this emphasized their contrasts. He blended with their surroundings in a way she couldn't.

He'd grown up in the tropical forests of Drakar, an area famous for its warmth and humidity. The rich coloring of his skin and the tendrils of brown that meandered across it fit in perfectly with the foliage, as did the thick hair that flowed down to his shoulders in shades ranging from dark chocolate to caramel, adding to his natural camouflage. Only his golden eyes gave him away, revealing the sharp intelligence within the breathtaking exterior.

Aurora unhooked the bio-scanner from her utility belt and panned it across the surface of the water, checking for signs of life. The device registered various aquatic creatures, but nothing larger than her hand. Definitely no rock monsters. She glanced at Jonarel. "See anything?"

Drakar teemed with life, some of it of a very large and predatory nature. While Jonarel's race had learned long ago how to thrive in their environment, they still maintained their survival instincts and had an uncanny knack for sensing danger. Their keen eyesight and hearing didn't hurt, either. If he'd been with her on the beach two weeks ago instead of Kire, she probably wouldn't have taken more than a couple steps onto the sand before he would have hauled her off the ground and rushed them back to the shuttle. Hence his presence with her today.

He met her gaze. "No."

She smiled. "All righty then." Pulling a small vial from her belt, she approached the water and crouched on one of the damp boulders. Lowering her hand, she allowed the liquid to run into the glass tube, caressing her fingers in the process. She was a water addict, and the tactile pleasure of the coolness gliding over her skin made her whole body tingle.

Lifting the full tube, she slid it into a compartment on her scanner and waited a few moments while it analyzed the results. "Wow. No bacteria or contaminants of any kind. I wonder if this is what water used to be like on Earth. You could drink this stuff straight from the river." She returned the scanner to her belt and stood. "Star said this was one of three water sources within walking distance?"

Jonarel nodded. "There's a large waterfall to the northeast that feeds a river about a kilometer away, as well as a small spring located about the same distance to the south."

So fresh, clean water would not be a problem. That was a major plus. She glanced at the sky, where pale grey and white clouds were thinking about having a meeting of the minds sometime soon. Judging by the surrounding greenery, it was a daily event. "Let's scope out possible building locations."

She led the way through the overgrowth, climbing

uphill as the sounds of the river faded into the background. The terrain was fairly easy to traverse thanks to patches of rock and sand that created natural pathways.

When the ground began to level off, she paused and did a slow three-hundred-and-sixty-degree survey of the surrounding topography. This section was elevated from the rivers that ran on either side, and the incline continued to the west, rising to the peak that housed the dormant volcano that had created the large island. Visible through breaks in the foliage, the coastline stretched like a tan ribbon along the ocean's edge five kilometers to the south.

It was...perfect. She couldn't imagine a more ideal setting. Unfortunately, she also didn't want to get her hopes up. This was their first day, so there was still plenty of time for the planet to show its ugly side.

Jonarel ran his hand along the trunk of one of the trees, then gripped it and gave it a good shake. The tree's branches swayed, creating a subtle whooshing sound. "This would make good structural material." He glanced at her. "What type of design did you have in mind for the buildings?"

The question caught her off guard and she stumbled over her answer. "I...I don't know." She honestly hadn't given it a moment's thought. She'd been focusing on finding the location, not planning out what would happen afterward. That had been shortsighted. She'd have to oversee the development of the settlement as well. But she had no idea where to begin. "I've never built a house before, let alone designed an entire community." She shrugged. "You're the engineer. You tell me."

He leaned against the tree trunk and folded his arms, the muscles in his biceps bulging. "It should be something that pleases you."

"I suppose so." She gazed at the trees as they swayed in the gentle breeze. "We definitely won't be replicating the treetop design you use on Drakar." Even though a part of her would love to. She'd always enjoyed spaces that were up high, whether it was in the trees, the mountains, or out in space. She'd been enchanted by the Kraed dwellings on Drakar for that very reason.

"I'd like to camouflage the community as much as possible." She stroked the leaves of the nearest plant and felt its energy pulse in sync with hers. The sensation felt like a gentle caress. "We'll need to integrate the native vegetation with the interior and exterior, so that the structures blend in with the foliage." The longer she stood surrounded by the greenery, the more the sensation of deep nurturing grew.

The low rumble of distant thunder brought her attention to the clouds. They were gathering momentum, and the scent of rain carried on the breeze. She breathed it in, exhaling on a sigh of happiness. This could work.

She glanced at Jonarel. He was watching her. "What?"

"It's good to see you enjoying yourself." He pushed away from the tree and rested his hands on her shoulders. "You've been working too hard."

The tenderness of his touch warmed her through the material of her tunic. "We've all been working hard. Including you." She tapped him lightly on the chest for emphasis and he caught her hand in midair.

"Perhaps. But you never slow down."

She shrugged. "Comes with the job description." As if to emphasize her point, her comband pinged. Jonarel released her and she opened the connection. "Yes?"

Celia sounded almost giddy, which was not a tone

Aurora heard from her friend very often. "I've identified at least thirty plants that should be edible, and that's just to start. I've gathered samples to take back to the ship. After Mya and I analyze them, I'll test them out in the kitchen to see if they're palatable."

Cooking was one of Celia's secret pleasures, and this mission had provided her with an excuse to experiment. The large galley kitchen that was housed between the observation lounge and the greenhouse on the *Starhawke* had become her unofficial domain. The crew ate well on the days she had time to make use of it.

"Mya has roughly the same number of plants to take back for her medicinal studies. We'll both have plenty to keep us busy for the next few days."

A flash of light and a loud rumble brought Aurora's head up. The afternoon rains were getting serious. "Then let's pack it in for now. We'll meet you at the shuttle."

"On our way."

Five

The *Nightingale* had turned into a prison.

After more than two weeks on Burrow with nowhere to go and nothing to do, the feeling of claustrophobia was beginning to wear on humans and Lumians alike.

Cade was no exception. The spacious box canyon where the ship rested had dwindled to the size of a thumbnail. He'd decided to climb to the top of the surrounding rock formations to trigger endorphins and get some breathing room. He'd left Justin in charge and set out before dawn, when the temperature was still bearable. This hemisphere of Burrow was in midsummer, with long, sweltering days, and nights that seemed to go by in a blink.

When he reached the peak, he stretched out on his back and gazed at the blanket of stars. Somewhere up there, one of those beacons of light represented the planet Aurora was currently investigating. He'd received a brief communication from her yesterday. She'd estimated her crew would finish their assessment in about a week. If everything checked out, they'd head to Drakar to gather supplies. That was the good news.

The bad news was that even if things went according to plan, building the settlement would take four to six weeks. Minimum. And until it was completed, his team and the Lumians would have to remain on Burrow. Given the current level of tension, another month of confinement and inactivity might stretch them to the breaking point.

What they needed was a distraction, something to keep everyone occupied while they waited. But so far, he'd come up with zip.

The rattle of pebbles alerted him to the presence of visitors headed his way. He sat up and glanced over his shoulder, expecting to see Reynolds or Gonzo. Instead he spotted a familiar trio of teenagers climbing the steep incline in the dim light of dawn.

Raaveen, the current de facto leader for the Lumians, was in front, her dark hair standing out in sharp contrast to the beige and tan of the surrounding rocks. Paaw was right on her heels, her blue-eyed gaze focused on the summit as she pulled herself up. She reached back to offer a hand to Sparw, a brown-haired boy of fifteen who was the smallest of the three.

Cade lifted a hand in greeting. "Good morning."

The teens returned the gesture as they reached the top. "We join you?" Raaveen asked in Galish, folding her hands in front of her.

Justin had uploaded the Lumian language translation into all the team's combands the previous week, which had solved the ongoing communication issue. But Cade's translator wasn't turned on at the moment. Raaveen, Paaw and Sparw were all learning Galactic English, or Galish as it was commonly referred to, from Justin.

Cade nodded. "Of course."

Raaveen stepped around him and settled on his right while Paaw and Sparw sat to his left. The teens mimicked his posture, ankles crossed and arms around their knees as they gazed at the vista.

"Pretty." Raaveen nodded to where the sun's first rays painted the rocks with streaks of gold.

It was pretty, in a stark way. But compared to what

the teenagers were used to, any sunrise would be considered pretty, even one as bland as the one before them. Burrow wasn't a beautiful planet, particularly in this arid region, but the early morning light gave the harshness of the landscape a softer look that brought out the subtle variations in color of the rocks and the mountains in the distance.

Raaveen turned her head, the sunlight revealing the faint lines between her brows and around her eyes. The adult Lumians were still recovering from the physical and emotional wounds inflicted during their long imprisonment, and Raaveen had stepped into the void. She shouldered a heavy responsibility, taking care of the Lumians and coping with the recent death of her mother and her father's permanent catatonic state. Her expression often looked as it did now.

She cleared her throat. "We talk idea."

He should have guessed this wasn't a social call. He tapped his comband to turn on the translator. "Go ahead." The nearly instantaneous translation allowed him to follow her words and gestures as she spoke.

"We are grateful for all that you and your team have done to help us," she said. "We know that without your intervention, we would still be captives on the Setarip ship."

He acknowledged the comment with a nod.

"But after such a long confinement, we want to be productive and useful, not a burden."

He could certainly relate to that sentiment.

"We have a plan that will allow us to do that, but we need your assistance and approval."

Her tone indicated she wasn't certain she'd receive either. He hoped he wouldn't have to disappoint her. "What do you want to do?"

Raaveen glanced at Paaw and Sparw before

continuing. "Build a growing structure for plants."

A growing structure? It took him a moment to figure out what she was describing. "Do you mean a greenhouse?"

The translator apparently couldn't come up with a match for "greenhouse" in the Lumian language, because Raaveen frowned. "What does that word mean, *greenhouse?*"

"It's an enclosed structure for protecting and growing plants."

All three teens smiled and nodded. "Yes," Raaveen said. "A greenhouse."

A greenhouse. It was an intriguing idea, except for one major problem. "Where would you get the plants?"

A shadow of doubt passed over her face. "We would need your team to help us gather them from the surrounding area. It would mean leaving the canyon." Hope lit her brown eyes, as well as the fear of rejection.

Cade *really* didn't want to douse that flame. But as the person in charge of everyone's safety, he had to be practical. He rubbed the back of his neck, the dampness he encountered reminding him of how hot it was getting now that the sun had taken control of the day. "I don't know, Raaveen. It's a creative idea, but there are a lot of potential problems."

She dropped her gaze and nodded in acquiescence. But when she started to rise, he grasped her arm.

"Hang on. Give me a minute to think about this."

She immediately resumed her seat and kept her gaze averted, as if she didn't want to invade his personal space.

All the Lumians took consideration of others to a whole new level, and dammit, he wanted to reward that. There had to be a way to make this work. Constructing and populating a greenhouse would certainly keep everyone busy. The building materials could be obtained from items in the freighter's storage systems. And trading emergency rations for fresh fruits and vegetables would be a big bonus.

But gathering the plants could be tricky. They hadn't seen any sign of the Meer since arriving, but his team hadn't ventured very far from the canyon, either. He didn't know how big a project the teenagers had in mind, but even a modest greenhouse would require several trips, especially since they'd have to locate suitable plants first.

Gonzo could oversee construction, and Williams could supervise selecting and gathering the plants. The good doctor would certainly approve. Cade had been on the receiving end of Tam's philosophy regarding nutrition for years. He affirmed that diet was the number one source of good health, and he'd turned identifying what would benefit a particular person into an art form. If there were edible plants nearby, he'd find them.

If they used the stealth pods for transport and worked at night, they could bring the risk factor to almost zero. He wouldn't be sending the teens out to gather the plants, which they clearly wanted to do, but he didn't need to tell them they'd be staying in the canyon until his team agreed with the basic idea of building the greenhouse.

Cade stood. "I can't make any promises, but let's see what we can do."

Six

"That looks promising."

Jonarel glanced up from the drafting table in his cabin. Tehar, or Star as the rest of the crew knew her, stood beside him, studying his preliminary sketches.

He was used to her sudden appearances in his room. Tehar had gained sentience shortly before his birth, so they had grown up like siblings. The projected image of her non-biological essence, with her long dark hair, hunter green skin and honey-colored eyes, was as familiar to him as the face he saw in the mirror. More so, in fact, since he did not waste time looking at his own reflection.

She peered at the drawing of the proposed settlement, her voice drifting to him from everywhere and nowhere, the ship acting as a speaker. "The layout is lovely. Aurora will like it."

He hoped so. "I want to please her." In fact, pleasing Aurora was his top priority.

Tehar rested a ghostly hand on his shoulder. "You will."

As the sister of his heart, if not by biology, Tehar knew all his secrets, all his dreams...and all his fears. She was his closest confidant, the only one who truly understood the powerful emotions that had driven him to build the *Starhawke*. And the real reasons he had given the ship to Aurora.

He had always expected to hand the ship over when it was completed, but he had assumed it would be missing the one key element that made all Kraed vessels unique—the presence of a Nirunoc integrated into the ship's systems. But Tehar had shocked him when she had chosen to bond with the ship the day before he had left Drakar.

The ship *was* Tehar in every sense that mattered, and her decision indicated the depth of her love for him, and her loyalty to the woman whose name she had accepted when she had joined with the ship. She had become Star, and the ship had become the *Starhawke*. He could not have asked for a greater gift.

It was a selfless act. She had given up her intimate connection with the other Nirunoc and the rest of the clan on Drakar. Like Jonarel, she had chosen an unconventional life among humans in order to serve something greater than themselves—their half-human, half-Lumian captain, the woman who had the power to change the course of history.

"Aurora sent me to fetch you," Tehar said. "She suspected you had lost track of time."

A quick glance at his chronometer indicated he was late for the crew meeting. He had not been this absorbed in a project since he had finalized the designs for the *Starhawke*. But it made sense. Like the ship, the settlement was a gift for Aurora. That made it special. And important.

"Tell her I am on my way."

Thankfully the conference room was only one level above the crew cabins.

The intricate colored panels that opened into the room parted silently as Jonarel approached. Aurora and Kire were seated at the far side of the massive circular table in the center of the room, with Kelly on Kire's left, and Mya and Cardiff to Aurora's right. A chair had been left vacant next to Aurora, and he settled into it.

Aurora smiled at him. The light caught the golden

highlights in her braided hair, making it look like a crown.

"I apologize for keeping you waiting."

She shrugged. "No problem. This week has been intense for all of us."

That was certainly true. But he suspected their efforts were about to be rewarded.

"I appreciate how hard you've all been working." Aurora rested her forearms on the table. "Now we have a decision to make. We'll start global and work our way down. Kire, tell me about the planetary geology and climate. Any concerns?"

Kire shook his head. "Nothing we can't plan for. The planet has active tectonics, but the volcano that created the island has been dormant for centuries. It shouldn't pose a threat. And the abundant rainfall provides a stable source of clean water in the freshwater aquifer."

Aurora shifted her attention to Kelly. "What about long-term sustainability?"

"I compared our readings to the historical data the Kraed survey team recorded four hundred years ago," Kelly said. "The information is nearly identical. Everything past and present indicates a healthy, stable ecosystem. Nothing that is cause for concern."

"That's good news." Aurora turned to Cardiff. "What about dangers from the local fauna?"

"You mean are there any walking mountains with teeth?"

Aurora's gaze flicked briefly to him. "Something like that."

Jonarel clenched his jaw. Aurora had been vague on the details of that encounter, but Cardiff's question indicated it had been more hazardous than anyone had admitted.

"Nothing that I could find," Cardiff said. "No large

animals of any kind, either predator or prey, and the smaller ones are relatively harmless. It's a very benign location."

"And a pretty one." Mya added.

Aurora snorted. "So was the one with the rock monsters."

Mya's brown eyes twinkled. "Pretty is as pretty does?"

Aurora nodded. "That's right."

"Well in this case, you can have both. The lack of aggressive fauna means the plants haven't needed to create potentially lethal defenses. Most of the plants on the island are edible in one form or another, and thanks to Celia, we know they're tasty to boot." Cardiff had spent most of the week preparing meals crafted from the local vegetation, which she had offered to the crew. The tastes were foreign, but enjoyable.

"So the planet and island are solid prospects." Aurora's green-eyed gaze met his. "Which brings us to the question of potential building sites."

He touched the control panel built into the table and projected his preliminary sketches. "I have identified several options, but this elevated location is the most advantageous for camouflage. There is plenty of concealing vegetation and easy access to water sources." He enlarged one of the images. "The ground is level and a rock promontory nearby could function as a shuttle landing platform."

Aurora studied the images. "That location was my favorite, too. It has a nurturing feel to it." She smiled, warming him from the inside out. "I think the Lumians would be happy there."

"As do I." And if the Lumians were happy, Aurora would be happy.

She glanced around the table. "Does anyone have concerns we haven't addressed?"

"Not me," Kire said. "I like it."

"Me, too," Cardiff replied.

Kelly nodded.

Aurora propped her chin on her hands as she focused on Mya. "So, do you think we've found their new home?" The look in Aurora's eyes belied the casual way she had posed the question. The success of their mission hinged on Mya's answer.

Mya held Aurora's gaze. "Yes, I do."

Aurora grinned. "So do I."

"Hallelujah!" Kire cheered as he smacked the table with his palm.

Mya and Aurora laughed, and even Kelly smiled at Kire's enthusiasm.

However, Aurora's grin faded as she turned to Jonarel. "But we still have one more hurdle. This planet is within the boundaries of Kraed space. We'll need approval from your father and the rest of the Kraed Elders before we finalize anything."

"That is not a concern." Every planet they had investigated as a potential homeworld had been within Kraed territory. Tehar had engineered the search that way. The Elders wanted to keep the Lumians close. "The Elders have already given approval for any suitable location. The Lumians are welcome to settle here."

Aurora frowned, her gaze searching his, but if she had any questions, she kept them to herself.

Kire leaned back in his chair. "You know, I hadn't thought of the planet's location as a bonus, but being close to Drakar will reduce the chance of the settlement being discovered. Fleet ships and Earth transports won't go anywhere near it."

"Or Setarips," Kelly added. "They usually avoid Kraed territory."

And with good reason. After his race had learned of the opportunistic and violent nature of the Setarips, they had taken a much more aggressive stance in their engagements, always to the detriment of their adversaries. Setarips who wanted to live gave Drakar and the other Kraed systems a wide berth.

Aurora pushed back her chair. "Then if everything is settled, will you contact your father and let him know we're on our way to Drakar?"

"Of course." And his clan would have quite a homecoming prepared by the time they arrived.

Seven

Aurora had found a homeworld.

Cade leaned back in his chair and reread the short message.

C -

Location confirmed. On our way to gather supplies. Will keep you posted as work progresses.

A -

He tapped his fingers on the console as he stared at the lines of text. During the weeks of waiting, he'd kept telling himself he'd be relieved when light appeared at the end of the tunnel. Instead, he was viewing the change as a proverbial oncoming train.

Not that he wasn't thrilled that the Lumians would have a new home soon. They deserved a fresh start and a chance to experience true freedom.

But their new beginning was his finale, at least where Aurora was concerned. As long as he was in charge of the Lumians, he had a connection to her. After she came for the Lumians, that connection would be severed. Probably for good.

They'd agreed before she'd left Gaia that he wouldn't be the one to deliver the Lumians to their new home. For one thing, he was flying a decommissioned Fleet medical freighter. The Admiral had done everything he could to guarantee the *Nightingale* was clean, but there was always a chance someone might find a way to track its whereabouts. Taking this ship to the new Lumian homeworld would be a monumental mistake. He didn't want to risk leaving a trail that could be followed.

That's why the *Starhawke* would be coming to him. Aurora would transport the Lumians to their new home, and he would report back to the Admiral for his next assignment. After that, his path might never cross Aurora's again. What a depressing thought.

With a sigh of frustration, he stood and headed outside. As he exited through the *Nightingale*'s main hatch, the soft glow of lanterns outlined the greenhouse to his left. The Burrow climate was intense during the day, so everyone preferred to work at night and sleep during the day. His team had set a rotating schedule, taking overlapping twelve hour shifts with eight hour breaks in between so that at least four members of the team were on duty at all times.

Construction was nearly finished, and the hum of activity ran through the community like the steady drone of a beehive. Williams stood in front of the greenhouse, his arms crossed over his barrel chest and his shaved head gleaming in the lantern light. He lifted a hand in greeting when he spotted Cade heading his way. "Almost done here," he called out, his gentle tenor voice at odds with his solid physique, but ideal for calming anxious patients requiring medical attention. "The shading materials are in place and irrigation from the well is completed."

"Glad to hear it. All we need now are plants. When are you making your first run?"

"Tomorrow night, as long as the weather holds."

They'd had a few nights of gusting winds recently that had slowed their progress. If the wind returned, it would prevent any attempts at transporting vegetation, too.

Reynolds appeared in the greenhouse doorway and Williams motioned her over. "Reynolds and I have mapped out three locations with sufficient plant density to meet our needs. And two of them are large enough for multiple runs."

Reynolds's short blond hair was streaked with dirt. She swiped at a trickle of sweat at her temple. "We've also rigged up a harness between two of the stealth pods." She gestured to the shadowy objects to their right. "We'll be able to bring back more plants that way and also avoid leaving any tracks."

Good plan. They certainly didn't want to draw attention to their presence. "How will you remove the plants without making it obvious they've been dug up?"

"We'll have to be very selective in what we take. And we'll bring a couple of the Lumians along to help."

Cade stared at her. "You want to take Lumians with you?" He'd nixed that idea during their initial discussion. Apparently she and Williams disagreed with his decision.

"Definitely. Their abilities will enable them to unearth the specimens without damaging them or disturbing the surrounding vegetation."

Williams nodded. "And the work will go quicker that way." His hands dropped to his hips and his stance widened, like a gunslinger preparing for a shootout. "We need them on this."

Cade's gut said no. As long as the Lumians remained in the canyon, he could protect them. But Williams made a good point. Taking the Lumians would minimize the overall risk. And that *was* the goal. However, if they were going to do this, Cade would be the one leading the team. "Then I'll ride point on the third pod."

Williams relaxed. "That's a good idea."

"Who did you want to bring along?"

"Raaveen, for one," Reynolds said. "And Paaw. After all, the greenhouse was their idea."

"And with you on the third pod, we could bring Sparw, too," Williams added.

More hands would mean less time out in the open. That was definitely a bonus. "Okay. As long as the weather holds, we'll head out tomorrow night."

Eight

"The Clarek clan is awaiting our arrival."

Aurora pulled her gaze away from the tantalizing image of Drakar on the bridgescreen and focused on Kire. "Let them know we're on our way. Kelly, take us down."

"Aye, Captain."

As the ship began its descent, Aurora's body tingled with anticipation. She'd been captivated by the homeworld of the Clarek clan when Jonarel had brought her here two years ago to attend his succession ceremony. Little had she known how much that event would alter the course of her future.

From space, Drakar reminded her of a Monet painting of water lilies. Lots of blues and greens interspersed with patches of white. The Kraed homeworld contained a diversified climate, but the plant life in most areas grew to a lushness that far surpassed Earth's most verdant rainforests, in part because the Kraed had never attempted to alter the landscape. They'd chosen adaptation over conquest.

Star shimmered into place next to the captain's chair, her expression revealing her eagerness as she gazed at the image on the bridgescreen.

"You look exactly the way I feel whenever I return to Earth."

Star's honey-colored eyes glowed as she met Aurora's gaze. "I suppose I do. I had expected to wait years for a chance to reconnect with my clan."

"Years? Really? I'd assumed we'd need to return at

regular intervals for maintenance and upgrades."

Star looked amused. "Unless we suffer structural damage to the exterior, I can maintain all my other systems."

Wow. Every time Aurora thought she understood the extent of the *Starhawke's* abilities, Star and Jonarel surprised her with something new.

The image on the screen shifted as the ship dropped into the lower atmosphere, revealing the stunning landscape that stretched to the horizon. The Clarek clan lived close to the equator, where a seemingly unending vista of trees and other plant life resembled a bayou combined with a redwood forest. Most of the tree species that thrived here were massive, with trunks that could easily grow to twenty meters in diameter and stretch up a hundred meters into the sky.

It was these trees that had enabled the Kraed to thrive in an environment where large predators patrolled the skies above and the waterways below. The Kraed's razor sharp claws served as both climbing tools for reaching the safety of the canopy, and weapons against creatures looking for a tasty meal. She'd thought the claws on Jonarel's hands were impressive until the day he'd shown her the ones on his feet. A well-placed kick from a Kraed could be lethal.

Of course, the advanced technology of the Kraed race made such life and death struggles almost non-existent. But that didn't mean their skills had dimmed. Every Kraed child was taught how to survive outside of the safety of the clan's compound. Only fools picked fights with the Kraed.

Kelly pivoted to face Aurora. "Captain, we're getting close to the landing coordinates, but I'm not seeing any sign of a platform."

"That's because the Kraed compounds and ship ports are camouflaged."

A line appeared between Kelly's auburn brows. "Then how am I supposed to dock the ship?"

Star's image vanished from beside Aurora and re-materialized next to Kelly. "When we get closer, the Nirunoc will guide you."

One of Kelly's brows quirked up. "Meaning what?"

"Maintain the heading I gave you and follow the ship's motion. You will be fine."

Kelly gave Star a long look, her reluctance obvious as she turned back to the console. Star was asking her to make a leap of faith. Not an easy task for the tech-minded navigator.

"What are *those*?" Kire's eyes were wide as saucers as he stared at the bridgescreen.

Aurora followed has gaze and spotted a dark mass of shapes in the sky. Their leathery wings and long tails were a dead giveaway. "Trebolks."

Kire gawked as the creatures glided through the air, momentarily blocking out the late afternoon sun. "They're *huge*!"

Celia watched from the tactical console, her hands hovering over the weapons controls as the flock swung in their direction. "Are they dangerous?"

"Not to us. They don't bother ships. They spend most of their time nesting in the upper canopy or hunting in open water."

"Good to know," Kire murmured as the creatures drew alongside the ship.

They kept pace with the *Starhawke*, like dolphins swimming in the wake of a boat, giving the bridge crew a close up view of their thick bodies and refined heads. But as the ship descended toward the canopy, the trebolks changed course, heading off to the east.

Kelly decreased their speed, a look of apprehension on her normally placid face as she glanced at Star.

"Trust me," Star reiterated.

Aurora could only imagine how challenging that request was for their navigator. Based on the image on the bridgescreen, it looked like they were about to smash into the upper branches of the nearest trees, which were close enough to make out the shape of individual leaves. But they wouldn't crash. Star and the other Nirunoc were guiding the ship into an invisible web of tethers that would direct the ship's motion.

Like a bird returning to its nest, the *Starhawke* glided through a break in the trees, continuing to slow as they approached an alcove that was the perfect size to accommodate the ship's bulk. The greenery of the surrounding trees filled the screen as the ship's forward movement ceased. A moment later the engines powered down. The *Starhawke* was home.

"Well done." Star beamed at Kelly.

Kelly blinked. "I've never seen anything like that." An uncharacteristic grin spread across her face. "That was stellar."

Celia looked similarly impressed with their unconventional landing procedure.

Jonarel's deep baritone boomed over the comm. "All docking connections are secure."

"Acknowledged," Aurora replied. "We're on our way." She rose from the captain's chair. "Who's ready to see Drakar?"

Nine

Jonarel stood on the starboard side of the main deck, waiting for the rest of the crew to join him. Or to be more specific, for Aurora to join him.

His body hummed like the interstellar drive. He finally had an opportunity to reveal a facet of the ship she had never seen. Watching her reaction as the *Starhawke* transformed would be a memorable experience.

He had designed the ship's hull according to Kraed tradition. Large sections of the exterior could slide into specially constructed compartments, converting the starship that protected the crew from the vacuum of space into an open-air communal hub that integrated with the pathways and structures of the compound. When the transformation was complete, it would be virtually impossible to distinguish the ship from the surrounding trees and permanent features.

Camouflage was a skill his ancestors had cultivated for millennia. Originally they had needed the talent to avoid predators. Later, they had adapted the techniques for space travel, which helped them to prevent unwanted encounters with other interstellar beings. As an added benefit, the few visitors who were invited to Drakar had no way of knowing how many ships were actually docked at the compound.

For this visit, the bridge and upper decks would remain sealed so that the crew would have a haven from the heat and humidity. But the five lower decks would be opened for the transfer of supplies.

Tehar appeared next to him. "They are exiting the

lift now."

The rest of the crew rounded the curve of the med bay a moment later.

Aurora's green eyes sparkled like emeralds. "Okay, you two. Show us what you've got."

"Remain in the middle of the corridor, and prepare for a wave of damp heat when the seal is broken," Jonarel warned. He met Tehar's gaze, her excitement as palpable as his. And then the exterior walls began to move.

The moist air that pushed inside felt like heaven, but Aurora gave a little gasp as she took a step back. However, the movement seemed involuntary since her attention was going everywhere at once.

The hull split into sections that disappeared into slots above the ceiling and below the floor, revealing the thick trunks and the deep greens and browns of the trees outside. A pathway connected snugly along the ship's side, flowing seamlessly in perfect alignment with the floor of the corridor.

Aurora had commented the day he had brought her to the *Starhawke* that she loved the beauty of the walkways with their rich natural grain. Now she would understand how precisely he had matched the ship's decor to the design of the Clarek compound. In addition to the pathways, the textured surface of the ship's interior walls perfectly mimicked the bark of the surrounding trees.

The look on Aurora's face as she stepped onto the shaded walkway and pivoted in a slow circle captivated him. It was everything he had hoped for and more.

Ten

Incredible.

Nothing in Aurora's line of sight indicated she was standing outside her ship—she could be anywhere in the Clarek compound. The illusion was perfect.

Which begged the question of how many ships the Clarek clan had hidden in plain sight. Ten? Fifty? A hundred? Had some of the places she'd visited during her last trip to Drakar been ships in their docking ports? It was certainly possible. She wouldn't have been able to tell the difference. "This is...unbelievable."

Her reaction must have been exactly what Jonarel was hoping for. His lips parted in a rare smile that transformed his handsome face into a work of art. He had a wry sense of humor, but like all the Kraed she'd met, he rarely smiled and almost never laughed. It always caught her off guard when he did.

The intensity in his golden gaze also ratcheted up the temperature a few degrees. "Thank you."

Kire slapped Jonarel on the back. "Pretty impressive, big guy. I know camouflage is a Kraed skill, but this is above and beyond."

Jonarel broke eye contact with Aurora. "It was necessary for survival. Our world poses...challenges."

Kire chuckled. "No kidding. Like those dragon-looking creatures we saw during our approach. What did you call them?" he asked Aurora. "Tree bolts?"

"Trebolks."

"Yeah. I'd describe those things as more than challenging."

"So would I." Celia crouched at the edge of the walkway, inspecting the perfect alignment of the ship with the nearby tree trunk. "But the illusion you've created here is perfect. If you didn't know where the ship was docked, you'd never find it."

Kire nodded. "Speaking of which, how do we keep from getting lost? Will we have guides while we're here?"

Star gestured to the path. "You will have me." A curving line of blue lights glowed in the center of the walkway leading directly to where they stood.

"Are you controlling those?" Kire asked.

Star nodded. "You can contact me from anywhere in the compound, just as you can on the ship."

"You're kidding." Kire stared at her in disbelief. "You mean the entire compound is interconnected so you and the other Nirunoc can go everywhere?"

"Correct."

"Wow. That's cool."

Aurora had to agree. She'd learned a lot about the Kraed culture and their advanced technology over the years, especially with Jonarel as one of her closest friends, but the revelations since they'd landed indicated she'd only scratched the surface.

"Greetings!" a deep voice called out.

Siginal! Even amongst his own people, Jonarel's father was an impressive presence as he strode toward them, with arms like tree branches and a mass of dark hair that fell past his shoulders. Aurora had compared him to a grizzly bear once, and the image fit. Jonarel's mother, Daymar, was shorter than her mate, with the lithe grace of a cheetah. She also bore a striking resemblance to Star. The

Nirunoc had clearly patterned her projected image off the Kraed female who'd been a mother to her.

Jonarel stepped forward and embraced his father while Daymar and Star touched palms in the traditional family greeting between Kraed and Nirunoc.

When Jonarel turned to his mother, Signal reached for Aurora and enveloped her in a bear hug. Being accepted as part of Jonarel's family had been an incredible blessing in her life. She hugged him back with equal enthusiasm.

"You are looking well." His large hands gripped her upper arms with gentle strength as he gazed at her, his golden eyes so like Jonarel's.

She smiled. "As are you."

His attention shifted to Kire and Mya, who patiently waited their turn with their friend and mentor. "I recognize these faces as well." Signal motioned them forward.

During their years together at the Academy, Jonarel's parents had routinely invited Aurora, Mya and Kire to dine in the Clarek family's quarters. Many spirited discussions and fascinating tales had been shared during those meals. Not only was Signal Clarek a brilliant scientist, but he was also a gifted storyteller. He'd had them alternately laughing themselves silly or sitting on the edge of their seats.

"Kire. Mya." He pulled them each into a warm hug. "Welcome to our home."

"Checala." Daymar's melodious voice reached Aurora a moment before her slender green-skinned arms wrapped around her from behind. "It has been too long." Daymar's voice hitched as she pressed her cheek against Aurora's.

Moisture gathered in Aurora's eyes as she placed her hands over Daymar's and squeezed. Checala was a Kraed term of endearment that roughly translated to *beloved one.*

and was used predominantly to refer to one's own children. But Jonarel's mother had always treated her as the daughter of her heart. "I know. But we're here now."

Daymar released her. "Yes. And we will make the most of our time together." She greeted Mya and Kire while Aurora gestured for Celia and Kelly to join them.

"Daymar, Signal, I would like to introduce you to Celia Cardiff, our security chief, and Bronwyn Kelly, our navigator. Celia, Kelly, these are Jonarel's parents, Signal and Daymar Clarek."

"It is an honor to meet you," Signal said as he and Daymar shook hands with Celia and Kelly.

"Celia's the best hand-to-hand fighter I've ever met," Aurora said. "If you want a challenge, you should spar with her."

"Indeed?" Signal looked intrigued. "Then we will find a time to do so."

Celia's eyes gleamed. "I look forward to it."

Aurora knew that look. She'd seen it every time they met on the mat—right before Celia knocked her on her butt.

Daymar was studying Kelly with interest. "You must be an exceptionally talented navigator for one so young. Piloting a Kraed vessel is not an easy task."

High praise, indeed, especially from Daymar, whose background was in navigation.

"She's a beautiful ship. And I'm fascinated by your landing technique. I've never seen anything like it."

Good move on Kelly's part. One of the quickest ways to earn the admiration of the Kraed was to show appreciation for their technology.

"Then perhaps you would enjoy a tour of our other ships?"

Kelly looked positively giddy, an out of character expression for the stoic navigator. "That would be wonderful."

Siginal flashed Aurora a look of approval. "Aurora has chosen her crew well. Our clan shall enjoy the opportunity to meet you all. Come."

They left the *Starhawke* behind and moved deeper into the compound, following the curving path through the trees. "Mya, I have arranged for two of our botanists to take you on a tour tomorrow," Siginal said. "I assume you will want to add specimens from Drakar to your collection."

Mya and Celia exchanged a look. "Would it be possible for Celia to join me?" Mya asked. "She's a specialist in pharmacology. And an amazing cook."

"Of course." A sparkle showed in his eyes as he glanced at Celia. "And perhaps when you return you will meet me in the training arena."

"I would be delighted."

Aurora made a mental note to be in attendance. She hadn't been joking when she'd warned Siginal that Celia could probably beat him. He'd definitely need to stay on his toes if he wanted a chance to win the match.

"And what can I offer you, Kire?" Siginal gave Kire a friendly thump between his shoulder blades that nearly knocked him to his knees.

Kire staggered as he regained his balance. "I understand that you have quite a language library here, with documents from all the Kraed clans on Drakar. Would I be allowed to look over them?"

Siginal nodded. "You are welcome. I will see that you are given access." His attention shifted to Aurora. "And what would you like to see while you are with us, checala?"

"I was hoping Jonarel would give me a lesson on the

glider." Ever since the near disaster on Gaia when she and Mya had been forced to leave their glider behind, she'd vowed to become more proficient with the Kraed device.

Jonarel stopped his conversation with his mother in mid-sentence. "I am yours to command."

His tone indicated he was teasing, but the look in his eyes said something else entirely. What was going on with him? His attitude had shifted ever since they'd landed, and it was knocking her off balance. She didn't like it.

Mya must have picked up on her discomfort, because she redirected the conversation by pointing to the massive trees with the bright purple and yellow flowers at the tips of the branches that swayed in the breeze. "Is this the same species that you used to construct the tables and chairs in the *Starhawke*'s observation lounge and conference room?"

"Yes," Jonarel replied, breaking eye contact with Aurora. "The root structure acts like a bulb, but without the dormant phase. Each year the trees generate new sections. If they are not thinned, they choke the waterways, causing pooling and flooding issues that kill off other plant species. By carefully harvesting the pods for use in construction, the tree and surrounding vegetation remain healthy."

Mya frowned. "But you have predators in the waterways, don't you? That would be dangerous work."

Jonarel's calm words belied the seriousness of the answer. "We manage."

Mya's brows lifted. "I see." She shot a questioning look at Aurora.

Aurora shrugged. Mya might be curious how the Kraed dealt with the hazards of their world, but she wasn't. That side of Kraed life, particularly as it pertained to Jonarel, always made her a little twitchy.

The pathway curved to the left, leading them through a collection of towering structures that rose into the canopy in graceful, flowing lines. Technically they were tree houses, but the term tree cathedrals hit closer to the mark. Part of their breathtaking beauty lay in the way they blended with the surroundings, turning the entire community into a living work of art.

The path opened before them, revealing their destination. The majestic clan lodge nestled at the heart of the compound, a multi-level structure that appeared rustic to the unobservant. Five trees grew in a nearly perfect circle, their branches supporting the foundation and their trunks forming the interior walls. A woven network of smaller branches enclosed the roof. However, as with all things Kraed, looks were deceiving. The lodge might resemble something from a fantasy story set during the Middle Ages, but technological wonders were carefully concealed and easily accessible.

As they entered through the wide archway, the murmur of conversation faded out. Every member of the Clarek clan, including a large contingent of Nirunoc, seemed to be gathered in the tiered expanse, some leaning over the railings of the upper levels, while others sat around the circular tables that spread across the room's interior.

Aurora felt like an actor walking onto a stage, a sensation that intensified when Siginal raised his arms wide, the corded muscles in his back and shoulders rippling.

"My clan. Our own have returned."

Roars of approval greeted the announcement, followed by a surge of bodies. Aurora was enveloped in hugs from many of Jonarel's kin, some of whom she'd met before, but many that she hadn't. It didn't seem to matter. She and every member of her crew were welcomed like long lost relatives.

Eventually they made their way to one of the larger tables near the center of the lower level and settled into their chairs. The younger Kraed, who stood out in contrast to the adults because of their diminutive size and the paler green and brown of their skin and hair coloring, picked up platters of food from the side tables.

Celia leaned toward Aurora, bringing her mouth close to her ear. "They make the small children do all the serving?" Disapproval threaded her words. Clearly she was disturbed by what she saw as an injustice. "I thought the Kraed were culturally advanced."

Aurora smiled. "They are. These aren't children. Kraed don't begin adolescence until they're near their twentieth year. You're seeing teenagers who are close to adulthood."

Celia frowned, her gaze following the petite Kraed.

"Jonarel was the same size when I met him thirteen years ago, and he's two years older than I am."

"Huh." Celia watched the young boy who had appeared at their table and was busy filling mugs from a large pitcher. She didn't look convinced.

Aurora turned to Daymar for backup. "Your clan has a strong tradition of service, correct?"

Daymar nodded. "It is a core belief. From childhood we learn the importance of serving others, both literally and figuratively." She paused to thank the youth as he handed her one of the full mugs. "We think of the needs of the clan first, rather than focusing on self. Every member is valued and respected, no matter what tasks they perform, what age they have achieved, or what family line they are born or mated into."

"So you did this same work when you were their

age?" Celia asked.

Daymar nodded. "Of course. As did Siginal and Jonarel."

"Interesting." Some of the tension eased from Celia's shoulders as she viewed the situation with a fresh perspective.

The attitude of service and respect the Kraed modeled was a large factor in why their culture had been so successful for millennia. It was a dynamic that humans still struggled to achieve in their interactions with one another. But Aurora believed they would get there one day.

She took a sip from her goblet. The delightful flavor of Kraed *tenrebac* slid along her tongue. She'd been introduced to the beverage by Jonarel, who'd served it to celebrate the day she and Mya had joined him as members of the crew of the *Excelsior*. Tenrebac had a flavor and texture similar to red wine, but with twice the alcohol content. Aurora had learned that last part the hard way.

Daymar's family line cultivated the fruits that produced the beverage, and she'd stocked the pantry on the *Starhawke* with cases of it before the ship had been delivered to Earth.

As she lowered her goblet, she met Jonarel's gaze. He was watching her from across the table. No, not watching. Staring. Staring as though he was studying a beautiful painting or gazing at a breathtaking landscape. She didn't qualify as either.

She glanced away, completely flustered. What was going on with him? Had something happened she wasn't aware of? This was the third time she'd caught him looking at her like he had something very intimate on his mind.

Or maybe it wasn't him at all. Maybe it was her. That was certainly possible. Drakar was an intense experience, and she'd arrived super-charged from the excitement of locating the new Lumian homeworld. It was probably all in her head, seeing things that weren't there.

She glanced in his direction just to make sure. He was still staring. He lifted his goblet and nodded at her before taking a drink, his gaze never leaving hers.

Nope. It wasn't her imagination. Something was very different. If she didn't know better, she'd swear that her chief engineer was flirting with her.

Eleven

Jonarel was caught in a waking dream. And he never wanted it to end.

He watched Aurora all evening, mesmerized by the way she interacted with his clan like she had been sharing meals in the lodge all her life. She was a perfect fit. True, her blonde hair and pale skin made her stand out among the greens and browns of his race, but that only made her shine all the brighter.

Of course, if she ventured away from the compound, that coloring would make her a target for Drakar's predators. But Aurora did not need protection from the creatures of his world. She could handle herself just fine. And he would never allow any harm to come to her.

His emotional state must have telegraphed to her empathic senses, because her attention shifted from the conversation she was having with his mother and Celia. She gave him a quizzical look, her brows drawing together in a tiny frown. She seemed vaguely uncomfortable, but she did not look away. Neither did he.

His father's voice broke the connection. "We need to talk."

Jonarel glanced at him, irritated at the interruption.

His father's knowing look did not help matters. "Join me in my study after the meal."

He knew what topic they would be discussing. She was sitting across the table. And she had shifted her attention away from him to his mother. He bit back a growl of frustration.

After the feast wound down and the rest of the crew, including Aurora, had returned to the ship, Jonarel walked the short distance to his family's dwelling. The trees that formed the exterior had matured over the centuries, and the enveloping structure had grown with them, adding vertical levels to accommodate the changing needs of the extended family.

Jonarel's chamber was located on the upper level, which he had loved as a child. He had spent countless nights lying on his back, looking up through the oculus in the ceiling to catch glimpses of the stars above the canopy. He had stared until dawn on the night his father had accepted a position as the head of the Astrophysics department at the Galactic Academy on Earth.

Jonarel's parents had offered him the option of remaining with the clan. They had mistakenly thought it might be difficult for him to leave Drakar. But they had been wrong. His entire life he had dreamed of traveling off-planet and exploring the galaxy. His father's decision had been an unexpected gift.

But he had not counted on Aurora. Or on the plans his father and Admiral Schreiber had for her future. When his father had first asked him to befriend Aurora, he had not given a reason for the request. But the admiration his father had expressed for his most talented student and her many accomplishments had been reason enough for Jonarel.

He had learned that Aurora often hiked one of the trails near the Academy in the early morning hours, so he had planned a route that would intersect hers. By a twist of fate, when he had arrived at the spot where their paths would cross, he had discovered three ruffians from the local town passed out after a night of drinking. He had decided to take advantage of the opportunity to learn how Aurora reacted to conflict. He could have slipped past the boys easily without drawing attention, but he had purposely made noise to rouse them instead. Predictably, they had viewed him as easy prey, since at the time he had been the size of a human child of seven or eight.

He had kept their attention on him while he listened for the sound of Aurora's footsteps approaching from the opposite direction. From the information his father had provided about her character, he had expected her to confront the bullies. He had not counted on her risking her life to save him when one of the boys had suddenly shoved him over the cliff edge. Or that the resulting fall and rockslide would force her to reveal her secret ability to manipulate matter and energy.

That moment had changed everything. Until then, he had been more than willing to go along with whatever his father had planned, viewing the entire situation as a science experiment. But as he had gazed into Aurora's dirt-smeared face and seen the fear of discovery in her beautiful green eyes, the urge to protect her had overwhelmed him. He had become her ally and friend, pledging to guard her secret with his life.

As a result, the past thirteen years had been a continual struggle as he walked a tightrope between his loyalty to his clan and his loyalty to Aurora. Most of the time the two sides were in alignment. After all, his parents loved Aurora almost as much as he did. How could they not? He had told them about her heroic efforts to save his life, but her innate charm and compassion would have won them over without that added incentive. It was one reason she had easily convinced her friends to join the *Starhawke* crew, even though it meant leaving their posts in the Galactic

Fleet. Very few people said no to Aurora Hawke.

Except one. Heat seared his chest. One man had dared to turn his back on Aurora. Jonarel would gladly slit Cade Ellis wide open for the pain he had caused her. But Aurora would never allow it. She had made that very clear at the Academy when he had tried to do just that, and she had reiterated her position on Gaia when Ellis had unexpectedly reappeared in their lives. That had been an unpleasant surprise, one that had placed a strain on Jonarel's self-control.

He reached the arched entrance to the house and the doors parted in invitation. Needing to burn off some energy, he bypassed the open-air lift in favor of the winding staircase, moving as quickly and silently as possible, a habit he had developed as soon as he had been old enough to climb the planks alone.

He reached the upper landing and walked to the doorway to his father's study. He had patterned the entrance to Aurora's office after this one, the gracefully curving panels and the rich brown of the wood grain practically glowing from within as the doors opened to reveal the compact room.

He had always loved his father's study, with the solid desk that faced the entrance and the high-backed chair behind. The branches of the tree that gave form to the space had been coaxed into creating natural shelves for his father's collection of family mementos. The wooden chess set Jonarel had carved for him held a place of honor on a table beneath the room's only window.

Jonarel had given a portable version of the same set to Aurora for her eighteenth birthday. She had introduced him to the game during their days at the Academy. He had been fascinated by the history and mathematical quality of the game and had quickly developed into a skilled player. But Aurora was always a worthy opponent. She approached chess from a more intuitive sense, and could be unpredictable in her methods. They both loved the challenge of facing off against each other.

During the two years Jonarel had been living on Drakar and working on the *Starhawke*, he and his father had spent many nights seated on opposite sides of the chessboard. His father had appreciated the game's intricacies as much as he had. Jonarel had been forced to adapt his playing style, however, since he was used to Aurora's more unconventional approach. His father thought more like him, and had quickly learned to anticipate his strategies.

His father came around the desk, pulling him into a loving embrace before stepping back and resting his hands on Jonarel's shoulders. "Are you well, my son?"

It was a question his father would not have asked in front of the crew. But as a parent, he would want to know. Jonarel nodded. "Yes, I am very well, father."

"I am glad to hear it." His father folded his arms over his broad chest and leaned against the edge of the desk. "And how is Aurora? She looks happy."

"She is." Although she had faced more challenges on Gaia than he cared to remember.

"She has taken to her captain's role with grace."

"Would you expect anything less?"

His father shook his head. "Of course not. She was born to lead." His expression darkened. "I heard from Will."

His father was the only person Jonarel knew who called Admiral Schreiber by his first name. Aurora had not received any word from the Admiral since they had left Gaia. She was also under orders not to contact him until their mission was completed. The Admiral feared that his communications were being monitored, and he had not wanted to risk revealing Aurora's whereabouts.

The Admiral and Jonarel's father, however, had set up a system of coded communications years ago that allowed them to keep each other informed without the hazard of discovery. Even if someone intercepted one of their messages, it would look like a personal message between old friends, nothing of importance.

"The decoy ship disappeared."

A couple of Kraed swear words sprang to mind, but Jonarel kept them in out of respect for his father. This was not good news for Aurora. Or the Lumians. "Does the Admiral have any idea what happened to it?"

"Unfortunately, no. The ship abruptly shut down all communications. The Elders sent the *Fasnaborel* to investigate, but they were unable to locate any trace of the ship. Someone set a trap to capture it."

"Setarips?"

His father shook his head. "Doubtful. This was a precision strike with no evidence left behind. Setarips could not pull that off. Not without help."

"Which was also true for the attacks on Gaia." Aurora's supposition that someone else was involved appeared to be correct. "Does the Admiral know who is behind the attacks?"

"Not yet. And that concerns me."

It concerned Jonarel, too. The Kraed had been the acknowledged power in the galaxy for their entire interstellar history. Even the warring Setarips gave them a wide berth. But this new challenger could pose a legitimate threat. "Does the Admiral have a plan?"

"For now, getting the Lumians settled somewhere he and the rest of the Council will not find them." His father's gaze grew speculative. "How is Aurora handling the realization of her true heritage?"

"With grace, as you would expect. She is eager to help the Lumians. And excited about the new settlement."

"So she does not yet understand her importance?"

Jonarel stiffened. His father loved Aurora, but sometimes he talked about her like she was a chess piece. It was an attitude that made Jonarel's claws itch. "She knows she is important to the Lumians. And they are devoted to her. Right now she is focused on helping them. She does not have time to contemplate what else is at stake."

"Good. The longer she remains unaware of the true circumstances, the easier it will be to achieve our goals."

Irritation gave way to a flame of anger. He ground his teeth together. "Do not talk about her as if she does not have feelings, father."

Genuine surprise showed on his father's face, and a trace of hurt. "I know she has feelings. I love her. And respect her." He frowned. "But you act as though something has changed. It has not. We have been on the same path since the day you confirmed her identity."

"I know. And I have regretted it ever since."

His father's expression clouded. "Regretted it?" He spread his arms wide. "How can you be angry about this? You want her. That has been clear since the beginning. One day you will pair bond with her and everything else will fall into place."

"And what if she does not want that same future?" He hated the words, but they had to be said. "What if she chooses something else?" Or some*one* else.

The hard look in his father's eyes was all the answer he needed. "This is bigger than her. Bigger than either of you. The Elders have decided. She must become a part of our clan. Jonarel. There are no other options."

"*No other options?*" The feral side that lived just under the surface of his skin roared at the implied threat to the woman he loved. "She is not some pawn in your chess game!"

He expected his father to roar right back. He didn't. "You are correct."

For one moment, hope flared.

But his father's expression did not change. "She is not a pawn. She never was." His father crossed the room and picked something up off the table.

When Jonarel saw what his father held in his hand, his body went cold.

"She is the queen, Jonarel. The most powerful piece in the game. And we cannot win without her."

Twelve

Justin Byrnes slapped a hand over his mouth to hide his smile. He certainly didn't want the teens to think he was laughing at them. But the fall Sparw had just taken off the stealth pod as he'd tried to make a banking turn had rolled the teenager like a tumbleweed. Not that it mattered. He'd popped right back up.

Justin trotted over to where the boy stood.

Dirt covered Sparw from the top of his coffee-colored hair to the toes of his boots, but his brown eyes sparkled as he brushed himself off. "Not right." He flashed a smile.

Justin grinned back. Nice to know the kid wasn't beating himself up about the fall. "Not exactly. But you're getting there." They walked to where the pod had stopped. "Give it another try."

The boy nodded and straddled the pod once more, tucking his feet into the toeholds on either side. Raaveen and Paaw watched from their own pods, their arms draped over the handgrips. They'd both completed the maneuver successfully, and they called out words of encouragement as Sparw accelerated the pod and began the curving arc that would bring him back in their direction.

This time he maintained control of the pod, with only a few wobbles as he came out of the turn and raced back to the waiting group.

"Great job!" Justin gave the kid a high-five, a gesture he'd taught them while they'd been working together digging the irrigation for the greenhouse. He'd made a point of encouraging a sense of fun and playfulness, and it was paying off. Laughter was now a regular occurrence at the campsite, usually from the children, although even some of the adults had surprised him with a chuckle or two.

When he'd first met them on Gaia, smiles were unheard of, let alone laughter. In fact, many of the adults had barely spoken. But the longer they remained on Burrow, the more everyone looked and acted like a gregarious family.

Getting past the language barrier had been huge. He was continuing to refine the translation protocols he'd written, working in the nuances of their language as best he could, but his team could now communicate freely with everyone. Raaveen, Paaw and Sparw had put a lot of effort into learning Galish, which meant he didn't even need his translator most of the time.

Of course, it helped that he was learning their language, too. It had a very lyrical quality that was pleasing to the ear, with long vowel sounds and a softness to the way the words were spoken that made everything they said sound like an endearment or lullaby. Getting the accent right was his biggest challenge, but he was working on it.

He'd also learned the name of their race. Suulh. The root was related to their word for peace, which spoke volumes for how they had developed as a species. So very different from humans, and yet physically almost identical. He still liked the term Lumians, because they were a race of bright spirits, but he was making the switch to calling them Suulh.

The teens gazed at him expectantly, waiting for their next instructions.

"You're getting the knack of guiding the pods

individually. Now I'd like to see if you can do it as a team."
He gestured to Raaveen. "I want you to fly point." He
created a triangle with his index fingers and thumbs. "With
Paaw and Sparw on either side but slightly behind you." He
pointed to a spot about fifty meters away where several
large boulders formed a natural wall. "Head in that direction.
Make the same arc that you just did, but do it while holding
formation."

The teens gazed at each other for a moment in
silent communication. He could almost hear their thoughts.

"Don't worry about being perfect. In fact, this first
time, the important thing is to not run into each other.
Raaveen, you're in charge of setting the pace and telling the
others when to begin the turn. Go easy, and don't rush it."

Raaveen's dark eyes revealed her excitement. It was
a welcome change from the sadness that had haunted her
for so long.

The trio set off on the pods. As they began their
approach, he could tell they weren't going to make it at the
angle they'd chosen. They figured that out as they started
the turn and nearly collided. He waited to see what they'd
do.

Raaveen led them back about halfway then turned
them to try again. This time the angle was perfect, and they
made the turn successfully. Paaw swung a little wide and
Sparw lagged behind, but it was an impressive achievement
for beginners.

He'd expected them to return to his end of the
small gully and stop, but they didn't. Instead, Raaveen began
leading them into another turn, and then another, weaving up
and down the channel in ovals and figure eights that grew
increasingly tighter and more focused. They executed a final
hairpin turn and then barreled down the open space to

where he stood. When they stopped in front of him, all three wore matching smiles of triumph.

"We did well!" Paaw shared a high-five with Raaveen.

He chuckled. Their enthusiasm was infectious. "Yeah. You caught on quickly." He folded his arms loosely over his chest. "We'll call it for today, but tomorrow we'll take the pods out on open ground. You're ready for a new challenge."

"Thank you. Good teacher." Raaveen nodded at him.

He smiled. That was something else about the Suulh. They were the most generous beings he'd ever encountered. They always showed gratitude and offered assistance. Which made the captivity and abuse they'd suffered from the Setarips that much harder to take.

Setarips were high on his personal hit list anyway, since they had no problem inflicting death and destruction on anyone they encountered if it served their purposes. However, they spent far too much effort trying to exterminate each other in their civil war to have masterminded the heinous plan that had led to the Suulh's presence on Gaia.

Which meant someone else was out there pulling the strings. He sincerely hoped that Admiral Schreiber's next assignment for the Elite Unit would be to uncover the identity of the mystery guest at the party and haul them to the Galactic Council so that justice could be served

.

Thirteen

Aurora slept like the dead. When the gentle alarm roused her, it took her a moment to get her bearings. Her cozy cabin looked the same, but the light was all wrong.

Then it hit her. This was the first time she'd seen sunlight flowing through the starports, rather than distant starlight. It cast a dappled glow over everything it touched, creating strange shadows that made familiar objects look slightly surreal. When they'd landed yesterday she hadn't paid attention to how different the ship's interior looked when lit from the outside.

Sliding to the edge of her sleeping nook, she placed her feet on the wood floor and stretched. She was the only crewmember other than Jonarel who chose to keep her bed platform in the traditional Kraed formation, with only one edge open to the room. Maybe it was from all the years of building tents and forts with Mya when they were kids, but she had always been drawn to cubbyholes. Sleeping inside what looked like an owl's nest in a tree suited her perfectly.

She padded over to the starport and peered out. Below her, the walkway connected to the main deck. Even though the thick foliage and large branches that surrounded the ship hid much of the area from view, she could still see the Clarek clan hard at work loading supplies. A glance at her comband chronometer told her she'd need to get moving if she didn't want to be late meeting Jonarel for her glider lesson.

After a quick breakfast and an even quicker shower

she pulled on the long-sleeved tunic and calf-length leggings Daymar had given her the night before. She'd graciously provided similar outfits for the entire crew.

The fabric was Kraed design, providing temperature regulation and absorption of excess moisture, which was a distinct advantage in the humid environment. Daymar had also given her a pair of fabric Kraed boots, which fit snugly to the foot, then wrapped and tied around the leg to just above the knee.

She wove her hair into her customary braid and then stepped out into the corridor. Kire's cabin was next to hers, and she paused at the open door on her way to the lift. He was seated on the floor, working on the laces of his boots.

"Need any help with that?" She'd worn them before during her previous visit to Drakar, so she'd already learned how to work the elaborate set of pulls and knots that held them in place.

He gave her a wry grin. "Oh, I don't know. I think in another couple of hours I'll have it done."

She laughed, stepping into the room and kneeling in front of him. "Here, let me."

He turned the laces over to her. She backtracked to the point where he'd gone wrong, then worked her way up slowly so he could see what she was doing. "Are you all set to visit the library?"

"Yep. Siginal introduced me to the custodian last night, so I'll be heading over there as soon as you finish helping me look respectable."

"That could take a while," she teased. She tied the last few knots then pushed back to her feet. "There. Now you're ready for a day of study."

He stood and shifted his weight back and forth,

testing out the new footwear. "Not bad. In fact, these might be the most comfortable shoes I've ever worn."

"They look good on you." The dark browns and greens of the boots blended with the matching leggings and tunic he wore, which suited his black hair and hazel eyes.

"You too."

"Thanks. But I'm never going to blend in with my surroundings like you will." She lifted her blond braid. "Maybe I should ask Jonarel for a cap to cover my hair while I'm out there."

Kire shook his head. "Don't bother. You and Jon will be fine. I saw how you handled that rock monster. Drakar's big, bad predators should be a piece of cake."

She stuck her tongue out at him and he chuckled.

They walked to the lift and descended to the main deck. Kire headed off to the library while she stepped inside the med bay where Mya and Celia were filling a couple of packs. "Are you two set for your tour?"

Mya nodded. "Our guides are meeting us here. They wanted to see the greenhouse first and take a look at some of the plants Celia and I brought from the new homeworld. How about you?"

"I'm meeting Jonarel at the main lodge in a few minutes. What about Kelly? Is she up?"

Celia laughed. "She was out the door before dawn. I swear, that girl lives, eats and breathes ships. Give her an opportunity to tour a few Kraed vessels and she's off like a shot."

Aurora smiled. Bronwyn Kelly was definitely in the right place, and the right occupation. She was never going to have a better chance to study ship design and interstellar navigation. The Kraed had written the book on both.

"Then I'll see you at the send-off celebration

tonight." Aurora turned to leave.

"Oh yeah, about that." Celia twisted her thick hair on top of her head and secured it with a clip that probably doubled as a weapon. "What exactly is this all about? Is it a party or a formal gathering?"

"More like a party. The clan has a tradition of getting together before any ship departs, no matter how long or short the journey may be. Since we'll be leaving tomorrow, and taking one of the Clarek ships along with us, the clan will gather tonight to give blessings for a safe return."

"That's a lovely tradition." Mya tucked a few more items in her pack.

"I think so, too." Aurora checked her comband. She was officially late. "Ack. I've gotta go. Have fun!" she called out as she headed for the door.

When she reached the walkway she picked up the pace, pausing just long enough to exchange greetings with the members of the Clarek clan she encountered along the way.

Despite the shade provided by the tree canopy, the heat and humidity were already building. Thank goodness for the clothing Daymar had provided. She had no idea what the fabric was made of, but it felt like she was wearing a full-body cooling system.

She spotted Jonarel standing by the lodge entrance, talking to Star. His outfit was similar to hers, but it looked entirely different on him. His rich skin tones and hair matched the fabric perfectly, and the fit showed off the contours of his upper body and defined his lean hips and muscular legs. Artists would fall over themselves to portray Jonarel in portrait or sculpture.

His surroundings emphasized the raw physicality of

his being. Among the crew, he stood out because of the way he looked. Here, he stood out because of his commanding presence. He drew attention, just as Signal did. And he could have easily chosen a life here on Drakar, following in his father's footsteps. Instead, he'd designed and built the *Starhawke* for her, and joined her crew. She still wasn't clear on why exactly he'd made that decision, but she was grateful. His selflessness and willingness to leave his clan to travel the galaxy with her still humbled her.

He turned toward her as Star's image faded away. The look in his golden eyes almost stopped her in her tracks. If he'd been intense yesterday, that was a pale shadow to the way he was gazing at her now. Almost like she was prey. Her stomach clenched as warning bells went off in her head. She might have made a mistake asking for this lesson.

Too late now. But she could change the dynamic. She halted in front of him and snapped off a perfect Academy salute. "Cadet Hawke reporting for training, sir."

Her attempt to lighten the mood worked. The intensity in his gaze dimmed. "Are you ready?"

"Lead the way."

He set off across the walkway and she followed, having to hustle to keep up with his long strides. It was easy to forget how quickly he could cover ground. On the *Starhawke*, everything was in easy reach.

"We will start in the practice arena," he said. "That way you can focus on the glider rather than your surroundings. If you get comfortable, we can head out into the forest."

"Stellar."

They continued down a narrow path that led away from the main compound and out toward the fringes of the community. The trees thinned, with a large opening appearing up ahead. The walkway continued out to the center of the open area. Stairs led down into a large sand pit surrounded by a three-meter-high thicket of what looked like thorny briar that had been sanded on the inside, creating a bowl effect, like a small stadium without any seats. "What's that?" She indicated the living barbed wire.

"*Greglar*. The thorns are poisonous, so it's an effective deterrent for predators."

Aurora halted on the walkway. "Deterrent? Do you mean some of your predators might pay us a visit while we're practicing?" Her shielding ability would protect her, but she'd planned to focus on the lesson. If they were likely to be attacked, she wanted to know.

Jonarel turned. "No. They have learned not to approach this area." He rested his hands on her shoulders and gazed into her eyes. "All you need to focus on is me."

There was that warning bell again. She pulled back slightly and he released her, continuing along the walkway. As she followed him down the stairway to the sand, the feeling of unreality grew, like she'd stepped out of time into an alternate universe. The way Jonarel kept gazing at her reinforced that concept.

She glanced around, surprised to find the place deserted. "Isn't anyone else practicing today?"

He shook his head. "Not at the moment. My father thought you might appreciate some time alone."

The warning bells turned into klaxons. She'd been alone with Jonarel thousands of times in the long years of their friendship, including an entire month that they'd spent working side by side to get the *Starhawke* ready for her first mission. And she'd never been the least bit uncomfortable. Today, everything was different. And it was making her jumpy as a frog.

Jonarel lifted a glider off one of the racks at the center of the circular space and set it on the ground between them.

It was a little wider and shorter than the ones they had on the *Starhawke*, and resembled a surfboard that had been stretched lengthwise. "Is this a different model than our gliders?"

"This is a training glider." He touched a panel and two sets of controls lifted out of the narrow base, one at the front of the device and a second set positioned about half a meter behind. "It will allow you to take the lead position but gives me dual controls from the center." He motioned for her to step up in front. "I will direct our motion so there is no risk of crashing."

"What about falling off?" she asked as she grasped the controls. That had been her major concern on Gaia, since balancing on moving objects was not her forte. She'd never tested whether her shield could protect her from injury following a vertical freefall, and she really didn't want to learn the answer today.

Jonarel's arms came around her from behind and she sucked in a breath. Then she realized he was reaching for the slim harness that was attached to the controls in front of her. *Overreacting much, Aurora?*

He slipped the harness around her torso and secured it. "You will not fall." His deep voice rumbled next to her ear. "I am right here."

She swallowed. This wasn't how she'd pictured the lesson going.

"Do you remember how to start it?" he asked.

She nodded, touching the ignition point with her thumb. Jonarel moved away from her as the lightweight craft lifted off the ground. She swayed as the glider shifted under her feet, but the harness helped her stay in position.

"Now what?" She glanced over her shoulder. Bad move. Her body followed the movement and she tilted to the left, pressing into the harness. She whipped her head back around and gripped the controls to regain her balance. "Sorry."

Jonarel cleared his throat before replying. "It is probably best if you do not look at me right now." He sounded amused.

Too bad she wasn't. His behavior had her wound up like a top. It had been a while since she'd been a beginner at something, and her tendency toward perfectionism was rearing its head, especially with Jonarel as her teacher. Tension wasn't going to help her balance or coordination, and she'd need both if she wanted to develop any level of competence. But she wasn't sure how to get her mind and body to relax.

Too bad Cade wasn't around. He had a knack for getting her to let go and laugh at herself. She could easily picture him standing in front of the glider, a taunting smile on his face as he teased her mercilessly until she loosened up and stopped taking everything so seriously. Learning from Cade would be a lot of fun. And he'd be a natural with a glider. After all, she'd seen first hand how well he handled his jetbike when he'd rescued her on Gaia.

"Aurora?" Jonarel's voice startled her out of her daydream.

Oh boy. Definitely not the time for those thoughts. "Sorry. Just trying to get focused." What the hell was wrong with her? Maybe the humidity really was going to her head. She took a slow breath, held it to the count of four, and released it, willing the tension and anxiety to flow out with the air. It didn't. Oh well. She'd work with what she had. She kept her gaze forward this time. "What's the plan?"

"To start, we will complete a few circuits around the interior. Stay as steady as possible. The circle will force you to balance while turning."

Unless she slid right off. She glanced at the harness. Would she be dangling from it in a moment? "Here goes." She released the stabilizers and the device crept forward. So far so good. But when she increased the speed beyond the sedate pace she'd experienced the last time she was on a glider, the muscles in her abdomen and shoulders tensed. She braced against the feeling of motion and unease, which only made everything worse. Her hands clutched the controls in a death grip and an involuntary moan escaped her lips.

The glider slowed immediately as Jonarel took over. "Aurora, are you okay?"

Good thing he couldn't see her face. "I'm fine. The motion just feels...weird."

"Your body tensed."

"I realize that."

He was silent for a moment. "How can I help?"

You can't. You're part of the problem. But she certainly wasn't going to tell him that. "I don't know."

More silence. Then the stabilizers engaged, bringing them to a halt. He appeared at her side a moment later. "Wait here."

Fourteen

Jonarel mentally berated himself as he approached the glider racks. His father's words from the previous night still echoed in his ears, influencing his thoughts and actions, and draining all the joy out of what should have been a fun experience with Aurora. Instead, she was so tense she could barely move.

Tehar appeared, her expression concerned. "What do you need?"

He briefly outlined his plan. He noticed the skepticism in her eyes, but she did not argue, just kept glancing at Aurora with a frown.

"As you wish," she replied before disappearing. A few moments later, one of the panels in front of him opened, revealing a small canteen.

He carried it back to the glider. "Drink this." He held the canteen out to Aurora.

She took it tentatively, inhaling as she brought it toward her nose. When she caught the scent of the tenrebac, she gave him a hard look. "Care to explain why you're offering me alcohol?"

He rested his hands on his hips and held her gaze. "Because you need to be relaxed if we are going to leave this arena. That is what you want, correct? To go explore in the forest?"

Her expression was wary. "Yes."

"Then unless you have a better idea, I recommend you drink that. It will allow you to stop fighting the motion of the glider."

She obviously did not like the idea, but there was no way he would allow her to operate a glider when she was tight as a bow. That would put them both in danger.

She brought the canteen to her lips and sipped. The alcohol took effect within moments. Her shoulders slowly relaxed and her posture became more fluid. The look in her eyes also indicated her brain had stopped trying to force a million conflicting commands through.

He plucked the canteen from her fingers. "That should be enough."

She grinned, another sign she was a little tipsy. "Let's do this."

Now he was the one feeling tense. He might have given her a bit too much. But she looked a lot happier to be on the glider. And with him. That was something.

He stowed the canteen in a compartment in the glider's base, then rejoined her. This time when she brought them up to speed, she remained relaxed. In fact, she looked like she was having fun.

By their fourth lap, she was moving with the glider, using it like an extension of her body rather than bracing against it. And he did not have to make adjustments to their course to keep them from crashing, either.

"I think I'm getting this," she called out.

"Much better," he agreed. "Ready for the next step?"

She slowed the glider but did not make the mistake of looking back at him. She was learning. "Which is?"

"Obstacles."

Thanks to her tenrebac-induced confidence, she responded with enthusiasm. "Sure!"

Tehar, who was keeping a close watch on the proceedings, activated the hidden compartments and the open space in front of them filled with sculpted tree trunks that lifted out of the sand, creating a mini forest.

Aurora engaged the stabilizers as she studied the terrain. "What exactly am I supposed to do?"

He rested his arms on the controls, a convenient excuse to get closer and breathe in her scent. "Circle the exterior first to get a feel for the layout, then begin weaving between a few of the trees as you go along. After you are comfortable with that, add a few more and perhaps change direction."

"So the goal is for me to be able to go wherever I want?"

"No."

"No?" That apparently surprised her, because she tipped her head up so she could see his face. "Why not?"

He struggled to focus on her question when she was so tantalizingly close. It would be easy to lean forward and brush her lips with his. He forced his gaze to meet hers, instead. "For one thing, it would take months to become that proficient." She looked adorably disappointed. It took all his willpower not to wrap his arms around her.

"Then what *is* the goal?" she asked.

That question touched a little too close to home, reminding him of his conversation with his father. He banished his father's voice from his head. "For you to become comfortable enough that we can take the glider into the forest. Out there, we will encounter obstacles, some of which will be moving. I will need to make quick adjustments, and if you resist, we will run into trouble."

She frowned, her gaze searching his like she was looking for hidden meaning in his words. He had not meant it that way, but his description was apt to their situation on many levels.

For the next hour they practiced weaving through the makeshift forest and changing direction. When he was convinced she had the basic feel, he switched the controls over so that he was directing their motion and she was following his lead. Then he pushed up the speed and took the glider in and out of the trees, which flashed by in a blur. The tenrebac was still doing its job, because Aurora's reaction indicated exhilaration rather than anxiety.

When they came to a halt, he tapped her lightly on the shoulder.

"What?" she asked.

"We have an audience."

She glanced up.

The walkway and stairs were now filled with members of his clan, mostly children and teens, as well as a few Nirunoc, who leaned on the railings, watching them.

"Do you mind if they join us?" he asked.

"Of course not."

He called out a greeting and the youngsters responded by pouring down the stairs or, in some cases, climbing down the support structure itself using their claws. They had the gliders off the racks and in position in a heartbeat, but no one moved. They simply waited with the anticipation of competitors at the starting line.

Jonarel leaned toward Aurora as he disengaged the stabilizers. "You ready?" he murmured.

"Absolutely."

Calling out a challenge, he kicked the glider into high gear. They shot forward, racing through the course with the kids chasing them like a swarm of bees.

Fifteen

Before leaving the safety of the practice arena, Aurora shared a light lunch with Jonarel and watched the children and teens racing around on the gliders.

The teens would be hitting their maturity soon, when they'd undergo the same painful transition Jonarel had endured shortly after she'd met him. He'd doubled his height in less than two years. Daymar had confided that it was the most vulnerable time in a Kraed's life, and she'd been thrilled Jonarel had gone through it while they were at the Academy on Earth rather than among the dangers of Drakar.

After they finished their meal, Jonarel lifted the training glider off the rack and she settled back into the front position. She was much more relaxed than she had been this morning. She took that as a good sign.

"I will handle the controls." Jonarel said as the glider lifted off the ground. "But you will need to focus on the motion and follow my lead."

"Okay."

Several of the kids waved as Jonarel navigated the glider toward the exterior fence. Aurora nodded in acknowledgment but kept her hands on the controls as the glider rose into the air. She'd never been this high on an open glider before, but thanks to the lingering effects of the tenrebac, her muscles weren't tying into knots.

As they cleared the outer fence, she glanced at the trees. The dappled sunlight danced through the swaying leaves, creating moving mosaics on the trunks and the brightly colored flowers. With only the thin plank of the glider beneath her feet, she had a panoramic view of her surroundings, including the waterways twenty meters below. It was exhilarating now that she was allowing herself to relax and enjoy it.

Jonarel set a leisurely pace along the exterior of the compound, no doubt because he wanted to give her time to adjust to their new surroundings. She turned her head slightly so she could see him out of the corner of her eye. "Do you use the gliders when you visit the other clans in the region?"

"No. We take shuttles, similar to the ones on the *Starhawke.*"

Of course they would. It was strange, but she kept forgetting how advanced their technology was. They'd created their world so perfectly to harmonize with the natural beauty around them, rather than putting their technology front and center, that her mind believed she really was in a rustic setting. Their method had a subtlety that enabled everything they needed to be hidden in plain sight.

"So tell me more about the predators we might see out here." She wanted to be prepared in case they had a face-to-face encounter.

"We have four in this region that pose a serious threat, but two of them are not a problem when traveling by glider. The velpar are raptor-like pack creatures that hunt the trebolks above the canopy, and the resheeks are slow-moving amphibians that resemble giant salamanders, but with a bite like a crocodile."

"Fun."

"Oh, they are. At least on the ground." He guided them closer to the compound's outer buildings as they made their way around the perimeter. "But we will need to watch out for the greewtaith and the relquirs."

"And what are they like?"

"The greewtaith look like thirty-meter aquatic snakes, with barbed fins along their backs and sides that they use to anchor themselves to the trees. And to their victims. If one grabs hold, nothing short of death will make it let go."

Aurora tightened her grip on the controls. "So don't get close. Got it."

"They rely on visual acuity to locate prey, so most of the time they float on the surface of the waterways where you can see them from above. However, if they use the barbs to twine around the root systems of the trees, they can lift out of the water, putting them on a level with the glider."

Aurora's heart rate kicked up a notch. "O-*kay*. How do you avoid that?"

"You listen for them. Their bulk prevents them from staying out of the water for more than a few seconds. When they lift up, they make a bellowing noise from the exertion."

"You *listen* for them? You mean they make this noise in the split second *before* they grab onto you?" She risked a glance over her shoulder. "I'm not a Kraed. I don't have your fabulous sense of hearing. Or your reaction speed."

He had the audacity to look amused. "Do not worry. I will be listening."

"Good to know." She faced forward again. "And the relquirs? What's their story?"

"They are the real danger." His tone indicated he wasn't kidding. "They look innocuous when they are resting against the trees. In fact, they can be mistaken for large chunks of bark when they are immobile. They have thin membranes that stretch from their upper limbs to their lower ones and a narrow torso, somewhat like enormous flying squirrels."

"Sounds interesting."

"Until you realize how deadly they are. Like a spider, they spin a thread that they attach to the tree before plummeting at incredible speeds to snatch their prey out of the air. They have a reach of almost three meters, and are very strong. They wrap their prey in the membranes like a cocoon and secrete a neurotoxin in their bite that immobilizes their victim. Then they climb up the thread to reach their nests in the lower branches to feed."

Aurora shivered despite the heat and humidity. "And how do we defend ourselves against that?"

"By staying alert. When they move, they are easy to see. Their underside is bright red and the membrane has an iridescent quality. As soon as they leave the tree, they stand out like a beacon."

"Uh-*huh*. I'm beginning to understand why Kraed have developed a sixth sense about danger."

"You are correct. But you and I would not be out here if I believed you were at risk."

Very true. He'd always made it clear that her safety and wellbeing were his primary concern. He'd made a pledge to that effect the day they'd met. Besides, the predators of this world probably had more to fear from her than she did from them. And wasn't that a sobering thought?

A flash of bright color in the trees off to their right caught her attention and she focused on it. Was she about to encounter her first relquir? But the shapes quickly resolved into a flock of winged creatures that somewhat resembled parrots, their brightly colored bodies creating a living rainbow against the backdrop of the trees.

"They are harmless," Jonarel said. "Would you like to take a closer look?"

"Absolutely."

The glider picked up speed and Jonarel maneuvered them so they were flying in perfect sync with the flock as it soared through the trees. The creatures didn't pay them any mind, even though they were close enough to touch.

"They're beautiful," she breathed on a sigh.

Jonarel's reply sounded a little husky. "Yes, they are."

The creatures changed direction but Jonarel didn't follow. Instead he headed toward a grove of trees that looked different than the ones near the compound. He slowed as they approached, the glider slipping up silently until they hovered next to one of the trunks.

She turned her head to ask him what they were looking for but he lifted a finger to his lips and pointed into the trees.

"Listen," he whispered.

Aurora strained to make out whatever she was supposed to be hearing. She heard the rustle of leaves and the burble of water below, but nothing that sounded like an animal. At least not...wait a minute. There. She finally caught a snippet of something in the distance. It sounded like someone drawing a bow over the strings of a cello. The deep resonant hum came again, playing over a few notes, up and down, before fading out.

She stared into the shadows, trying to spot any sign of movement. The hum began again, but this time it was coming from the other side of the tree closest to them. The notes were pitched higher than the first, more like a viola, and they continued for nearly a minute before fading away.

"What are they?" she whispered.

"Clestoks."

"Which are what?"

His golden eyes sparkled. "Furred herbivores that live off the leaves of this particular tree species. The music is how they communicate."

"What do they look like?"

"They resemble a cross between a sloth and a koala. But much bigger."

Aurora peering into the darkness. That was something she wanted to see. "Are any of them visible right now?"

"No. They are hidden under the cover of the leaves. They are more mobile at night."

"Is that to protect them from predators?"

"Not really. They have sensitive eyes, so they hate bright light. They can inflict a lot of damage with their claws, more than you might guess by looking at them. The predators tend to avoid them."

The low notes began again, some in the distance, some nearby as others joined the conversation. The voices melded and blended in perfect harmony, some fading while others picked up the melody and took it in a new direction. It was like listening to an impromptu orchestra rehearsal, especially when a high-pitched voice joined in, sounding for all the world like a squeaky fiddle.

"What's that?"

"The young. That is how they ask for food."

Aurora grinned. "And with a voice like that, I'll bet the parents are quick to feed them."

"No doubt."

They listened in companionable silence for several minutes, the music of the voices wrapping Aurora in a spell of enchantment. But the longer she held her position, the more aware she became of Jonarel's nearness. A quick glance confirmed he was watching her rather than the creatures in the grove.

"So, what else do you have to show me?" she asked, pulling back.

He studied her for a moment. "Would you like to see some of the aquatic creatures?"

"Is that safe?"

"You are always safe with me."

And if that comment wasn't loaded with double meanings, she'd eat her boots.

"Then let's go." She was determined to ignore whatever implication he was making.

They set off again, this time skimming closer to the water. "Look for flashes of silver," he called out as the wind rushed past them.

"What am I going to see?"

"Kritoks. They are shaped somewhat like tiny dolphins, and they travel in schools like fish. Their skin has a metallic sheen to it."

Aurora adjusted her grip on the controls to maintain her balance as she leaned forward and gazed into the clear water ahead of them.

"To your right." Jonarel banked the glider and followed a slightly different course.

She looked in the direction he'd indicated and sucked in a breath. He'd said they traveled in schools, but she hadn't anticipated that the waterway would look like it was alive. Thousands of small creatures streaked through the water, creating a ribbon that bent and flowed around the trees like molten silver. But that wasn't all. She couldn't tell whether they were doing it for fun, or whether it was an efficient way to move ahead in the pack, but at any given moment a dozen or more would leap out of the water and plunge back into the swiftly moving tide.

"Do they swim this fast to avoid the greewtaith?"

"No. They are one of the few creatures that can kill a greewtaith. They are too small and fast for the greewtaith to catch, and the bony protrusions on their heads are effective battering rams. When they are hunting, they slam into the greewtaith en masse, like being pummeled by a thousand hammers. They can kill one in less than a minute, and feed the entire pod off the one body."

She grimaced. "And I was going to call them cute."

"They are cute." Jonarel slowed the glider and the river of silver moved off into the distance. "And non-aggressive except when they are feeding. One pod stays fairly close to the compound, and some of the kritoks have become quite tame. We encourage it, because they keep the greewtaith away from the area."

And that was the strange dichotomy that was Drakar. It was home to the most advanced technological civilization in the known galaxy, yet the Kraed chose to live alongside the dangers of their world rather than trying to sanitize and control them. They could have cleared the trees and redirected the rivers so that they could insulate themselves, or killed off all the large predators, but instead they lived in small, integrated communities in the relative safety of the trees. And by working with their environment instead of against it, they'd maintained a connection with everything around them. It was a lesson well worth understanding.

As they continued to wind their way through the forest, she tried to imagine what it would be like to grow up on Drakar, with all its inherent beauty and danger. She had a hard time visualizing it. "Your way of life is so different from how most people live on Earth."

"Yes. But not that different from the way the Lumians live."

That gave her pause. She'd never really compared the Lumians and Kraed, but now that he mentioned it, she could see a lot of similarities. They were both community focused, and also nature based. They were polar opposites when it came to skill with technology, but that wasn't necessarily genetic. Come to think of it, Mya and her parents were all very adept with technology. The Lumians might be too, if they had the opportunity to learn. All kinds of talents might reveal themselves over time.

Her musings were interrupted by an abrupt shift under her feet.

"On the left!" Jonarel called out.

As she registered the command and responded by activating her energy shield, a low wail filled the air like the beginnings of a siren, followed by the patter of falling water as an enormous triangle-shaped head rose into view.

The greewtaith's skin was grayish-blue, but the spines on three sides of its body that were latched onto the bark of the nearby trees were dark brown and hooked like cactus thorns. The creature's forehead had a crest that flared upward as it opened its jaws, revealing thousands of jagged teeth.

However, it clearly wasn't going after them. They were at least thirty meters away from the aquatic nightmare and viewing it in profile. A flash of bright red and iridescence appeared just before the greewtaith's mouth snapped shut on its victim. The creature shrieked in pain, its head sticking out from the row of teeth.

"A relquir." The air punched in and out of her lungs. "It just caught a relquir."

The greewtaith's torso plummeted, the struggling relquir clasped firmly in its jaws. When it hit the water, the resulting splash sounded like cannon fire. The rest of the creature's long body followed as the barbs disengaged from the tree trunk and the greewtaith slid below the surface of the water.

Aurora stared at where the two creatures had disappeared. Her stomach churned. Intellectually she understood that predators hunted to survive, but she wasn't used to watching it first hand. And given a choice, she wouldn't have seen it this time, either.

Keeping a firm grip on the controls, she looked over her shoulder. "Did you know that was going to happen?"

Jonarel shrugged. "The relquirs like to hunt in this area and there was a good chance you would have a chance to see them dive. But I had not counted on the greewtaith waiting for them." His expression changed to one of concern as he tuned into her reaction. "Are you okay?"

Nope. Not even remotely. But that's not what came out of her mouth. "I'm fine."

The look in his eyes told her he didn't believe her. Not one bit. "Hang on."

He set the glider in motion and they flew in silence for a couple minutes, slowing as they approached a tree with a wide branch that jutted out parallel to the water far below. He maneuvered the glider next to it and engaged the stabilizers. Before she could react, he unsnapped her harness and slipped one muscular arm around her waist, pulling her with him so that they were standing face to face on the meter-wide branch.

She stumbled, but his arms locked around her torso, keeping her steady. He, on the other hand, was solid as a rock, no doubt because he was using the claws in his feet to grip the bark. She latched onto his biceps for stability, his muscles flexing beneath her fingers.

His expression was deadly serious. "Do not lie to me, Aurora." A deep groove appeared between his brows as he frowned. "You are not fine. And you know it."

She swallowed as her insides flip-flopped. He'd never really called her on her tendency to evade before, but then again, ever since they'd arrived on this planet, his attitude toward her had shifted. Apparently he was leaving subtle behind and going straight to direct. "You're right. Seeing that really upset me." She blew out a breath. "Saying I'm fine when I'm not is a very old habit. I've spent my entire life hiding the truth." And she wasn't just talking about her feelings.

She could sense the sadness that enveloped him. His grip tightened. "But why do you feel a need to hide from me?"

He was pushing her to be honest. Well, that was a two-way street. And he wasn't going to like her answer. "Maybe because I'm not the only one who's hiding something."

Direct hit. He flinched and his gaze shifted to a point just past her shoulder.

Obviously her instincts were right. He wasn't being completely honest with her, either. Ever since the day he'd given her the *Starhawke*, she'd questioned his motivations. And his change in behavior since they'd landed seemed to underscore the fact that there was a lot more to the story than he'd led her to believe. He was hiding something. His internal conflict was as tangible to her as his warm skin.

Which meant it was finally time to ask the question she'd been dancing around for months.

"What's the real reason you gave me the *Starhawke?*"

His gaze snapped to hers, his eyes widening. He clearly hadn't expected that question. And he was working just as hard as she was to conceal his emotions. She could feel it.

"You know why."

No way was she letting him off that easily. The time for evasion was over. For both of them. She needed an answer. "No, I don't. Not really." If he was going to make her bare her soul, he was going to bare his, too. "Jonarel, I have to know. What exactly do you want from me?"

A tornado of sensation swirled around her as his emotions broke free, but rather than giving her insight, it was a tangled jumble she couldn't decipher, full of chaos and contradictory information. She frowned, trying to get a fix on something...anything...that would provide her with a starting point. And then he gave her one.

Releasing his hold on her waist with his left arm, he sank his fingers into the braid at the back of her neck, pulled her flush against his body, and kissed her.

Whatever she'd been expecting, it sure as hell hadn't been that! In all the years they'd been friends, she'd been in countless situations where she'd sensed Jonarel's thoughts and emotions with regards to her went beyond friendship. But he'd never made the slightest move. Until now.

His lips settled over hers with assurance, but without force. In fact, she sensed that the slightest indication of reluctance from her would end the kiss. For a millisecond she considered doing just that. But curiosity got the better of her. She'd wanted an answer, and he was definitely giving her one.

Relaxing the tension that had gathered in her shoulders when he'd startled her, she shifted her arms so that she could wind her hands behind his neck, the silky strands of his thick hair brushing against her fingers. He pulled her in tighter and changed the angle to deepen the kiss. She let him, opening her mouth when he brushed her lips with his tongue.

But despite the pleasurable sensations his touch created, and the sensual nature of the embrace, she couldn't turn off her analytical side and enjoy the moment. Instead, she observed the interaction from an emotional distance, like she was having an out-of-body experience. Which made it impossible to tune into how she felt.

She loved Jonarel. That was never in any doubt. And she knew he loved her with equal devotion. Hell, he'd used his succession money to create a ship and then he'd given it to her without asking for anything in return. It was hard to imagine a clearer declaration of unconditional love than that. Building a future with him made perfect sense.

However, something kept tripping her internal alarms. She had no idea why, but until she figured it out, she couldn't allow things to go any further. She pulled back, ending the kiss.

He lifted his head, and they stared at each other as the emotional whirlwind faded away. He kept his arms around her in a loose grip but allowed her to put some distance between their bodies.

"We should go."

The look in his eyes was impossible to read. Then again, he probably wouldn't be able to make any sense of the look in hers, either. He'd forced her hand, and then she'd forced his. She'd hoped for clarity. Instead, she'd ended up more muddled than before.

"Very well."

He helped her onto the glider and secured the harness, then stepped up behind her. They set off, moving slowly through the trees, the shadows growing thicker as the sun continued its trek toward the horizon. Her feel for the glider had definitely improved, and she was able to anticipate the shifts he made as they wove their way toward the Clarek compound. Her feel for Jonarel, however, was blown to pieces.

What now? The question of Jonarel's ultimate intentions was answered, but regardless of whether she wanted the same thing or not, it still presented more problems than solutions. Had he created the *Starhawke* with the idea that they would try to raise a family together while exploring the galaxy? She wasn't even certain whether genetically that was an option. To her knowledge, no Kraed had ever taken a non-Kraed as a mate, so children might be impossible.

The more she pondered the interchange and the kiss, the more convinced she became that revealing the depth of his feelings was only one of many secrets he was holding. That meant she needed to be careful about making assumptions until she had more pieces of the puzzle in place.

By the time they returned to the practice arena, she'd worked herself into a mental tangle that left her on edge. She unsnapped the harness and stepped down before he had a chance to help her. It wasn't a good idea to have him touch her right now.

"Thank you for the lesson," she said as he stowed the glider on the rack. "And the tour. It was lovely."

He nodded, his eyes devoid of emotion. "You are welcome."

They stood facing each other for several long moments, the awkward silence becoming more oppressive with each breath. Her brain finally latched onto a neutral topic. "Celia and your father were scheduled to spar this afternoon. We might still be able to watch if we hurry."

She turned toward the stairway, but paused when he didn't move to join her. Instead, he stood like a statue carved in stone. "Are you coming?"

He shook his head. "I will see you tonight."

She licked her suddenly dry lips. This wasn't how she wanted to leave things with him. "Oh. Okay." She needed to say something, do something, before they slid into the chasm that was opening between them. But she had no idea what. "Thanks again." That was the best she could come up with. The words sounded as weak and pathetic to her as they must have to him.

And for the first time since they'd met, she felt relief as she walked away.

Sixteen

Aurora was avoiding him.

Jonarel tracked Aurora and Mya's movements as they circulated through the throng in the clan lodge. Aurora looked stunning in a blue dress with thin shoulder straps that made her pale skin and golden hair glow like moonlight. Mya wore a dress in a similar color but with dark accents that matched her hair. Both garments had been gifts from his mother, who had provided attire for the entire crew for the evening's event.

Aurora and Mya had greeted him when they had first arrived, but Aurora had quickly excused herself to go thank his mother for the dress, dragging Mya with her. Mya's behavior indicated Aurora had not told her about the incident in the forest, but the looks Mya had given him throughout the evening showed that she was aware of the unusual tension.

When the music had started after the meal and dancers had filled the open floor, Aurora had kept herself on the opposite side of the room whenever he moved toward her. The rest of the crew, however, appeared to be enjoying the festivities. Cardiff was engaged in a lively discussion with his father, who bore a few bruises on his face from their sparring match earlier in the day. To the shock of his clan but not the *Starhawke* crew, his father had lost.

Kire had talked Kelly into joining him on the dance floor, where they were being given a quick lesson by the other dancers. The normally placid navigator was grinning as much as Kire as they stumbled through the intricate steps. Apparently spending the day touring the clan's ships had unlocked a part of Kelly's personality that she normally kept tucked away.

Tehar appeared at his side. "Aurora has returned to the ship. She told me she was fine, but her behavior indicates otherwise. Is there a problem?"

How to answer that question? Tehar had admitted to him on numerous occasions that she found Aurora's behavior confusing. Well, so did he. And that left them both in a quandary.

She rested her ghostly hand on his arm. "Jonarel? What is bothering you?"

Her touch held no more substance than light, but it soothed him nonetheless. "I made a mistake this afternoon. And I upset her."

"Can you apologize?"

"An apology would not help."

Tehar frowned. "Are you certain?"

"Yes."

"Then what will you do?"

He sighed. "Give her time."

"And if the problem remains?" The look she gave him reminded him of his mother.

"Then perhaps I will apologize."

"Excellent idea." She placed her palm against his cheek in the Nirunoc equivalent of a hug.

As her image dissolved, he spotted Mya making her way toward him. He met her halfway.

"Are you going to join the dancing?" she asked as the musicians switched to a slower melody.

"It does not hold much interest for me." Especially now that Aurora had left. But Mya might enjoy it. "Are you looking for a partner? I am happy to teach you the steps if you would like."

Mya made a face. "Trust me, no one wants to see me dance. It's not pretty." She fanned herself with her open palm. "But I could use some fresh air. Care to join me?" She indicated the archway to their left.

"Of course." Her suggestion was obviously a ruse, since the lodge was temperature controlled and the outside air was not, but it was a welcome distraction. Talking to Mya might provide him with valuable insight regarding the situation with Aurora.

They strolled under the gently swaying branches of the trees, the breeze ruffling Mya's hair and carrying her familiar rose scent his way. He breathed it in, allowing her nearness to calm his agitation.

He led the way to one of his favorite spots in the compound, a covered platform overlooking the waterways below. The light from the lodge cast a warm glow on the alcove while still giving them the privacy of the shadows. He had spent many happy hours here as a child, studying every science manual he could get his hands on and dreaming of building the most amazing starship ever created.

Of course, at the time, he had not known he would be giving that ship to someone else. But he did not regret his decision. The ship was made for Aurora. In every way that mattered, it was hers and hers alone.

Mya sat on one of the carved benches and he settled next to her. She folded her hands in her lap. "So tell me what happened with Aurora."

Leave it to Mya to get right to the point. It was a quality he cherished. "I kissed her."

Mya drew in a sharp breath. "*What?*"

"I kissed her," he repeated.

Mya blinked once...twice...three times as she stared at him. Then she snapped her mouth shut and swallowed. "I see. And how did Aurora react?"

That was a harder question. "I am not certain." He believed that Aurora was attracted to him. She had looked at him with open appreciation on numerous occasions since their Academy days, though never with the heat of passion. And that was the problem. The deep love and affection of a friend was one thing. He wanted her to desire him as a lover.

Mya frowned. "What do you mean you're not certain? Did she kiss you back?"

"Yes."

When he failed to elaborate, Mya made a rolling motion with her hand. "And?"

And...Aurora's response had confused him. At first, he had startled her, but that had passed and she had relaxed into his arms and responded to his touch. At least, for a little while. Then her emotional wall had gone up. "She seemed to enjoy it."

Mya's frown deepened. "Really?"

A growl rumbled up from his chest. "Yes, really." He glared at her and she held her hands up, palms out.

"Sorry. That came out wrong. I know most women would be thrilled to be kissed by you."

That was good to hear. His battered ego needed a little reassurance right now.

"But if that's true, I don't understand why she's so upset."

He tilted his head back and gazed at the canopy. "I am not certain, either. But right before I kissed her, she asked me what I wanted from her." When Mya did not respond, he glanced at her. She looked like she was biting her tongue to keep from saying what was on her mind. "I know what you are thinking."

"I doubt it."

"I never should have kissed her in the first place."

Mya's dark brows lifted slightly. "Why not?"

"Because if we are to be together, she needs to be the one to initiate it."

"Why?"

Because forcing her into a choice she does not want will destroy us both. But he could not tell Mya that. Or Aurora. Admitting it to himself was difficult enough. The path that was laid before him was treacherous, and he hated where it was leading.

"Jonarel?"

She was still waiting for an answer. As he gazed into her warm brown eyes, his mind flipped back to a discussion they had had while they were still at the Academy. Aurora had just started dating Cade Ellis, and her infatuation with the man had made Jonarel's life a living hell.

He had been seriously considering stating his intentions as he had today in order to get her attention, and he had broached the idea to Mya. She had listened with patience and understanding while he had catalogued all the reasons Ellis did not deserve Aurora. Then she had gently reminded him that it was Aurora's choice to make, not his.

But the reality was not nearly that simple. It never had been. His father had made that clear. "I want her to choose me."

Now Mya was gazing at him with that same look of compassion she had had ten years ago. "I can understand that." She clasped his hand gently in her own. "But what if she chooses someone else?"

He growled, louder this time. Over the past few

weeks, he had been able to convince himself that the possibility of Aurora returning to Cade Ellis was remote. But he remembered the way Aurora had looked at Ellis. And the way Ellis had looked at her.

Today in the forest, Aurora had responded to his kiss, but she had not looked at him that way. Not even close.

And he needed to draw that response out of her. Soon. So much depended on it. Because if he failed, he was not certain just how far his father would go to insure Aurora would become a permanent part of the Clarek clan. And he did not want to find out.

Seventeen

Aurora felt like a snapping turtle on a rampage.

Her crew had given her looks as she'd stalked around the ship this morning in preparation for departure. Her foul mood reflected her roiling thoughts, but so far, her friends had kept their questions to themselves. She'd retreated to her office as soon as she could, desperate for some emotional sanity.

She dropped her head against the padded surface of her chair as she gazed out the starport. Normally she'd see the calming glitter of starlight, but the ship was still docked at the Clarek compound. She was staring at an opaque collage of brown and green tree limbs.

Kire was on the bridge, coordinating with the crew of the *Rowkclarek*, who would transport the members of the Clarek clan who would be helping build the settlement. Kelly was also on the bridge, deep in discussion with Star about the launch sequence for leaving the compound.

Celia was doing a final check of supplies in the cargo bay, and Mya was in the greenhouse, integrating the new specimens she and Celia had acquired during their outing with the Clarek botanists the day before.

That left Jonarel. Thankfully, he'd made himself scarce, remaining on the lower decks where they were less likely to run into each other.

Avoiding him was stupid. And childish. It also wasn't a behavior she could indulge forever. She had a ship to command and a mission to undertake. But she didn't have a clue what she was going to say to him.

They'd been friends for more than ten years, and he'd never made any kind of move. Then suddenly they'd arrived on Drakar and he'd hauled her into a liplock. How the hell had he expected her to respond? But it wasn't entirely his fault. She'd been the one to ask the fateful question that had set him off. She just hadn't liked his answer.

She sighed. Might as well focus on something productive. Tapping the controls on her desk, she brought up the message she'd received from Cade that morning.

> *A –*
>
> *Building a greenhouse to keep everyone occupied. Translators working well. Healing continues.*
>
> *C –*

A greenhouse. What a brilliant idea. No matter where Cade had taken the Lumians, it was unlikely they'd have much freedom of movement while they were in hiding. Constructing a greenhouse would provide them with a focus and a food source.

Cade's comments also underscored the urgency to get the settlement completed. Despite his assurance that all was well, she detected a subtle tension in the short message. Supervising three hundred refugees was hardly in his regular job description. She'd definitely need to thank him the next time they saw each other.

And she was really looking forward to that day. Probably way more than she should.

That was the other sticking point that had contributed to her foul mood. Thinking about yesterday's encounter with Jonarel had conjured the memory of another kiss, one that had taken place on a moonlit beach on Gaia.

But that memory didn't stir up feelings of confusion and agitation. No, it grabbed hold of her and pulled her into a whirlpool of rich and intoxicating emotions—passion, excitement, desire, connection.

The only problem? That kiss had been with Cade, not Jonarel. Their interaction on Gaia had exposed chinks in her emotional armor, weaknesses that revealed themselves as a flutter in her stomach every time she got a new message from him. Unfortunately, he didn't share her feelings. He'd rejected her at the Academy because she was half-human. Her new role as leader of the Lumian race certainly wouldn't improve his view of her mixed ancestry. The only reason he'd kissed her was because she'd asked him to.

What a mess.

Pushing back from the desk, she headed to the bridge.

Kire looked up as she approached, wariness in his hazel eyes. "Star and Kelly have worked out the departure sequence, so we're just waiting on the *Rowkclarek*." He continued to gaze at her, a question in his eyes.

Might as well get it over with. She propped her hip against the console. "Go ahead and ask."

He kept his voice low. "What's the deal with you and Jonarel?"

"We had an exchange yesterday that ended on a bad note."

His eyes widened. "You fought?"

"No. Not exactly." She glanced at Kelly and Star, who appeared to be completely engrossed in their discussion. "He kissed me."

That elicited a bark of surprise. "Oh, *ho*. Did he now? I was wondering if he'd ever take the plunge." Kire paused, his gaze assessing. "But clearly you're not diving in with both feet. Was it a bad kiss?"

And this was the downside of having a crew that consisted of friends. They didn't hesitate to ask you questions you weren't comfortable answering. "No, it wasn't a bad kiss. But I wasn't expecting it, either. I need some time to process."

"I see." His eyes narrowed. "Well, that explains the weirdness. I've never seen the two of you so uncomfortable around each other."

"That's because we've never been uncomfortable around each other." And she didn't want them to be now. But she had no idea where to go from here.

Kire clasped her hand in his. "You'll work it out."

"I hope so."

He released her as he brought his hand to his earpiece and shifted his attention to the comm panel. "The *Rowkclarek* is ready to depart. They'll follow us out."

And that was her signal. Time to shelve her personal problems and get back to work. She crossed to the captain's chair and settled in. "Then let's get this wagon train moving."

Eighteen

Cade slowed the stealth pod as he approached the thick grove of trees. Raaveen sat behind him, with Justin and Paaw on the second pod and Reynolds and Sparw on the third.

Two weeks had passed since the greenhouse had been completed, and this was their third trek to gather plants. The Suulh were doing an amazing job of nurturing the seedlings and smaller plants into flourishing food sources. This trip might yield everything they'd need to finish the project.

And they needed to wrap this up. None of the sites Williams had chosen were close to camp, so they'd had to travel more than an hour to reach their current location. Thankfully, there'd been no sign of the Meer anywhere in the area.

Despite his initial reticence, Cade had to admit he was enjoying the process. The teens had worked hard to become skilled with the stealth pods. Now they could serve as drivers as well as passengers. That had allowed for flexibility in the teams they sent out. On the first run, he'd had Williams and Reynolds with him, but on the second trip Justin and Gonzo had requested a turn, and Cade and Reynolds had stayed behind. For this journey, they were returning to a location they'd visited before, so Williams's discerning eye wasn't needed, allowing Justin and Reynolds to join Cade.

Drew had declined Justin's offer to let her take his

place on this expedition. She'd preferred to remain at the camp where she was busy teaching the Suulh how to use the various tech tools onboard the ship. They were a curious and eager audience, and Drew obviously loved the opportunity to share her knowledge.

Cade checked the scanners as his team approached the grove that marked their destination. The only creatures of note were a herd of cow-like herbivores that were grazing on the grasslands above the ravine. From this angle a few were visible along the ridge, their bodies showing as patches of darkness against the moonlit sky.

He led the way as the pods slid under the cover of the trees. The eastern end of the grove had already been harvested during the team's last trip, so he headed for the western half, halting in a small clearing near the tree line. Raaveen slipped off and joined Paaw and Sparw as they gathered their equipment. Thanks to their prolonged captivity in dark cells, the teens didn't require the visors that he, Reynolds and Justin wore. They already had excellent night vision. The pale light from the waxing moon was sufficient for their needs.

Cade walked back to where Justin and Reynolds were unpacking the carrying harness. He secured one corner of the harness to his pod with a clip, then slid the guide poles into place. Justin and Reynolds did the same on their pods so that the harness formed a triangle between the three to hold the plants in the center.

Initially they'd tried to keep the plants upright during transport, but the teens had assured them it was unnecessary. They could mend any damage the plants suffered, which meant the team could gather more plants in a single outing.

After two hours of work, the harness was filled with a mountain of seedlings, small shrubs and vines. Cade was hefting an unwieldy bush into place when Paaw gave a sharp cry. The plant tumbled from his fingers as he dropped into a defensive crouch, palming his pistol. He spun toward her but quickly realized the weapon was unnecessary.

Paaw lay sprawled on the ground partway up the hillside, her hands gripping her lower leg.

Even at this distance he could see the look of pain on her face and the odd angle of her foot. He sprinted up the incline, joining Justin and Reynolds as they crouched next to her. He didn't need Williams's medical training to know that the bone was broken. He flipped up his visor so she could see his face clearly. "What happened?"

Paaw bit her bottom lip as silent tears tracked down her cheeks. She drew in a shaky breath and indicated a spot to her left. "Hole."

A depression in the surrounding soil looked like the collapsed entrance to a rabbit's burrow, or whatever rabbit-like creatures this planet had. Apparently she'd sunk her foot into it while walking and had snapped her ankle like a twig.

"We need to get you to Williams. I have splinting material in the pod's emergency kit." He started to rise, but a firm grip on his forearm stopped him.

"Hang on," Justin said as Raaveen and Sparw knelt on either side of Paaw. "Let's see what they can do first."

"What do you—" But then a halo of yellow and red energy formed around Sparw and Raaveen. Right. He needed to remember who they were dealing with.

Raaveen clasped Sparw's right hand in her left and placed her other hand on Paaw's leg just above the break. Sparw did the same with his left hand while the yellow and red energy wove its way down their arms and pulsed around the injury. A moment later a faint blue glow joined the red and yellow and spread around Paaw's body. Her breathing slowed and evened out as her own energy added to the healing process.

Justin and Reynolds wouldn't be able to see the colors. Most humans couldn't. Cade was a rare exception. He still wondered if that ability had anything to do with the deep connection he'd always felt with Aurora. She'd been as surprised as he was that he could see the breathtaking pearlescent energy field she produced.

As the minutes ticked by, Cade's knees ached from the prolonged crouch, but he was hesitant to move too much and risk disturbing the teens' concentration. Besides, he was fascinated by what he was seeing. Not only were the energy ribbons beautiful to watch, but Paaw's ankle was rotating into proper alignment.

She flinched from time to time, and her blue energy flared and waned, but eventually the colors faded and Raaveen and Sparw stood. They grasped Paaw's hands and pulled her to her feet. She placed weight on her foot gingerly, but after a few shifts back and forth, she seemed confident that everything was as it should be.

"That's incredible." Reynolds's voice held a touch of awe.

"Sure is," Justin replied. His expression was hard to read in the darkness, but his voice sounded a little rough around the edges.

The teens seemed embarrassed by the admiration. Clearly they weren't used to being praised for an ability they'd been born with.

Cade glanced at the chronometer on his comband. They'd have to hurry to make it to the camp before sunrise. "We need to get moving." He held out a hand to Paaw. "Can I help you down the hill?" He didn't want her to reinjure the ankle.

She shook her head. "Almost new," she said in Galish. "Will finish when at ship."

He'd have to trust her on that. "Okay. But take it easy going down."

She nodded, stepping carefully over the rocky terrain until she reached the bottom.

They loaded the remaining items into the collection bundle and the storage compartments in the pods. After tidying up the site to remove any trace of their presence, they straddled the pods and made the slow journey to the camp.

Cade sent Drew a message to let the rest of the team know they were on their way. When they arrived, Cade called Williams over. "Paaw had an accident while we were out there. Broke her ankle."

Williams's brows snapped down as he glanced at Paaw, who was helping unhook the harness from the pod she'd shared with Justin. "Her ankle's broken? Then why the hell is she standing on it?"

He took a step in her direction but Cade laid a hand on his shoulder, restraining him. "It *was* broken. The kids fixed it. But I'd feel better if you'd do a follow up and make sure everything's as it should be."

He rubbed his hand over his shaved head. "The kids were able to repair a broken ankle? That's impressive. I've seen what they can do with scrapes and bruises. But a broken bone? That's a big deal." His gaze shifted back to Paaw. "How long did it take?"

"I wasn't timing it, but I'd guess thirty or forty minutes."

Williams's eyes widened. "You're kidding."

Cade shook his head.

"Damn." They watched as Paaw walked with the

other teens toward the freighter with only the slightest hesitation in her step. "I'd have trouble setting the bone and initiating a healing cast in that amount of time, let alone completely repairing the break." His brows lifted. "I'm beginning to wonder just how indestructible this race is."

Cade wondered the same thing. And how that knowledge would affect Aurora Hawke. After all, she was their queen.

Nineteen

The settlement was taking shape.

From his vantage point on the front porch of the main house, Jonarel gazed through the surrounding foliage to where similar structures rested in the shadows of the verdant green.

The designs for the settlement were based on the house Aurora and Mya had grown up in. It had seemed like a logical choice, since both Mya's parents and Aurora's mother were Lumians. From what Mya had told him, the house had been created to echo a traditional Lumian style. Aurora had invited him to visit once during an Academy session break, and the light and airy feel of the space had appealed to him, as had the careful integration with the surroundings.

The concept was based on a central circular room with two wings that opened off of it, so that from an aerial view, the design looked like a circle with two half moons attached on opposite sides. Windows and curved panels set at strategic points throughout the house and in the ceiling directed natural sunlight to fill the space without spotlighting any particular point. Guest accommodations and working spaces filled the lower level in each wing, while a curved staircase at the back of the central hub led to the family quarters on the top floor. An upper gallery followed the curve of the staircase, joining the two halves at the front of the house and providing additional seating and recreation spaces.

Aurora and her mother had lived in one of the half

moons, while Mya's family had inhabited the other. They had shared the central hub, with the kitchen at the heart of the space, surrounded by plush seating and a large wooden table for dining. A stone fireplace on one wall, a fountain that fed a miniature herb garden on the opposite wall, and several small trees that lifted their branches to the ceiling completed the sense of an indoor-outdoor space.

It was an unusual arrangement, with the two families so intimately connected in a communal existence, but it made perfect sense for the Lumian heritage. Having the two ruling families of the race in such close proximity was logical, considering how their abilities enhanced one another.

Mimicking that design here also made sense. He had made a few modifications in structure to follow the natural topography of the area and to anticipate the function of the space, but the basic layout was identical. The expansive main house sat at the center of the settlement on a slight promontory, with pathways leading to the eight smaller versions that circled it, each capable of housing up to forty Lumians.

The settlement was probably more ambitious than it needed to be, at least to start. The Lumians feared isolation after their long confinement, so there was a good chance they would decide to cohabitate in the main building rather than using the outbuildings, even if it meant being crammed together. Three hundred Lumians in the hub would be tight, but they might prefer it to spreading out.

Or they might surprise him. After all, it had been almost two months since he had last seen them. The healing power of time might have impacted their need for physical closeness.

"It's a beautiful setting."

He glanced over his shoulder as Mya strode toward

him from the arched entrance to the main house.

She stopped beside him, clasping her hands behind her back and gazing over the tops of the trees at the sparking water of the ocean in the distance. The sun had passed its zenith some time ago, and the afternoon clouds that were a daily occurrence were beginning to gather, breaking up the light into golden rays that danced on the air.

"I am glad you like it."

The corners of her mouth softened into a smile. "I really do. Your clan has done an amazing job. Thank you."

"You are welcome." He appreciated the kind words, but he liked the soft glow of joy in her brown eyes even more. Her patience and support over the past few weeks had helped him get through the awkwardness with Aurora.

"How much longer before we can bring the Lumians here?" she asked.

"The subsystems are in place, and the exteriors should be completed in a day or two. The interiors will take longer, perhaps another month, particularly if we furnish all the houses before the Lumians arrive."

"I know Aurora would like to. The Lumians have spent far too much time in ascetic surroundings, and I doubt their current living conditions are ideal." A small frown line appeared between her brows. "We want this place to feel welcoming when they arrive."

"It will." He forced himself to ask the obvious question. "Has she heard from Ellis recently?"

Mya's brows lifted, probably because he never, ever brought up Cade Ellis voluntarily. But Ellis was still in charge of the Lumians. The only way to find out how the Lumians were doing was to go through Ellis. Besides, Jonarel needed to keep tabs on how much the man was communicating with Aurora.

"Actually, she heard from him just this morning. He said everything's fine and the greenhouse has been a great success."

Jonarel really hated the admiration in Mya's voice. It was juvenile, but he wanted her completely on his side when it came to Cade Ellis, especially now.

At least Aurora had stopped acting skittish around him. The first few days of construction had been filled with stilted conversations and strange behavior from both of them. Kire and Mya had done their best to diffuse the awkwardness, which had helped immensely.

Things were far from normal, but to someone on the outside, it would be hard to tell Aurora was still keeping her distance from him. But she was. Every single time they were together.

She never got close enough to touch anymore. He had taken their casual interactions for granted until he had been cut off from giving her a hug or resting a hand on her shoulder. He was starved for physical contact. The hunger gnawed at him, becoming an acute ache whenever Aurora was nearby.

He heard her footsteps a moment before she appeared from around the side of the house and climbed the front steps.

"Stop loafing you two," she called out.

Mya laughed. "We weren't loafing. We were supervising. Very different."

Aurora smiled, and Jonarel's heart thumped painfully.

"Yeah, I've heard that one before." She glanced at him briefly, but her gaze quickly focused on Mya. "How are the gardens coming along?"

Mya and Celia were in charge of creating a network of kitchen gardens behind the outbuildings and stocking them with edible plants they had gathered from all over the island.

"Really well. I don't foresee any issues with sustainability, especially with the mild climate. Celia's worked up menus from the recipes she's tried. And she's having a ball experimenting," Mya said. "If she hadn't gone into security, she could have become a professional chef."

"And that would have been a great loss to us." Aurora's gaze shifted to Jonarel. "What's the status on the main house?" The way she spoke to him was still formal, more a captain to a crewmember rather than a friend to a friend.

It made his skin itch.

Aurora had placed him in charge of the construction for the main house. He had hoped the task might bring him closer to her, but it had not worked out that way. After she had approved the initial plans, she had found excuses to avoid spending much time on site, devoting her attention to the outbuildings and the pathway to the shuttle landing site.

"We are on schedule. The staircase was completed this morning. Would you like me to give you both a tour of the upper level?" He would enjoy seeing their reactions, especially Aurora's. After all, this was a replica of their childhood home.

Mya smiled. "I'd love that." She glanced at Aurora. "You coming?"

Aurora avoided looking at either of them as she shook her head. "You two go ahead. I need to check on Kelly's progress with the landing platform."

She was down the stairs and out of sight before he or Mya could respond.

"Can't stay still for two minutes at a time." Mya murmured, her gaze on the spot where Aurora had disappeared. She sighed. "But I'd still love that tour." She rested her hand on his upper arm, her eyes filled with understanding.

He took comfort from her touch. "Then follow me."

Twenty

"Mind if I join you?"

Justin looked up from his quiet contemplation of the campfire. Bella stood over him, a plate of food in one hand and a mug in the other.

He gestured to the empty space on the rock next to him. "Be my guest." He returned his gaze to the fire.

"Nice night." Bella sat down and settled her plate on her lap. "I'm glad the winds stopped," she added as she lifted her mug to her lips.

He gave a non-committal grunt.

She set the mug down with a thunk. "Okay Byrnsie, what's up with you?"

He glanced at her in surprise.

"You've been pensive and withdrawn ever since you came back last night."

Apparently she'd been watching him. "I've just been thinking."

"About what?"

"The teens."

"What about them?"

He rubbed the back of his neck, where steel rods had taken up permanent residence. "Last night, as I was watching Raaveen and Sparw healing Paaw's ankle, my brain was spinning. I kept thinking of all the implications, all that we'd learned about them over the past couple months. The enormity of what was happening in front of me." He paused, trying to put his feelings into words.

"Go on," she prompted gently.

He sighed. "I pictured their future. Then I pictured my future. And I realized how completely different those two realities will be." He stared at his boots as the tension rods extended from his neck down to his back. He met Bella's gaze. "After the new settlement is finished, we'll never see them again."

Bella's blue eyes filled with compassion. "And you hate that idea."

"Yes. No." He returned his attention to the fire. "I don't know."

"You've been spending a lot of time with them. It's understandable that you'd miss seeing them when they're gone."

"I know. But it's more than that. Working with them, first with the stealth pods and then gathering the plants, I've seen so much potential. They can do anything they set their minds to."

"And you want to see those abilities develop."

He rested his elbows on his knees. "Yeah. I guess I do." But he'd never have that opportunity. In fact, they probably only had a few weeks before the *Starhawke* crew would arrive, and that would be the end of that. The teens would vanish from his life like a puff of smoke.

"Because you care about them."

Immediately his brain spit out a denial. "No, that's not it. I mean yeah, they're great kids, but I'm not emotionally invested or anything. I just hate the idea that I'll never know how they turn out."

"Hate?" Bella peered at him. "That's a pretty strong word considering you're not emotionally invested."

The tension in his gut told him she was right, but he resisted. "Are you saying it doesn't bother you?"

"Of course it does. Some of them are becoming tech wizards. I've never had such attentive students. They want to know everything, and they follow instructions really well. I'd love to watch those talents come to fruition." She set her plate aside. "But that's not up to us."

"I know." He waved his hand in a dismissive gesture. "It doesn't matter. They'll be so happy in their new home they won't even realize we're gone." And he needed to start thinking in the same way.

Bella laid her hand on his shoulder. "Justin, don't do that."

He glanced at her. "Do what?"

"Cut yourself off from those kids."

"I'm not. It's the situation, not me."

She shook her head. "I'm not talking about the day they leave. I'm talking about right now. I can see the change happening already. You're shutting down, closing them out in order to save yourself from the pain of saying goodbye. That's selfish."

He frowned. "That's not what I'm doing."

She sighed. "Byrnsie, you know I love you, but you're so wrong. I've never seen you get emotionally invested in anyone except maybe Cade, and I think that's only because you expect to work with him until the day you die."

She was right about Cade. But she was wrong that Cade was the only one he was emotionally invested in. He couldn't imagine his life without her in it, either.

The corners of her mouth pinched. "Trust me on this. Please." Her hand gripped his forearm. "Don't shut them out. They love being around you and learning from you. It means a lot to them. They need you right now. And I think you need them, too."

Point. Set. Match. She was right and he was wrong.

Might as well be honest. "I'm going to miss them."

"Me, too." Her focus shifting to a spot over his shoulder. "You have a visitor."

He glanced to his left. Paaw was approaching, her steps tentative, like she didn't want to interrupt them.

"Hey, Paaw." He cleared his empty plate off the rock to make room for her. "Have you eaten? I could go get you something."

The teen shook her head as she perched next to him. "I eat earlier."

"How's your ankle?" Bella asked.

Paaw shrugged. "It is good."

"Does it hurt?"

Paaw shook her head. "More healing with mother and Maanee." She gestured to where her younger sister sat with a group of children across the way. "No damage now."

Bella smiled. "That's good to hear."

Paaw lapsed into an uncomfortable silence.

"Do you need something?" Justin asked.

Paaw folded her hands in her lap. "The plants. On the hill. We did not get."

It took him a moment to figure out what she was referring to. "You mean the shrubs you'd wanted to bring back for your mother?"

"Yes. We go get now?"

He should have anticipated this. Paaw had been a little agitated the night before after they'd unpacked the stealth pods and the plants, but he'd assumed it was about her ankle. He'd forgotten that the reason she'd started climbing the hill in the first place was to obtain a gift for her mother.

He frowned. "You want to make a special trip just to get the shrubs?"

She nodded, her pale blue eyes full of hope. "Yes. Go tonight."

Unfortunately, it wasn't a simple request. He seriously doubted Cade would agree to lead the team on a two hour round trip just to pick up a couple plants. Their main job was protecting the Suulh, and that meant keeping the team on site as much as possible. Gathering large quantities of plants for the greenhouse benefitted everyone and balanced out the risk factors of having three team members away from camp for several hours. But this situation didn't. "I don't know, Paaw. We don't really need to go on another run."

Paaw's disappointment showed in every line of her body, but she didn't argue. Her gaze shifted to the ground as she started to rise.

She looked so dejected that he reached out on impulse and grabbed her forearm. "Wait a minute. I have an idea." He wasn't certain Cade would go for his alternative, but he could probably talk him into it. After all, Cade had a soft spot for the teens, too. "If Cade will allow it, maybe you and I could take one pod and fetch the plants so we wouldn't have to pull the rest of the team off their regular work rotation."

Paaw's face lit up and she gave him an impulsive hug. His chest constricted as he hugged her back. He also said a silent prayer that Cade wouldn't shoot him down.

He found Cade on the bridge and explained his plan.

"I don't want to disappoint that kid, either," Cade said. "I feel bad that she got injured on our watch, even if she was able to heal the damage." He leaned back in his chair. "But if you're going to do this, you need to take two pods, not one. That way you can still use the harness rather than trying to balance the plants while you're driving."

"In that case, would you have any objection to my bringing Raaveen and Sparw rather than someone from our team?" Justin asked. "Raaveen's a damn good driver, and if she's in charge of the other pod, I can focus on the scanners. We'd also get the plants out of the ground and our tracks covered a lot quicker with the three of them working together."

Cade folded his arms across his chest. "I guess that's okay. The quicker you can get out and back the better. Just be careful."

"Always."

Raaveen and Sparw were thrilled with the opportunity. Within minutes they were retracing their path from the previous night. Raaveen flashed him a wide grin. She also drove the pod like she'd been born to it.

They made excellent time. As they drew close to their destination, he kept his focus on the scanners. The herd of cow-like herbivores had returned to graze on the plateau above the ravine, but otherwise everything looked clear. They took the pods up the hill rather than leaving them in the grove so they could minimize footprints and load the shrubs directly into the harness.

Paaw and Sparw worked on one plant while he and Raaveen teamed up to dig out a second one. The ground in this area was drier than in the grove, so it required more effort to free the root systems. Justin supported the branches of the shrub while Raaveen working to coax the plant out of the ground.

A sudden burst of pain like a solar flare cut into his right shoulder and his fingers clenched, snapping one of the branches in half.

He sucked in a breath as a second flash bloomed in

the back of his left thigh. In his peripheral vision, he caught a glimpse of a crude arrow sticking out from his leg. But that didn't hold his attention for long. His focus shifted over his shoulder as a dense pack of quadrupeds stampeded down the hillside toward them.

Several of the creatures rose onto their hind legs and took aim. Definitely not herbivores. The furred bodies underneath revealed the truth. The attackers were Meer wrapped in the skins of the cow-like hooved animals.

Raaveen bolted to her feet, raising her trowel like a dagger and snarling at the approaching figures as she placed herself in front of Justin.

But this wasn't the first time he'd been injured in a surprise attack. He was far from helpless. Ignoring the agony in his leg, he hauled himself upright and palmed his pistol in his left hand so he could cradle his right arm against his abdomen to keep his shoulder immobile.

Paaw and Sparw had also risen, although they seemed confused by the sudden turn of events. "Get behind the pods!" he shouted as he fired several shots at the Meer. He aimed for their legs rather than their chests in the hope it would halt their charge. It didn't. The ones he'd struck stumbled, but those behind sent a volley of arrows his way.

And they were definitely aiming at him. The teens followed his orders, crouching behind the pods. He lurched toward them but the two arrows embedded in his skin slowed his movements. A third nailed his left bicep. He lost feeling in his hand and the pistol slipped out of his grasp as he staggered.

That's when the teens took over. Raaveen and Sparw leapt on the pods while Paaw snatched the pistol he'd dropped and fired at the Meer. Sparw reached out a hand to help Justin up. The kid had surprising strength for his age.

Justin managed to sling his leg over the back of the pod, but a screech of pain and anger halted his movements.

Raaveen was clutching her left forearm with her right hand, an arrow protruding from her left wrist. Paaw made an attempt to reach the pod's controls around Raaveen's body, but four of the Meer intercepted the teens first, hauling them off the pod and pressing sharp claws against their throats.

They barked at Sparw and flashed their pointed teeth. Sparw raised his hands away from the pod controls.

The Meer moved in, one of them grabbing onto the arrow that poked out of Justin's shoulder. The resulting river of agony brought his upper body parallel to the ground. He caught a flash of movement out of the corner of his eye, and then everything went black.

Twenty-One

"How long have they been gone?" Cade stopped pacing as he waited for Reynolds to reply.

"Three hours, thirty-seven minutes."

Too long. Too damn long. And no communication from Justin.

He turned to Gonzo at the bridge's tactical station. "What about on the perimeter scanners?"

Gonzo was all business, devoid of his usual mirth. "Nothing. Wherever they are, they're not in range of the sensors."

"Drew, any sign of ships in orbit?" If their mysterious enemy had tracked them to Burrow, this could be the first move to reclaim the Suulh.

"Not that we can see," she said, "but we have a limited field of vision. If a ship approached from the other side of the planet, we'd never know."

Cade stared at the floor. Why had he agreed to let Justin take the kids out alone? It had seemed like a reasonable request at the time, but that was before his number one had failed to return. Now Cade had some hard decisions to make. "I need recommendations."

Gonzo rested his elbows on his knees. "We have one pod left, which could take two of us. Other than that, the only transports are the ship itself and your jetbike." Gonzo grimaced. "And that thing can raise the dead."

Very true. It was incredibly fast and could carry three passengers in a pinch, which was why he had it. But in this case, he might as well set off a cannon to announce their presence.

Williams crossed his arms as he leaned against the bulkhead. "Any chance they encountered the Meer and had to take an alternate route?"

Cade had thought of that, too. "Possibly, but Justin would have reported in if that was the case."

Gonzo nodded. "If they had a problem with one of the pods, they would have contacted us or sent the other one back for help. And the kids could handle any injury situation, just as they did last night."

"They're late *and* silent," Cade said. "We have to assume someone's detained them. No other explanation makes sense."

"Justin would have to be incapacitated before he'd break off communication." Reynolds's voice matched the flatness in her eyes. "They may be dead."

Cade refused to even consider that possibility. Justin was his closest friend, and he didn't want to believe that a generous impulse had led to his demise. "I don't want speculation. I want answers. We have one pod left. We need to make it count." He motioned to Reynolds and Williams. "I'm sending you two out first. Keep a channel open and report in at five-minute intervals. No exceptions."

"Got it." Reynolds rose from her chair and checked the weapons in her utility belt.

Cade placed a restraining hand on her arm. "No matter what you find, do not engage. Reconnaissance only. Understood?"

Her eyes narrowed, but she nodded. "Yes, sir."

As Williams and Reynolds left the bridge, he turned to Gonzo. "I want a physical perimeter check of our position. Look for any weak points we may have missed. If someone's figured out we're here, we need to be prepared."

"On it." Gonzo headed out the door.

That left Drew. "Gather everyone in the med bay. Let them know the situation and make sure they're ready for a quick departure on my command."

"They won't like the idea of leaving Justin and the kids behind." Her blue eyes reflected the same worry he felt. She was close to Justin, too.

"That's not my plan, but we can't allow the Suulh to fall into enemy hands, either. See if you can boost the ship's scanners to locate Justin's comband or the pods. Alert me immediately if you pick up any signals."

Less than an hour later, Williams and Reynolds checked in from the grove where Justin had taken the teens.

"No sign of them here," Williams said, "but there's a mess of footprints coming down the hill that don't belong to Justin or the kids. And Reynolds found blood on the ground."

Cade's jaw tightened. He'd been expecting something like this, but having it confirmed didn't help. "Setarips?"

"Definitely not. That's the good news. The shape and size looks like Meer."

At least they weren't dealing with an enemy from above. But why would the Meer attack Justin and the teens? "What about the pods? Are they there?"

Reynolds replied. "No. We can see Meer tracks heading off to the east but no boot prints. It looks like they took Justin and the kids on the pods."

"Are you picking anything up on scanners?"

"Not yet, but these tracks should be easy to follow," Reynolds said. "And that opening that Paaw stepped into last night? I examined it more closely. It's actually a spyhole. I've located half a dozen just like it along this hill. They're connected to a series of narrow tunnels that lead to the plateau above."

So the Meer could have been watching them last night, and then planned an attack for tonight. But why? "Stay alert. They obviously managed to sneak up on Justin. Don't underestimate them."

"Understood."

Cade glanced at Drew. "Any luck tracking the pods or Justin's comband?"

She shook her head, frustration evident in the lines of tension around her eyes and mouth. "I've boosted the range as best I can, but our location limits our ability to get a clear signal. If we were airborne, it would be a different story."

"Then we'll keep that as a last resort." No telling how violently the Meer might react to the appearance of the freighter in the sky.

For the next hour and a half, Cade waited on the bridge with Drew and Gonzo while Williams and Reynolds followed the trail. The first rays of dawn were beginning to lighten the sky when they finally reached their destination.

"You wouldn't recognize this," Reynolds said. "The Meer have built a small fortification on the edge of the cliff face. They've cleared the surrounding area so there's no way to approach without being exposed. The aerial view is nearly three hundred sixty degrees."

An image appeared on the bridgescreen, revealing a landscape cast in the shadowy light of dawn. The Meer fortress consisted of a block wall topped with sharp wooden spikes that encircled the predominantly stone buildings inside. Five years ago that type of architecture would have been outside the scope of Meer understanding, but clearly necessity had sparked invention. They'd learned a harsh lesson from the Setarips. And they'd adapted to make themselves less vulnerable.

"How high are those walls?"

"Five meters, minimum."

Gonzo let out a low whistle. "Hard to imagine how long it took them to move that much rock to that location."

"They were highly motivated," Drew murmured, her gaze locked on the image.

"Something else you should know." Williams panned away from the fortress. "I found something." The image shifted to his hand, where a crude arrow lay across his palm, the shaft broken. "They weren't using bows and arrows before, but it looks like they've figured out the concept."

And a bow and arrow could be lethal. "Any sign of Justin or the kids?"

"I'm picking up an electrical signal that indicates the pods are still turned on," Reynolds said. "But I'm not getting any transmissions from Justin's comband."

Cade paced behind the captain's chair while he considered his options. He still had no idea why the Meer had taken Justin and the teens captive, but until he knew otherwise, he would act on the assumption that they were alive. The teens could heal their own injuries, and as long as they were in physical contact with Justin, they might be able to help him, too. "Set a transmission booster so that we'll receive any message Justin is able to send. Then get here as quickly as you can. We'll have some ideas for our next move ready when you arrive."

"Roger that."

"At least we know where they are," Drew said as the transmission ended.

But not whether they were okay. And that answer was far more critical.

Twenty-Two

A nest of wasps had taken up residence in Justin's head. He drew a few slow breaths and waited for the buzzing to settle down. Then he worked on peeling his eyelids open.

They felt gritty, like they'd been glued together with cement. And he got blasted with a new shot of unpleasant when light pierced into his retinas. Wow. So not the kind of wake-up he would have hoped for.

He stifled a moan and closed his eyes. *Breathe in. Breathe out. Breathe...wait a minute.* Someone was calling his name. A female voice, barely a whisper. *Bella?* Lifting his head off the floor took a monumental effort, but he finally brought his gaze over to the left far enough to see the speaker.

Blonde hair framed a pretty face smudged with dirt. Not Bella. Paaw. Her wide blue eyes were shadowed with concern. "Justin?"

She was seated next to him, but judging from the angle of her shoulders and arms, her hands were bound behind her back. He tried to lick his dry lips but couldn't quite get his mouth open wide enough to accomplish it. Apparently the cement had been applied there, too. Talking was out of the question, and her image began to waver the longer he kept his head up. He blinked a few times, but that really didn't help.

A frown creased her brow and she shifted her body, giving him a view of the leathery ropes that bound her. A moment later her fingers brushed against his calf. A soothing coolness began creeping up his leg to his thigh, but a bright flash of pain caught him off guard, successfully prying his lips apart as he sucked in air.

He forced his head up higher and gazed down his torso. A nasty wound was visible through a long tear in the fabric covering the back of his thigh, punctuated by a halo of blood. The arrow. Apparently someone had removed it, but without bothering to clean or cover the area.

The coolness pooled there, and the pain retreated somewhat. But then two more ribbons snaked their way up his back to his right shoulder and down his left arm to his bicep, creating flares of pain at the other impact points, like a hundred red-hot needles being inserted under his skin.

The wave continued upward to his head. That's when a drum line began playing between his ears.

He moaned out loud this time as his body fell back to rest on the floor. His thoughts scattered like leaves on the wind. He was vaguely aware that his hands were tied behind his back and his feet were bound together, but he just couldn't summon the energy to care. Tiny gremlins were pushing and pulling him apart, so a little extra tension really didn't matter.

He lost track of time, his consciousness of his surroundings fading in and out over what could have been minutes or hours. Eventually he realized his breath was coming easier, and the searing pain in his body had faded to a dull ache. This time when he opened his eyes, the room came into sharp focus almost immediately, and without the resulting discomfort. He glanced over his shoulder and found Paaw facing him again, her expression hopeful.

"Better?" she asked.

He frowned as he realized that the skin of his

bicep was no longer shredded. It was red and raw, but looked more like a bad burn than a serrated flesh wound. A glance at the rip in his pant leg revealed a similar improvement to the skin underneath. And his shoulder didn't screech as he levered himself onto his back.

Best of all, his head had stopped pounding out a Sousa march. When he met Paaw's gaze, he figured out why. She'd been sending healing energy into his system to help repair the damage inflicted during the attack. Drawing in a steadying breath, he nodded. "Much better. Thank you."

Relief flashed in her eyes and her lips tilted in a tiny smile.

He glanced around the empty room. "Where are Raaveen and Sparw?"

The smile disappeared. "They took outside." She nodded toward the wooden planks that covered the low door.

"Were they hurt?" He had a vague memory of Raaveen being hit with an arrow to her wrist, but he had no idea what had occurred after the Meer had knocked him unconscious.

Paaw shook her head. "Raaveen heal fine. Sparw okay."

That was something. He couldn't imagine what the Meer wanted with the two teens, but most likely he'd find out soon enough. In the meantime, he had to figure out a way to get them all out of here.

First things first. He needed to get upright.

Taking a deep breath, he contracted his abdominal muscles and hauled his torso off the floor. The bindings on his wrists shifted, but remained tight. Okay, he could work with that, especially if some of the rocks that lined the walls were as rough hewn as they appeared.

He began shuffling backward, but halted when the low door to the room opened. Raaveen and Sparw crawled inside, followed by four male Meer armed with short spears.

"Justin!" the teens cried in unison.

Raaveen took a step toward him but stopped abruptly when the Meer brandished their weapons and snarled. Their pointed teeth glittered in the firelight. Justin had no problem picturing them sinking those teeth into anyone who crossed them. Not exactly reassuring.

"Hey guys. Glad to see you're okay."

Raaveen looked frantic. "We fine. You?"

"Thanks to Paaw, I'm much better."

Raaveen and Sparw shot Paaw a look of gratitude. Obviously they'd all been worried about him.

The Meer pushed the two teens toward the opposite side of the room, making space for a male who entered with an air of authority. He was taller and stockier than the four guards, the short fur that covered his body blending with the earth tones of the sand on the floor, while the dark patches around his eyes stood out in sharp relief. His gaze focused on Justin, intelligence shining in his black eyes. And anger. Lots and lots of anger. This was a very hostile Meer.

Four more guards entered behind him, their bodies twisted sideways so they could hold onto the corners of a stretched animal skin. Something heavy weighed down the middle of the skin. As they carefully lowered it to the ground, Justin got a good look.

A Meer female lay within. Judging from her size, she was an adolescent. And she was in bad shape. A bone protruded from her right leg, the skin and pale gray fur around the wound matted with dried blood and swollen with infection. Her eyes were half-open and glazed with fever, her breath alternating between long, raspy draws and panting.

That's why we're here. Somehow the Meer must have witnessed Paaw's injury and the resulting healing to repair the broken bone. He glanced at Raaveen. "They want you to heal her, don't they?"

Raaveen nodded. "But we say no. Help you first, then her."

Justin stared at Raaveen in shock. She'd successfully negotiated with the Meer despite the language barrier? Impressive. With a few years of training and experience, she would make one hell of an addition to the Elite Unit. That is, if her heritage hadn't already sentenced her to a life of isolation on the new homeworld.

The leader barked a command. The words were unintelligible but the demand for silence came through loud and clear. Then the male got right up in Raaveen's face—or as much as he could considering she was a head taller than he was. Despite his height, the male looked imposing, the brown horizontal bands of fur on his torso making him appear larger. He pointed at Justin and then at the Meer female, his lips pulling back from his teeth in a snarl.

Raaveen and Sparw stepped forward, settling themselves on either side of the female.

"Can you save her?" Justin had seen them work wonders on Paaw's ankle, but healing a compound fracture that had already triggered a raging infection might be asking too much. Especially for a species with such radically different physiology.

"Nedale could," Sparw said, referring to the title of respect the Suulh used for Dr. Mya Forrest.

Justin believed him. He'd heard the stories from Williams about the power of the *Starhawke's* physician. But these two didn't have her talent or experience.

Raaveen met Justin's gaze. Worry lines etched her face, but determination, too. "We try."

He gave a brief nod. They'd do their best. That was all anyone could ask.

Paaw shifted next to him, her entire focus on the Meer female. She began using her feet to push herself toward Raaveen and Sparw. "I help," she said when one of the Meer stopped her. She looked up at the leader, her gaze steady. "I help," she repeated, nodding toward the female.

The leader seemed to understand her, but his rigid stance didn't change. He seemed reluctant to trust her. However, when the Meer female let out a pitiful moan, his concern won out over his fear. He crouched behind Paaw and untied the bindings around her hands and feet.

She rolled her shoulders and flexed her fingers before moving next to Sparw. She placed one hand on the female's foot and the other on her knee. Raaveen rested her hand alongside Paaw's and clasped hands with Sparw over the female's torso. Sparw placed his other hand alongside Paaw's, completing the circuit.

The leader stared down at Justin, his gaze shifting to the locations where the arrows had struck. Then he gestured at the female and barked something that was clearly a question.

Justin didn't need his communications training to know what the male was asking. Unfortunately, the leader wouldn't like the answer.

Allowing the compassion he felt to show in his voice and eyes, he shook his head. "I'm sorry. I don't have their abilities."

The leader's dark eyes narrowed.

Justin worked hard not to focus on the male's very

sharp teeth. "I'm sorry. I didn't heal myself. She healed me." He nodded to Paaw. "I would help if I could."

The leader growled in warning before glancing at the female. His throat moved in a convulsive swallow, his mask of anger slipping for a moment to reveal the terror and anguish that lay beneath.

The injured female was his daughter. That explained a lot.

Raaveen, Paaw and Sparw held their hunched positions for what felt like an hour but might have been half that time, their breathing evening out until it was in perfect sync. Their gazes remained locked on the Meer female as silence hung heavy in the room, broken only by the whimpering and harsh breathing of the female. Then without a word to each other, they pulled on the female's leg from both ends. The bone disappeared under the pale fur covering her skin as a blood-curdling shriek shot out of her lips.

The leader swayed and took a lurching step forward, but stopped before he reached them. He stood, trembling, but didn't attempt to interfere.

Tears slid down Raaveen's cheeks and dripped onto the ground. Paaw and Sparw's hands shook. Clearly the female's suffering bothered them, but their concentration never waved.

The female mewled pitifully as the teens continued to work. The shadows cast by the light coming through the slats in the door shifted across the floor, marking time. Eventually the female grew quiet.

The teens didn't stop, but they began to show signs of fatigue. Sparw's entire body trembled, and Raaveen's skin glistened with sweat. Paaw's head hung almost to her knees, like the energy had drained right out of her.

Apparently the type of injury they were healing

made a big difference in how it affected them. The healing
session Paaw had done for him hadn't appeared to cause her
any stress, and the teens had all been fine after healing
Paaw's ankle. Then again, her break had been clean and
they'd worked on it immediately. Here they were dealing
with a major trauma that had festered, as well as an
unfamiliar species. Judging by the toll it was taking on them,
that increased the difficulty exponentially.

The teens weren't giving up, though. And when they
did finally stop, it wasn't by choice. Paaw simply slumped
backward, sinking to the floor in a prone position with her
arms and legs akimbo. Raaveen and Sparw toppled over a
moment later, lying motionless on the floor.

Justin got his first good view of the female since
the healing had begun. The results were astounding. Her leg
lay in perfect position. The skin and fur had knit back
together to form a seal over the wound, although the
surrounding tissue was still livid and swollen.

But the most telling sign of the teens' success was
the female's expression. Her mouth had relaxed, eliminating
the permanent grimace of pain, and her eyes were closed in
sleep, her breathing slow and steady.

The leader knelt and touched his child's face,
stroking her dark gray fur with reverence.

It was a poignant moment. But Justin was concerned
about the toll the healing had taken on Raaveen, Paaw and
Sparw. He used his bound feet to push his body toward
them. One of the guards brandished a weapon, stopping him.

Justin frowned. "I need to make sure they're okay."
He nodded at the teens.

The guard lifted the blunt weapon and snarled, the
crescent moon scar that cut along his muzzle and cheek
giving him a particularly vicious appearance.

Justin glared, refusing to back down.

A sharp command echoed in the chamber. One of the other Meer, this one as tall as the leader but lighter in coloring, stepped forward. He made a chittering sound and flashed his teeth.

Bowing slightly, the hostile guard retreated to the far side of the room, where he glowered in Justin's direction.

Interesting. Justin made a mental note to keep an eye on that one. Thankfully, the scar made him easy to identify.

Judging by the exchange, Justin pegged the other Meer as the captain of the guard. The captain sat on his haunches in front of Justin, his expression wary. He glanced at the teens and the leader, who still hadn't left his daughter's side, and then at Justin.

Justin gazed back, his expression as calm and unthreatening as he could make it.

The guard pulled his lips upward ever so slightly, revealing the tips of his teeth in a subtle warning. Then he stepped behind Justin and removed his bindings.

Justin's shoulder and forearm let out a loud protest, the dull ache that he'd been able to ignore ratcheting up a notch now that the muscles were back in motion. He slowly stretched his shoulders as the blood started circulating through his arms and fingers, making them tingle and throb.

He shifted onto all fours and crept to where Paaw and Sparw lay side by side, their eyes closed. He touched their wrists to check for a pulse. That became redundant as both teens gazed up at him.

"Are you okay?"

"Tired." Paaw whispered.

"Thirsty." Sparw added.

Justin nodded. He was thirsty, too. They had water in

the stealth pods, but he had no idea where those were. He glanced at the captain. "Water?" He cupped his hands and lifted them to his lips to mime drinking.

The captain immediately issued a command to one of the guards, who left the room and returned a few moments later with a bowl. The captain took the bowl and approached Justin cautiously, placing the container on the ground and then stepping back. Apparently Meer physiology precluded drinking from cups. They probably lapped like cats.

Justin started with Paaw, slipping a hand under her neck and lifting her up so that she could sip from the edge of the bowl. After a couple swallows, he did the same thing with Sparw before moving over to check on Raaveen.

She was slower to respond, and when she finally opened her eyes, she seemed to be having trouble focusing on him. "Here, drink this. It should help." He lifted her torso off the ground and held her against him so he could support her weight. She felt like a ragdoll, but at least she was able to take in some of the cool liquid.

Seeing how much the healing had drained the teens gave him a whole new appreciation for the abilities of Dr. Forrest. He had little doubt she could have fixed the child's injury without breaking a sweat. No wonder the Suulh held her family in such high esteem. She was, quite literally, a lifesaver.

Raaveen sagged against him and closed her eyes, sighing softly. He took that as his cue to satisfy his own thirst. He lifted the bowl to his lips, taking several long pulls, the liquid a balm on his parched throat.

Paaw and Sparw still slumped on the ground, nearly comatose. They probably needed food almost as much as water.

Justin noticed the leader and the captain watching

him. They spoke in a series of barks and chatters and then the captain left, returning a few minutes later carrying a large platter. He set it on the floor within easy reach.

The aromas that drifted up made Justin's stomach growl. The enticing smells must have reached Sparw and Paaw, too, because they lifted their heads. They managed to pull themselves into seated positions before they each grabbed something off the platter and shoved the food into their mouths.

Raaveen, however, was still unresponsive.

Justin snagged some fruit he recognized. "Eat this," he coaxed, touching the fruit to her lips.

She had to work to open her mouth, but after the first bite she gave a little start and came to life. She snatched the fruit out of his hands and tore into it while juice dribbled down her chin.

The next time he saw Williams, he needed to tell him that the healing session triggered intense hunger. He would want to add that information to his growing reference notes about the Suulh's abilities.

After a couple minutes the teens began to slow down their headlong rush for sustenance, and Justin decided he could allow himself a little as well. But as he reached toward the platter, his gaze fell onto the comband on his forearm. *The Meer hadn't taken it.*

Twenty-Three

Cade sank into the captain's chair and faced his team. "What do we know?"

"The Meer learned a harsh lesson from the Setarips." Williams ran a hand over his shaved head. "The fortification they've constructed is basic but effective. There's no way to approach from the ground without being seen."

"And an approach from the air would create panic," Reynolds said. "It could get Justin and the teens killed."

"In the eyes of the Meer, we're the invaders." Gonzo leaned back in his chair. "They may have kidnapped our people, but launching any kind of attack against them is morally wrong."

Cade sighed. "Agreed. We need a more diplomatic solution." He turned to Drew at navigation. "It would help if—" He paused when her console chimed.

She whirled around. "It's an incoming message from Justin's comband." She tapped the control panel and an image appeared on the bridgescreen.

"What the heck are we looking at?" Gonzo tilted his head to the side.

It took Cade a few seconds to make sense of the image, too. Everything was at an odd angle. But he caught sight of two faces he recognized. "Raaveen and Sparw."

They were eating, their focus on the food in their hands. The image moved up and to the right and revealed a sideways view of Paaw, her blond hair falling away from her face as she lifted a bowl to her lips.

"They're okay." Drew's shoulders slumped in relief.

The visual rotated to show the left side of Justin's face and his raised right forearm, as though he was clasping his arms over his head. He was filthy, and his hair stuck out in all directions, but as his gaze shifted to look into the camera, Cade swore he saw a flash of amusement.

"I'm surprised the Meer didn't take his comband," Drew said.

"They wouldn't have any idea it was a communication device." Gonzo stroked his goatee. "But we'll have to be careful how we talk to him. We don't want to alert the Meer."

The image moved again, this time away from Justin and the teens, revealing at least eight Meer in the room with weapons strapped to their bodies. Then the image stopped, focusing on a young Meer female lying on the ground.

Cade leaned forward. "Freeze frame."

"Sure." Drew touched the control panel. The video continued to play in a smaller panel while the still image took center stage. "Why would they have a female lying in the middle of the room?"

"Whoever she is, she's injured," Williams said. "You can see swelling and dried blood on the fur of her right leg."

Drew studied the image. "Why's Justin focusing on her?" She glanced back at Cade and her blue eyes suddenly widened. "The Suulh."

Of course. It explained everything.

Gonzo looked between them, a puzzled expression on his lean face. "What am I missing here?"

Cade cleared his throat. "If the Meer witnessed Paaw's fall and recovery at the grove, they'd assume, correctly, that the teens have healing abilities." He nodded toward the screen. "Whatever's wrong with this female, she's probably the reason they were kidnapped."

Gonzo frowned. "But what about Justin? He doesn't have that ability."

"They wouldn't know that. At least not for sure." This changed things considerably. "But they've probably figured it out by now. The question is, what are their long-range plans? Assuming they have any." Cade glanced around the room. "Thoughts?"

"We have to get Justin and the teens back," Reynolds said. "But we can't leave the rest of the Suulh here alone. We're shorthanded for a rescue mission."

Gonzo nodded. "Good point. We're limited to four people for the rescue. And only one stealth pod."

"I could stay behind," Drew offered. "But if anything went wrong, you wouldn't have backup."

Which was a major problem. With their limited transportation, just getting to the location would be tricky. Getting away safely would be even tougher.

Williams spoke up. "I have a thought, but you might not like it."

Any ideas were welcome at this point. "Shoot."

"Contact Captain Hawke."

Contact Aurora? The idea hadn't even occurred to him, but it didn't take long to realize the benefits. Her crew could provide additional transportation options and take charge of the Suulh while his team got Justin and the kids out. And if Aurora joined the rescue team, her presence would virtually guarantee that no one would get hurt, including any of the Meer.

But there were cons, too. She'd have to halt work on the settlement, causing further delays. And she'd be making the trip to fetch the Suulh before everything was in place. This situation would cost her, one way or another, and that knowledge stung.

He was supposed to be helping her. Instead, he'd ended up sabotaging her. Jonarel Clarek would have a field day eviscerating him. His ego rebelled, but he wasn't about to let his ego make the decision. "Any objections?" he asked the team.

Drew shook her head.

"Hell, no," Gonzo said. "We could use the extra muscle."

Reynolds nodded. "It would solve our transportation issue, too."

Cade pulled up the communications panel on his console. "Then let's see how quickly they can get here."

Twenty-Four

"Did you have to pick the heaviest tree on the island for your focal point?" Kire asked.

Keeping a firm grip on the tree's base. Aurora glanced over her shoulder.

Sweat rolled down Kire's face as he hefted the trunk of the palm-like tree on his shoulder. He sounded grumpy, but the teasing light in his eyes gave him away.

They'd been working on one of the green spaces in the central room of the main house since early this morning. "It's not the heaviest. It's the prettiest. Besides, this kind of work builds character."

"I already have lots of character."

"No, you *are* a character. Different thing." She laughed when he stuck his tongue out at her.

She shifted the root ball to her other shoulder so that she was facing him and prepared to back up the stairs. She halted when her comband chimed. "Saved by the bell." She gently eased the tree to the ground.

Kire set his end down with an audible groan.

Aurora opened the channel to the ship. "Go ahead, Star."

The Nirunoc sounded concerned. "I'm sorry to interrupt you, Captain, but you just received an urgent message from Commander Ellis."

An urgent message from Cade? That wasn't a good sign. Her pulse sped up. "Forward it to me."

The message appeared a moment later.

A-

Issue with local tribe. Justin, Raaveen, Paaw and Sparw taken. Need transport and crew backup ASAP. Burrow.

C-

Cade had taken the Lumians to Burrow?

Aurora had been with the *Excelsior* at the time of the Setarip attack against the research station. Her ship hadn't been called in, but she'd read the official reports. Most of the scientists hadn't survived, and at least one of the Meer tribes had been caught in the resulting battle.

Every member of the Fleet had been informed that the planet was strictly off limits. Which, of course, made it the perfect place to hide a ship and three hundred refugees that weren't supposed to exist. But apparently the Meer had found them.

The good news was that Burrow was relatively close. They could probably get there in less than two days if they pushed the *Starhawke's* limits. And her crew wouldn't be going alone. Cade wanted backup, and she would tuck an ace up her sleeve.

She met Kire's gaze. "Gather the crew."

Twenty-Five

Aurora was on her way.

Cade braced his forearms on the console and stared at the brief message.

> C-
>
> *Bringing backup. Estimate forty-six hours to arrival.*
> A-

He ignored the tingle of anticipation that danced over his skin. After months of separation, he couldn't stop his instinctive response to the idea of seeing her again. Unfortunately, her opinion of him would drop to an all-time low as a result of his failure to protect her people. He expected a wall of disappointment from her. And an avalanche of hostility from Jonarel Clarek. That would be challenging.

The timetable she'd given meant Justin and the teens would be stuck with their captors for another two days. Not ideal, but at least the Meer were taking care of them.

Justin had confirmed that the Meer had pressed the teens into service to heal the injured female. Drew had sent Morse code messages to him using a pulse signal that tapped on the inside of his forearm. He could respond to yes or no questions by turning on the video feed and rotating his arm left for yes and right for no.

The Suulh hadn't needed any encouragement to return to the ship after learning of the abduction of the three teens. However, Zelle and Maanee, Paaw's mother and younger sister, had been frantic. They probably would have stolen the remaining stealth pod to go after Paaw if they'd had any idea how to operate it. Williams and Reynolds had spent most of the afternoon trying to calm them down.

Raaveen's father and Sparw's parents were a different story. Ever since they'd been freed from captivity on Gaia, they'd existed in a catatonic state, unresponsive even with their own children. They had no idea who their kids were, let alone that they were in trouble. Sadly, that made this situation a lot easier.

Cade left the bridge and headed to the med bay. The hum of conversation flipped off like a switch as he stepped into the room. The Suulh had gathered into a tight cluster at the center of the open space, with Reynolds seated next to Maanee and Zelle. Their expressions revealed a heavy dose of fear and anxiety.

He turned on his translator. "Aurora and Mya are on their way."

He didn't have Aurora's gift for sensing emotions in others, but even he could feel the wave of relief that swept through the room. Knowing their Guardian and Healer were coming to help would decrease the Suulh's stress level enormously.

Reynolds pushed to her feet. "How soon will they be here?"

"About forty-six hours."

Reynolds frowned. "That means two more nights for Justin and the kids with the Meer."

Cade nodded. "I know. But it's the best we can do."

Zelle reached out to clutch Reynolds's hand, her blue eyes pleading. Reynolds knelt and murmured something that seemed to soothe her. She relaxed her grip, but her gaze followed them as they joined Gonzo, Williams and Drew around one of the lab tables on the far side of the room.

Cade studied the projected surveillance images. "What have you come up with?"

"The structures within the fortifications are comprised mostly of stone and packed dirt," Gonzo said. "Scans indicate one low-profile entrance for each building. Getting inside will be a challenge."

"I used the images from Justin's comband to calculate the dimensions and layout for the room where they're being held," Drew said. "We believe it's here." She pointed to a small structure at the back of the settlement, right next to the wall that ran along the edge of the drop-off.

"Something else came up in the scans," Williams said. "The Meer have created underground tunnels that connect the fortress with concealed entrances in the hills beyond. They can enter and exit without crossing the cleared area."

Cade studied the map. "Could we use the tunnels as access points?"

Williams shook his head. "They're designed for Meer, not humans. You and I wouldn't fit. And even if we could, we'd be sitting ducks until we reached the outer wall."

"So they can't use the tunnels to get the teens or Justin out, either."

"Correct. They must have brought them through the main gate." He pointed to a stone arch with a wooden gate that looked like something from a medieval castle. "Also, the room they're holding them in isn't connected to the tunnel system. That might be why they chose it—to isolate their prisoners from the rest of the tribe."

Cade looked at Gonzo. "How do we get in?"

"One option is an aerial approach from the canyon

on the far side of the drop-off. If we used one of the *Starhawke* shuttles, its stealth capabilities would make it virtually invisible to the Meer. We'd just need to wait for the right moment to exit the shuttle and make our way over the wall."

"Do you think we can get in and out without being noticed?"

"Getting in, yes. Getting out will be a lot harder, especially since we don't want to hurt any of the Meer. They're keeping Justin and the teens heavily guarded."

"What about using an inhalant to knock them out like we did with the Necri and Setarips on Gaia?" Not that it had worked the way they'd planned, but it might be more effective here.

Gonzo shook his head. "Those fortifications are an open air maze. We'd have to hit a hundred different spots at exactly the same time to provide full coverage. And even if we could, the Meer physiology is radically different from our own. An inhalant that is safe for us might accidentally kill them. We don't want to harm them if we can help it."

True. With the Necri and Setarips, they'd been dealing with a hostile invasion. The risk was acceptable. This situation was very different.

"But I have a suggestion." Drew pulled up several images from the video feed. "The Meer leader and all the guards we've seen are male. I don't think that's a coincidence. The injured Meer is the only female who's been allowed in the building, and they're fiercely protective of her, especially with Justin. I think we can use that to our advantage."

"How?"

She brushed a lock of hair behind her ear. "By sending an all female team to the front gate to negotiate with the Meer."

Cade blinked. "Negotiate? But we don't have a translation for their language."

Drew arched one brow. "We didn't have one for the Suulh, either. That didn't prevent us from communicating with the children when we found them locked in their cells."

Cade frowned. She had a point.

"And Justin and the teens seem to be doing fine. The Meer exhibit a lot of the same body language cues we do. I think it would work."

"I like this." Reynolds's brown eyes gleamed with anticipation. "Who were you thinking for the team?"

"Lieutenant Cardiff for sure. Her non-verbal communication skills are off the charts. I figured you and I would go too, and Captain Hawke."

"Works for me," Reynolds said.

"So you're hoping they'll allow you inside the fortress?" Cade asked.

Drew nodded. "Or they'll bring Justin and the teens out. At the very least it should give the infiltration team better odds for getting in and out unnoticed. All attention will be on us."

"And what if the Meer attack you instead?"

"Then we'll defend ourselves. But I don't see that happening. They aren't likely to view four passive, unarmed females as a serious threat. If anything, it might be a relief. They've probably been anticipating a counterattack ever since they took Justin and the teens."

"And we'll take concealed weapons," Reynolds added. "The Meer don't wear clothes, so they probably won't search us."

Cade glanced at Gonzo. "Who did you have in mind for the infiltration team?"

Gonzo and Williams exchanged a look. "That depends on whether you want to work with Clarek."

Ah, yes. The fly in the ointment. Guaranteed Jonarel Clarek would insist on being on the shuttle, either as the pilot or part of the infiltration team, especially if Aurora led the negotiations. "Unless Aurora objects, I'll be on the shuttle."

The corner of Gonzo's mouth turned up in a knowing smile. "Figured that. And we were both planning to join you."

"Then who's staying with the Suulh?"

"We were thinking Dr. Forrest and Emoto," Gonzo said. "She can keep them calm and he can oversee communications between the two teams."

Cade nodded. It was a solid plan that would play to everyone's strengths. "Let's hope the *Starhawke* crew agrees."

Twenty-Six

As prisons went, the Meer fortress wasn't terrible, but Justin's patience with the continued confinement was wearing thin.

He really shouldn't complain. The Meer treated them well. In addition to the food and water, they'd been given the opportunity to clean up and wash out their clothes.

The pseudo-bath had given him a chance to check on his injuries. He'd been amazed by how thoroughly they were healing. He'd anticipated feeling a sharp sting when the wounds came in contact with water, but instead he'd only felt a minor ache, like a bruise. Pretty impressive considering how banged up he'd been before Paaw's healing session.

And he wasn't the only one who was on the mend. The teens had worked on the Meer female again the previous morning. Afterwards she'd been able to sit up without assistance and bend her injured leg. She'd flinched at first, but the more she'd moved it, the better she'd seemed to feel.

She'd gazed at the teens with a look of wonder, but they'd been comatose on the floor by then and hadn't noticed. The captain of the guard had carried the female out of the room not long after, and she hadn't returned. The leader had sent in another robust meal, which the teens had devoured before falling into a deep sleep for the remainder of the day.

Justin had held onto the vain hope that the leader would release them the following morning. Instead, he'd brought in three males for healing. Justin had recognized the wounds, since he'd inflicted them with his pistol during the initial attack. The scorched skin and fur hadn't been treated in any way. Apparently the Meer didn't have any knowledge of healing.

With the exception of the captain, all of the guards were now treating him with thinly veiled contempt. The hostile guard with the scarred face who'd threatened him the first day seemed eager to be rid of him. In a lethal manner, if possible. The only thing stopping them seemed to be the visits from the leader and the presence of the teens. He doubted they wanted to risk upsetting their newfound healers. But that didn't mean they weren't plotting a way to terminate him that would look like an accident.

Bella's last message had informed him that the *Starhawke* was en route and due to arrive the following day. He'd debated whether to tell the teens, but had decided against it. The kids were brave, but they were utter failures at hiding their emotions. Their reactions to the news might alert the Meer.

Turning his attention away from the guards, Justin stretched out on the floor facing the teens. Paaw slept with her head tucked down and her body curled up, like an armadillo, so all he could see was her back. Sparw lay next to her, his left hand resting lightly on her knee as they faced each other, their breathing in perfect sync.

Raaveen lay closest to Justin, her body sprawled sideways, her long legs bent and her dark hair falling like a curtain over her face. The thick mane hid the dark smudges that held permanent residence under her eyes. Her cheeks, which had always been thin, looked hollow. Even her skin tone was changing, losing the olive undertones and growing sallow. The healing might be helping the Meer, but it was taking a heavy toll on Raaveen, Paaw and Sparw.

A gentle tapping started against the inside of his forearm. Another message from Bella. He turned on the video feed and closed his eyes, focusing on the Morse code message. Bella always sent each message twice, giving him a chance to confirm he'd understood it clearly. After a few minutes, the tapping stopped.

Plan in place. Negotiate and extract. Will see you tomorrow night. You okay?

He'd be willing to bet a year's salary that the negotiate part had been Bella's idea. The extract sounded like Gonzo. Either way, they had a plan. That was comforting. He slowly rotated his arm to the left. *Yes.*

Her confirmation tap came through, followed by a short personal message. *We miss you.*

He allowed himself a small smile. Leave it to Bella to lift his spirits. He stretched his arms up so she would be able to see his face and winked, then switched off the camera. He rolled to his side.

Raaveen was staring at him. Her gaze flicked to his forearm. Her lips barely moved but he caught the one word question. "Rescue?"

He kept his voice low. "Yes."

A flare of hope erased some of the weariness from her face. She glanced at Paaw and Sparw, but Justin gave a subtle shake of his head.

Her lips pursed and lines appeared across her forehead. Clearly she didn't like his response. But a moment later her expression cleared. "Secret."

He nodded. "Yes."

An understanding that was heartbreaking in one so young shone in her dark brown eyes. She drew in a deep breath and her body relaxed. Within moments she was fast asleep.

He was glad she was able to rest. He couldn't. He'd been battling insomnia ever since they'd arrived, and he had a good idea why.

He'd never been in a position like this before, where he felt responsible for people he cared about but was helpless to do anything to save them. He couldn't take out a dozen armed Meer by himself, especially if he didn't want to hurt them. And even if he could, he had no way to get the teens to safety. That meant he had to sit and wait.

But that was almost preferable to what would follow after his team rescued them. His personal torment wouldn't end. Oh no. His reward for escaping this prison would be saying goodbye to Raaveen, Paaw, and Sparw. Forever. They'd board the *Starhawke*, and he would never see them again.

He'd had ample time during the long days and nights of wakefulness to play out that charming scenario in his head over and over in a hundred different variations. It always ended the same way—with his heart being ripped right out of his chest.

Rock, meet hard place.

Twenty-Seven

By the time the *Starhawke* shuttle touched down in the canyon beside the *Nightingale*, Cade felt like he was standing in the middle of an anthill.

The graceful, clean lines of the shuttle provided a strong contrast to the sharp angles and worn hull of the dust covered medical freighter. The two ships served as a visual metaphor that reinforced the fact that the *Starhawke* crew was here to clean up his mess.

Aurora and Mya stepped off first. Cade's gaze locked with Aurora's for a brief moment before the Suulh surrounded her. The intensity of his reaction hit him hard. Apparently absence did make the heart grow fonder. Bad news for him.

The rest of the *Starhawke* crew descended and were swallowed up by the crowd as well. It took more than a minute for Aurora to extricate herself from the press of bodies and head in his direction.

Breathe, Ellis. Years of training kept his body from locking up, but he couldn't help bracing for a blow. He knew how deeply her words could cut. And she had every reason to blast him into next week.

As she stopped in front of him, worry lines bracketed her eyes and mouth. But the anger he'd expected to see in her green eyes was conspicuously absent. "How are they?"

No hostility or condemnation in her tone, either. Huh. "They're okay. Drew's kept in contact with Justin through his comband. The Meer are treating them well."

Some of the tension eased from her expression. "That's good to hear. Ever since I got your message, I haven't been able to get the image of those Setarip cages out of my mind."

And he'd been the cause of her anxiety. He was lower than a dung beetle. "I'm sorry. This snafu is my fault. I should never have given them permission to leave the camp." He didn't expect her to forgive him, but he'd take the blame he so richly deserved. Especially if it helped her feel better.

She gave a subtle shrug. "Things happen." The slightest hint of a smile touched her lips. "It's good to see you."

The comment shocked him so much he stammered his response. "Y-you, too." This wasn't the reaction he'd expected. Fury? Yes. Resentment? Sure. But she almost looked happy to be here. That made no sense.

She started to say something else but paused when a shadow fell over them. Clarek.

Cade was no slouch when it came to height, but Jonarel Clarek had him beat, something the Kraed seemed to enjoy putting to advantage whenever the opportunity presented itself.

Cade shifted to the side so that he was out of range of his rival. "Clarek."

Clarek's expression remained completely neutral. "Ellis."

Cade blinked. That was it? A banal greeting? No snide comments? No scathing remarks? This situation presented the Kraed with a perfect opportunity to cut him down to size, and yet Clarek wasn't taking the bait. In fact, Cade would go so far as to say Clarek had never looked so completely non-confrontational in his life.

What the hell was going on here? Was he dreaming? The sensation of having fallen into an alternate reality intensified as the rest of Aurora's crew joined them and Aurora deliberately moved away from Clarek.

But solving the mystery wasn't his priority. Right now they had a job to do.

After greetings were exchanged all around, the group headed to the *Nightingale*. The bridge was too small to fit a dozen people, so Cade led them to the compact lounge that opened off the kitchen. Drew and Gonzo positioned themselves on either side of the central monitor and Cade settled into the chair next to Drew. Reynolds and Cardiff stood by the kitchen, while Aurora, Emoto and Kelly chose the seats facing the screen. Williams, Mya and Clarek filled out the loose circle on the opposite side.

Cade was surprised to see Kelly with the group. He glanced at Aurora. "Who did you leave on the *Starhawke*?"

"Star."

Ah yes, the mysterious Star. He'd yet to meet the ship's elusive crewmember, although apparently Gonzo had while he'd been temporarily stationed on the *Starhawke* following the Gaia incident. Gonzo had been very evasive when Cade had questioned him. Whoever she was, Aurora obviously had tremendous faith in her if she'd left the ship in orbit under her command.

He shifted his attention to Drew. "Let's start with the surveillance images and the first video feed."

For the next few minutes Drew took everyone through the details of what the team had learned. Aurora and Mya both flinched when they saw the images from Justin's comband of the injured girl and the way the teens wolfed down the food they'd been provided. They'd have a unique understanding of what the teens were being asked to do, and the effect it would have on them.

When Drew finished, Gonzo took them through the rescue plan.

Emoto glanced at Cade. "Any chance you have a basic translation for their language?"

"Unfortunately, no. The scientists who were studying them never cracked it."

"So we'll be negotiating non-verbally?" Aurora asked.

"That's right. Hopefully the Meer will be reasonable. If not, then the extraction team will assist you in getting everyone out with as little confrontation as possible."

Cardiff and Reynolds exchanged a look of solidarity. They'd worked together to rescue the Suulh children from the Setarips on Gaia. He suspected they'd start discussing contingency plans after the meeting broke up.

"And you'll be leading the extraction team?" Clarek's voice was toneless, not even a hint of challenge in his yellow eyes.

In some ways that was more unnerving than when the Kraed was openly hostile. Cade held his gaze. "Yes. If Kelly pilots the shuttle, that will leave four of us for the infiltration."

"You'll have more than that," Aurora said.

He glanced at her. "What do you mean?"

"We brought four members of the Clarek clan."

Her statement caused a ripple of surprise from his team.

Cade's brain flipped into overdrive. More Kraed. They could be an asset in this situation, but if they knew about his feud with Jonarel Clarek, their clan loyalty might create unwanted conflict during the mission. However, Aurora must trust them, or she wouldn't have brought them. He would have to put his faith in them, too. "Where are they?"

"On the shuttle. They didn't want to alarm the Lumians with a sudden appearance." She lifted her comband. "But they've been listening in."

Cade stood. "Then let's go meet them."

Twenty-Eight

Good thing Aurora liked challenges.

Her thoughts had been rather dark ever since she'd received Cade's message. Visualizing the teens as captives again had made her break out in a cold sweat. They'd been through too much already.

But her worries hadn't prevented her stomach from giving a telltale flip when she'd spotted Cade standing in front of his ship, watching her. Her reaction should have made her uneasy, but she'd had too many other concerns claiming her attention to waste time thinking about it.

The first hurdle had been introducing Cade to Jonarel's kin. It had been impossible to predict how either side would react, but Cade had treated the Kraed with great respect, and they'd responded in kind. Apparently the Clarek clan didn't know that Cade was public enemy number one in Jonarel's book.

Or at least he had been. Jonarel's behavior since their arrival had been even more unnerving. Aurora couldn't remember a time when he'd treated Cade with such civility. She questioned the purity of his motives, considering the tension that still existed in his relationship with her, but if it meant the two males could work together without getting into an altercation, that's all that mattered.

She'd left the campsite with Celia, taking two of the *Starhawke*'s gliders to reach the Meer fortifications. Drew and Reynolds rode shotgun behind them. The rocky terrain of Burrow was a snap to navigate compared to the forest of Drakar, especially without any large predators to avoid. They'd made good time. The sun was still an hour from the horizon when they'd halted at an outcropping near their destination.

They had hidden the gliders in a narrow crevice and were going through final checks of their combands and weapons while they waited for the signal from Cade. The shuttle team would head in at twilight, taking advantage of the shadows for their infiltration.

When her comband pinged, she read the short message. "Showtime."

Aurora took the point position as they walked onto the cleared plateau, with Drew and Reynolds just behind her and Celia guarding the rear. Sensor sweeps had indicated the Meer were currently inside the walls, but there was no reason to take any chances.

Craters littered the open area, left behind by the boulders that had been pulled from the ground to build the fortress. Deep grooves scored the dirt, the fading scars indicating how much effort had gone into the construction.

As anticipated, their approach did not go unnoticed for long. Within minutes, a cry from the fortress carried over the warm breeze.

"Movement on the wall," Reynolds murmured. Gonzo had outfitted her with inconspicuous magnification goggles that doubled her visual range. "The gate's opening."

They were still too far away to distinguish individual shapes, but Aurora could make out the gate and a brown mass emerging from it.

"Here they come," Reynolds said. "Eleven Meer heading our way."

"Any sign of weapons?" Aurora asked.

"Strapped to their bodies, but they're on all fours."

Which meant they wouldn't be able to fire those weapons unless they stopped. In the videos Drew had shown them, most of the Meer had been walking on two legs, but they probably ran faster on four. It was a good sign that they'd chosen speed over defense.

The Meer might also be confused by what they were seeing. A small group of females approaching on foot over open ground would be a puzzle.

The Meer pack continued at a brisk pace, fanning out when they were about a hundred meters away. They rose onto their hind legs, weapons at the ready. Aurora halted and engaged her shield as the Meer formed a rough semicircle that placed them between Aurora's team and the fortifications. Celia and Reynolds moved up to her right side and Drew shifted to the left, all three remaining slightly behind her so she could keep them covered by the shield.

Two of the Meer left the semi-circle and approached Aurora's team. The rest of the guards kept their weapons aimed in warning.

Aurora lifted her hands with palms out as the two Meer drew closer, a non-verbal gesture of pacifism that also helped her to extend her shield. This close, she could see why the scientists had named the Meer after meerkats. The resemblance was striking, if a bit unsettling, considering their size.

One of the males was nearly her height, with pale fur that looked like burnished wheat in the light from the setting sun. His eyes were the color of caramel, outlined in smudges of dark brown. She saw wariness in those eyes, but also curiosity. That was a good sign.

The smaller male wasn't the least bit curious. A crescent shaped scar cut across the fur on his nose and cheek, framing eyes that were nearly black with suspicion and menace. He stopped a couple meters in front of her and puffed out his chest.

Aurora didn't need a translation to understand the content of the short barking sound he made.

Go away!

"Bow your head," Celia murmured.

Aurora followed the cue. Unfortunately, that brought her face closer to level with the hostile Meer. His lips peeled back, giving her an excellent view of his sharp teeth.

She kept her voice soft. "We're here to see our family." She shifted her gaze to the fortress in the distance. "We have come to ask for their release."

The male glared at her, fear and anger pouring off of him in equal measure.

"He *really* doesn't want us here," Celia said. "Watch him."

He snarled, an ugly, violent sound, then pointed out toward the hills.

Aurora held perfectly still. "We can't leave without them."

The male's snarl turned into a growl and he took a step toward her.

She countered by moving to her left in front of the pale-furred male. "Please." She filled her mind with thoughts of Raaveen, Paaw, and Sparw. The emotions that welled up were real, causing her throat to constrict. Her voice sounded foreign to her ears. "We're worried about them."

She could feel the pale Meer's conflict. Even without understanding her words, he couldn't fail to know what she was asking. After all, four people who looked just like them were currently being held captive in the fortress. But would he help her?

The scarred male growled again, stretching out a

clawed paw to grab onto Celia. Aurora pulled in her shield so he wouldn't make contact with it, but before his claws touched Celia's arm the taller male barked at him.

He froze, the scar on his face twisting as he shot Aurora a look of pure malice. But apparently the pale-furred male was in charge. Another command sent Scar-face stalking over to join the semicircle of guards.

Aurora kept her focus on the tall male before her.

"He's listening," Celia said. "Convince him."

She tuned into his emotions, searching for the best way to make a connection. This one moment would decide whether their mission failed before it even started. She'd beg if she had to. "Please. I'm worried about them."

The male's gaze shifted to her right, where Celia, Drew and Reynolds waited, heads bowed, arms open in supplication.

A trio of "please" echoed hers.

His focus returned to her, analyzing, weighing his options.

She kept her thoughts on the three teens. She had to get them out of this prison, and the Meer in front of her held the key.

His emotions shifted a moment before he motioned to the four of them to follow him.

Aurora bowed and dropped her shield. "Thank you."

The Meer in the semi-circle didn't seem to know what to make of the change in plan. But a barked order from their captain got them in motion. They quickly surrounded her small group, but kept their distance, casting anxious glances at her team.

Heavy silence marked the walk to the fortress. Dust clouds swirled around their feet as the breeze swept over the barren landscape. As they approached the walls of the fortress the sun dipped below the ridge. The shuttle would be closing in on their location soon.

Aurora glanced at the walls. As predicted, all attention was focused on the front gate. But standing just outside, barring their way, was a huge male with an unmistakable air of authority. His striped fur accentuated his bulk and his dark eyes shone with intelligence.

"That's the Meer leader," Drew confirmed.

And he definitely did not look happy to see them.

The captain motioned for the group to halt. He approached the gate alone, facing the leader without a hint of fear. The tone of the conversation that followed reminded Aurora of debates she'd had with her former captains when they'd been deciding on a course of action. Intense, but respectful.

Clearly the Meer captain had authority, too, which could help her cause. The Meer leader wasn't acting like a dictator. And the captain seemed to be making an effective argument. She could feel the leader's resolve weakening.

He shot her team a look of warning before barking an order. The heavy gate swung open and Aurora's team was ushered inside, bookended by eight of the guards. Thankfully, Scar-face wasn't one of them.

The Meer led them through the labyrinth of narrow alleys between the buildings. After several twists and turns, they arrived at a large central fire pit. Cooking utensils of various descriptions lay by the hearth, the smells of partially cooked food indicating that a large communal meal had been abandoned in mid-preparation.

The leader motioned her group toward the cleared area beside the fire circle, then turned to leave as the guards took up positions surrounding them.

"We can't go with you?" Aurora asked, gesturing to

the leader.

He motioned her toward the fire circle again and lifted his paws with palms out.

"You'll bring our people here, to the fire circle?" Aurora mimed four figures walking toward her.

He barked something that might have been an affirmative, then disappeared down one of the narrow corridors in the direction of the back wall.

"Did you get that?" Aurora murmured, although the question wasn't directed at her team. All of their combands had been set to broadcast to Kire, who could respond through the receivers attached to their ears.

"Uh-huh," Kire replied. "And so did the shuttle team."

Now they'd have to wait for the Meer leader's next move.

Twenty-Nine

Well done, Aurora. Cade smiled. Not only had she alerted his team that someone was coming to fetch Justin and the teens, but she'd told them where they were being taken.

His position on top of the wall gave him a good view of the alley, and his night visor allowed him to study the Meer male as he approached the building where Justin and the teens were being held. The Meer's body language radiated tension and unease, but also power. As he drew closer, Cade recognized him. The Meer leader.

The leader dropped onto all fours as he entered the small doorway. Not long afterward voices rumbled inside, dissent clear in the tone of the barks and yips. The leader's voice quickly silenced the din. Scuffling sounds drifted out of the opening, indicating movement. A few minutes later the leader exited, followed by six Meer guards and the three teens.

The teens had to crawl through the opening with their hands tied in front of them. The guards quickly flanked them, their weapons drawn.

Four additional guards slipped out and then Justin was shoved unceremoniously through the doorway by a guard whose face was marked by a scar across his nose and cheek.

Justin's arms were tied behind his back. He landed hard on his side as the scarred Meer continued to push him.

The other guards hauled Justin to his feet before

taking up positions to his right and left. They caged him in as the scarred Meer who'd shoved him swung a blunt weapon that connected solidly with the side of Justin's head.

Justin stumbled, his knees buckling. The guards kept him upright and propelled him forward.

Cade gritted his teeth. That was a coward's move, perfectly timed so that the Meer leader hadn't seen a thing. A low growl made him glance to his right. Clarek crouched beside him, his gaze following the group as they retreated down the alley. From the look on the Kraed's face, the scarred Meer was now on his hit list, too.

As Justin and the guards disappeared from view, Cade and Clarek returned to the back wall where Williams, Gonzo, and the four Kraed waited. "They're taking Justin and the teens to see Aurora at the central fire pit."

"I thought they'd turn her down flat," Gonzo said.

Clarek puffed up like a rooster. "Do not underestimate Aurora."

Cade chose to ignore Clarek's proprietary tone. Now wasn't the time for a verbal duel. "They'll reach Aurora's team in a couple minutes. We need to back her up."

Gonzo checked the scanner. "The majority of the Meer are clustered in the outbuildings or in the tunnels. Hiding, from the look of it. What's our next move?"

Cade glanced at Clarek. He needed to make smart use of the Kraed's abilities. "We need to get to the fire circle as quickly as possible. Recommendations?"

Clarek's yellow eyes glowed in the dim light. "We'll cover from above."

Of course he would. "Then Gonzo, Williams and I will head to the ground level." He tapped his comband. "Emoto? Did you get that?"

"Relaying to Roe and the team now. Kelly has the

shuttle ready on your command."

Cade nodded to his team. "Let's go."

Clarek and the four Kraed slipped along the wall, moving like panthers stalking prey. When they reached the roofline, they leapt over the alleyway to the next building and disappeared into the darkness.

"That's a little unnerving," Gonzo muttered.

"Yeah." Cade unhooked the grappling gun from his utility belt and shot a zipline that would take them into the alley. "But there's no way I'm letting them get there first."

Thirty

Justin's head hurt. Again. And no wonder. That scarred bastard of a Meer had clobbered him from behind. He'd had a feeling something was coming, but with the guards surrounding him and his arms bound, he'd had no way to defend himself.

His ears were ringing and his vision was a little blurry. It felt like he had a concussion, thank you very much. He didn't want to take the mistreatment personally, but the pain made that difficult. That sneaky SOB had had it in for him since day one.

He stumbled into the circle of warm light from the central fire and sank to his knees. When he lifted his head, his gaze met Bella's. She was the most beautiful sight he'd ever seen.

Her face scrunched up. "Justin!" She rushed toward him, but two of his guards stepped forward to block her.

In the process they cleared a line of sight to the leader. The male glanced his way, and his lips pulled back from his teeth. Apparently the knock on the head hadn't been his idea. He took several menacing steps toward the guards, cowing them. They released Bella, who slipped past them.

"Hey," Justin murmured as she knelt in front of him. She placed her hands on either side of his face, her gaze assessing. "Had a little accident." His tongue was starting to feel thick in his mouth.

"So I see." She tore a piece of cloth from her tunic

and held it against the side of his head.

It hurt like hell, but her concern was a welcome balm. "Thanks."

A commotion started up to his right. Raaveen was struggling against the hold of the guards, her gaze locked on him. "Justin," she called out, her voice filled with concern.

Paaw and Sparw were similarly focused on him. And they weren't the only ones.

Captain Hawke was glaring daggers at the Meer guards. "It'll be okay," she said. "We're going to get you out of here." Her gaze shifted to the teens. "All of you."

That's when he realized he and Bella were the only two who'd been allowed to get close to each other. Reynolds, Cardiff and Captain Hawke were being held back by a group of guards on the opposite side of the circle.

Captain Hawke faced the leader. "Let them go." She motioned toward the teens. Her voice was respectful, but there was no mistaking the tone of command underneath.

The Meer leader replied in a similar tone, but with a clear *no* in the undercurrent.

Which confirmed what Justin had suspected all along. The Meer leader had no intention of releasing them. Ever.

Thirty-One

Count to ten, count to ten.

Aurora used every calming technique she knew to keep from reacting to the Meer leader's denial. But the blood on Byrnes's face made that difficult.

She understood the leader's motivations. After all, she'd recently become the guardian of three hundred tortured souls who'd been kept as prisoners in filthy cramped cages. She remembered her horror as the truth of what had happened to them, and who they were, had been revealed. She'd been strongly motivated to help them ever since.

The Meer had suffered at the hands of Setarips, too. Now their leader had stumbled onto a way to protect his tribe from more pain. Unfortunately, he didn't see the irony that his actions were inflicting pain on others.

And his attitude was trying her patience.

The captain of the guard stood near the leader, his gaze on the teens, who were still struggling to get free. His emotions indicated he disagreed with his leader's actions. He'd already talked the leader into allowing her to see that Justin and the teens were alive. Maybe he'd help her again.

"This is my family." She stretched her arm toward the teens. "You must let them go."

The captain looked uncomfortable, his gaze shifting from her to the leader. Taking sides against his own would be a supreme act of courage. It wasn't one he was likely to make.

The leader's focus zeroed in on her like a laser. He

strode forward, stopping when the tip of his muzzle was centimeters from her face. He pointed at her with one paw, then at the teens with the other, before bringing the two paws side by side. He barked something that was clearly a question.

Aurora frowned. "I don't understand."

The leader repeated the gesture.

"He wants to know if you're related to them," Celia murmured.

Of course. Thank goodness for her friend's non-verbal skills.

Aurora mimicked the leader's gestures and then nodded. "I am their kin."

The leader's eyes took on a speculative gleam. Then he pointed at Byrnes with one paw and Aurora with the other, before bringing them together and asking his question again.

"Oh boy," Celia muttered.

Aurora had a nanosecond to consider her response. Clearly they knew Byrnes was different from the teens. If she claimed him as well, she'd give lie to the truth she'd just spoken.

She held Byrnes's gaze as she shook her head and let her arms drop to her sides. "No, he's not my kin. But he is my friend."

A small smile appeared on his lips. But a moment later he started blinking rapidly like he couldn't quite focus.

That worried her. The blow to his head might be more serious than it looked. And it looked pretty bad. They needed to get him out of here.

The leader's gaze fixed on Drew, who continued to hold the makeshift bandage to Byrnes's head. He pointed at Drew and the teens, repeating the familiar gesture.

He'd probably already guessed that Drew wasn't a healer. If she were, she would have started working on Byrnes's injury already. Aurora shook her head. "No, not kin."

Then he pointed at Reynolds and Celia, and Aurora shook her head again. He stared at her, suspicion clouding out every other emotion.

She kept her expression neutral. She'd told him the truth. Either he'd believe her, or he wouldn't.

Finally he turned to the guards next to her and gave a command. They gripped her upper arms, holding her in place.

She didn't resist, even when the Meer leader extended the tip of his sharp claw towards her skin. He couldn't hurt her unless she let him.

He said something that she interpreted as *show me* before grabbing her hand and bringing the claw down on her open palm. She suppressed the instinct to shield as the sharp tip sliced across her skin, opening a gash that slowly seeped red. It stung, but if this was what it took to convince him she was trustworthy, so be it.

He gestured to her hand, where blood had created a small pool in the indentation in her palm.

If he wanted a demonstration, he'd get one. But she'd have to make it quick. Another glance at Byrnes told her he needed to get to Mya. Soon.

She engaged her energy field, but kept the healing energy isolated to her hand. The Meer leader had unwittingly done her a favor. Her hands acted as a focal point for controlling her energy, naturally coalescing there, so it was an easy point to heal. Stopping the bleeding and sealing the skin on top took only a minute. The damage he'd done to the soft tissue underneath could wait until later.

Tipping her hand up, palm out, she offered it for

inspection.

The look of wonder on the leader's face as he examined her hand was a good sign.

"Please." She poured the depth of her emotions into that one word. "Let them go."

The crackling of the fire beside her sounded like the roar of an engine in the utter silence that surrounded them. But instead of releasing her, the leader's paw clamped down on her wrist.

He turned to the guards that held Cardiff and Reynolds, and barked an order. The guards grabbed them and started pulling them toward the alley that led to the front gate. The leader gestured toward Drew and Byrnes as well, dismissing them.

Aurora's patience washed away like water through a sieve. The Meer leader's behavior was tripping every emotional trigger she had. When he ordered the guards to take her in the opposite direction, she shifted from irritation to anger. Which is why it took her a moment to register that the rage she was feeling wasn't her own.

She gave her empathic abilities free rein, tracking it. The feeling was familiar. Was it Jonarel? Or Cade? No. She sensed them, too, their anger shining like bright spots of red in the sea of emotion. But they were both separate from the dark malevolence. This was someone else. And she'd felt it before. When she'd...

Whipping her head to the right, she searched the shadows for someone she couldn't see but knew without a doubt was there. A Meer guard with a scarred face.

The firelight reflected off the tip of an arrow. An arrow aimed directly at Byrnes's chest.

"Byrnes! Down!" she screamed.

Two blasts from Kraed rifles raced across the open

area from opposite directions, slamming into the guard, toppling him off the wall.

Negotiations had just ended.

Thirty-Two

The bastard had been about to kill Justin.

Cade kept his weapon up and his focus on the Meer guards closest to him as pandemonium erupted around the fire circle.

The Kraed had dropped from their hiding places at the perimeter and were doing a great job corralling the Meer who were near them. Shrieks of terror carried on the breeze as the Meer stared in horror at the fearsome intruders.

Cardiff and Reynolds were busy at the far side of the clearing dealing with the guards that had been trying to haul them to the gate. Ordinarily, the fight would have been over in a heartbeat, but since the two women didn't want to inflict permanent damage, they were obviously curtailing their defensive strategy. Gonzo was making his way toward them to offer assistance.

Unfortunately, no one had reached Drew and Justin, who were trapped at the center of the cyclone. Justin was prone on the ground, and Drew was trying to shield his body with her own. But they were in the open, completely exposed to the Meer guards who had started turning weapons in their direction.

Cade targeted the nearest guard and fired.

At the same time, the guards who had been holding Aurora suddenly shot back two meters and crumpled to the ground, twitching like they'd been hit with a high voltage charge.

Cade was willing to bet they had. Courtesy of Aurora Hawke.

She raced toward Justin and Drew, her pearlescent shield blooming to life around her. Small flares of light appeared where arrows struck the shield but she didn't seem to notice as she dropped to the ground in front of Drew and Justin and enveloping them in the shield's protective glow.

On the far side of the courtyard, Clarek and the other Kraed stood like menacing trees at the edge of the firelight. The Meer guards had converged around the three teens and the leader, caging them at the center of the tight mob as they backed up against the nearest building.

But it was what Cade saw through the press of bodies that made his blood freeze in his veins. The Meer leader and two of the guards had their paws wrapped around the teens' throats, the sharp edges of their claws pressing into the tender flesh.

Thirty-Three

The teens were in danger. Whatever Aurora had envisioned with this negotiation, she hadn't expected the Meer leader to threaten the lives of the healers he coveted. Apparently he was that desperate, which made him extremely dangerous.

"Don't hurt them." Her voice carried through the din created by the whining of the frightened Meer, who were staring at the Kraed like they were demons from Hell.

The leader's gaze found hers over the heads of his guards and he snarled.

She understood the impulse. A part of her wanted to snarl right back. But he was terrified, and with good reason.

This mess was exactly what she'd been trying to avoid. She needed to get closer so she could talk to him, but she couldn't leave Byrnes. Now that her shield surrounded him, she could feel just how weak he was. She didn't have Mya's gift for diagnosing injury, but she feared the blow to his head had caused a major concussion and may have triggered an internal hemorrhage. She'd placed her foot against his leg and was feeding him as much energy as she could while maintaining her shield, but she needed to get him out of here.

"We've got him, Aurora."

Cade's voice at her elbow startled her. She snapped her head around and discovered Dr. Williams was with him.

"Go help the teens." Cade held her gaze. "We'll get

Justin out of here."

His strong presence calmed her. "He needs Mya. Now. Don't wait for us."

Concern flashed in his green eyes, but he didn't argue. "Okay. We'll be back as quickly as we can."

She stepped forward but kept her shield up so that it was forming a barrier between the Meer and Byrnes as Drew helped Cade and Dr. Williams lift him to his feet. The look on Drew's face made it clear she'd happily shoot anyone who dared to challenge them as they headed for the alley. None of the Meer did.

Aurora returned her attention to the Meer leader.

Jonarel and the other Kraed remained motionless, silent sentinels ready to take action on her command.

Without moving or shifting her gaze, she called out to Celia. "Celia? Any suggestions?"

Celia's voice came from behind her. "Take it slow."

Right. Slow. She lifted her hands, palms out, her gaze on the three teens, who looked remarkably calm. The Meer surrounding them did not. Every weapon was drawn, with half of them aimed at the Kraed and the other half at her.

"It's okay." She used her most soothing voice, keeping her hands well away from her body. "We're not here to hurt you. We only want to take our people home."

The leader barked what sounded like a threat and tightened his grip on Raaveen's throat, drawing blood.

Aurora stopped. "It doesn't need to be this way. I know you want what's best for your tribe. But this isn't it."

A growl was his only reply. And Aurora really didn't like the twitchy way the guards were holding their weapons.

Celia had said to take it slow. She could do that. She'd give them as much time as they needed to calm down and return to rational behavior. All night, if necessary.

But a loud screech took her by surprise.

Out of the corner of her eye Aurora saw a petite female Meer stumble into the light from the fire circle, her movements unsteady as she hobbled on all fours, heading straight for the cluster of Meer guards.

Unfortunately, several of the guards panicked at the unexpected noise. Spinning toward her, they released their arrows.

Thirty-Four

Jonarel wanted to rip the Meer leader into a million little pieces. He had hurt Aurora and threatened the teens. His senses were on full alert, his body quaked from the effort of maintaining control.

Which is why he heard the odd shuffling noise of the Meer female's stumbling approach before she opened her mouth and screamed. Acting on the sixth sense that was his birthright, he leapt across the courtyard.

She failed to see him. Her gaze was locked on the teens. But when her cry echoed off the walls, it had a predictable effect on the terrified Meer.

Several arrows streaked toward her.

Jonarel got to her first. He tackled her, turning his back to the incoming projectiles. They struck full force, driving the air from his lungs as he collapsed on the ground, his body wrapped like a cocoon around the female.

Two cries of anguish ripped through the air as an avalanche of pain swept over him. But his focus remained on the bundle of fur trembling in his arms. Lifting his head, he gazed into the largest brown eyes he had ever seen. They seemed to swallow the female's entire face. Her lips were pulled back from her teeth in a grimace that was either pain or terror.

He wanted to assure her she was safe, but breathing normally was not an option. The searing pain in his chest might be from a lack of oxygen, broken ribs, or an internal injury. Or all three.

But his anxiety vanished when a familiar warmth enveloped him in a loving embrace. *Aurora.*

She knelt beside him, her beautiful green eyes filled with fear. Fear for him. "Jonarel?"

When she placed her hand on his shoulder, he almost wept. Stellar light, he had missed that connection.

She glanced at the trembling Meer female before returning her gaze to his. "How bad is it?"

He forced air out, although the effort made his body burn. "She...is...fine."

Aurora's brows snapped down. "I wasn't asking about her. How are you?"

Consumed by fire. But he did not care. She was with him. Touching him. Loving him. And for such a gift, he would gladly face a greewtaith with his arms bound behind his back. "I...will live."

Her gaze shifted to his back and her frown deepened. "Are you sure about that?"

"Yes." Because there was no way he was leaving this life while Aurora still drew air. The pain was excruciating, but he refused to think about whether the arrows had hit anything vital.

"Celia, we need that shuttle back as soon as they drop off Byrnes."

"Already on it."

Aurora rested her hand on his back. The gentle warmth of her energy field soothed him, pushing against the pain and making it a little easier for him to breathe.

Her gaze held his, and unshed tears shimmered in her eyes. "I'm sorry," she whispered. "Jonarel, I'm so sorry."

She was not referring to the arrows. And given a choice, he would have found a less painful way to break their emotional stalemate. But he would gladly take the blow of a hundred arrows if it brought her back to him. "As am...I."

The corners of her mouth quivered in a tremulous smile. Her gaze shifted to the Meer female, and a flicker of curiosity crossed her face. But then her expression changed to something darker. Her hands slid away from his body and closed into fists. A ferocity he had never seen before glowed in her eyes as she rose to her feet and pointed one accusing finger.

"You!"

Thirty-Five

Aurora had tried to be patient. She'd tried to be understanding. She'd tried to keep everyone safe. But look where it had gotten her? Byrnes and Jonarel badly injured and the teens still in the clutches of the Meer with no resolution in sight. She'd hit her limit.

She kept her shield wrapped around Jonarel and the Meer female as she faced the leader. He'd released his grip on Raaveen and had shoved his way through the circle of guards.

"You!" She pointed a finger at his chest and he stepped back like she'd struck him, his eyes white with fear. "You're the reason for all of this!"

He whined softly, but that didn't stop her from yelling at him.

"Why couldn't you just let them go? They'd already healed your child."

The leader's gaze jumped from her to his daughter and back again, almost like he understood her words.

Her teeth ground together as she fought to control her temper. "Do you think you're the only one who's suffered? Do you think you're the only one who's known pain and loss?"

His paws curled and uncurled in front of his chest as he stared at her.

Her anger built up steam. "What about the teens? And Justin? What about their pain?" Pain that this arrogant male had inflicted on them without a second thought. "You *hurt* them. *Enslaved* them. *You forced them to do your bidding!*"

Her breath shot in and out of her lungs. Too much suffering. Too much heartache. Too many lives destroyed because of a selfish belief that one group had the right to impose their will on another. Would it never end?

"Do you have any idea what those kids have been through?" she snapped, pointing at the teens, who stood frozen in place, their eyes wide. "They've suffered in ways you can't possibly imagine. And they're still suffering." Because she could feel their pain. Had in fact been surrounded by it ever since the day she'd first come in contact with them.

"Nothing gives you the right to control them. Or anyone else." She stalked the Meer leader and he shrank from her. Her energy field whipped around her, creating a cyclone of energy that mirrored her emotional state, but she held onto her self-control. She wouldn't hurt him. But she would make him understand.

"You took away their freedom. You separated them from their families. Families that love them as much as you love your daughter." She brought her face within centimeters of his. "You. Will. Let. Them. Go."

He whimpered, his gaze locked on her. His fear was tangible. But it wasn't fear for his own safety. His gaze darted to his daughter, and the whimper turned into a pitiful mewl. He feared what Aurora might do to his child. He loved his daughter so much that he had put his entire tribe at risk in order to save her. His actions had started from that place of love and compassion. Unfortunately, he'd allowed greed to twist his intentions into something more insidious. And had unwittingly put his daughter in danger again.

Comprehension shone in his dark eyes. She'd made

her point. Now it was time to end this. "Enough." Her gaze drifted to the teens. They looked as emotionally strung-out as she felt. "You've all suffered enough."

The Meer leader remained frozen, although he was trembling hard enough his teeth chattered. The captain of the guard stood behind him, his body tense as he watched her. And waited. The rest of the Meer had lowered their weapons and were staring at her. In fact, she had everyone's full attention right now. And she knew exactly what she needed to do.

"Come here." She motioned to Raaveen, Paaw and Sparw.

None of the guards tried to stop them as they made their way to the front of the group.

She returned to Jonarel and knelt beside him. "I've got her."

He relaxed his hold and she scooped the leader's daughter into her arms. The petite creature remained curled into a protective ball.

Shame washed over Aurora. Her anger had made the situation worse. She allowed a flow of soothing energy to surround them both. "It's okay. Everything's going to be okay." She stepped around Jonarel and walked toward the captain, who met her halfway. She shifted her grip on the female so he could take her.

The leader stayed rooted in place, as if he feared any movement would bring down disaster.

As the captain carried the female to her father, Aurora turned to the teens. "I need your help with Jonarel."

They immediately joined her and dropped to their knees beside him. They clasped hands with her and each other. She winced when they connected with her energy field. They were more drained than she'd realized. She hated to ask them to give more, but Jonarel needed them. And she might be able to help them, too.

Taking a deep breath, she focused on the flow of energy. They responded, their energy blending with hers, growing stronger as she focused on building a nurturing web. This was what they'd been born to do. This was their gift. And it was a gift they shared willingly. The colors swirled, her pearlescent white mixing with their red, yellow and blue. As one, they lowered their hands and made contact with Jonarel's body.

He gave a jolt.

"Sorry." Apparently the teens didn't realize they needed to block the pain signals the healing process could cause. They did it instinctively for themselves, but Jonarel didn't have that ability. He'd need her help to suppress his body's natural reaction to the healing.

Her empathic senses allowed her to know when she'd succeeded. His anxiety faded and his breathing evened out. As they focused on containing his internal injuries, the flow of blood from his wounds slowed. When it finally stopped, she released the energy field. He'd have to wait for Mya to extract the arrows and repair the bulk of the internal damage, but they'd brought him out of danger.

And he was watching her. The look in his golden eyes wasn't hard to decipher. He loved her. It was as simple as that. He always had. And he always would.

And she loved him. Just not the way he wanted her to.

"The shuttle just arrived at the *Nightingale*," Celia said.

Aurora glanced up, surprised to find her friend standing behind her. Guarding her, she realized. Just in case.

Reynolds was doing the same with the teens, though

subtly, while Gonzo kept watch on the Meer leader and the captain of the guard.

"They'll pick us up as soon as Byrnes is transferred."

"Hang on." Aurora had an idea. "Tell them to wait until Mya has stabilized Byrnes. Then have Williams stay with him and send Mya back with the shuttle."

Celia frowned. "Why bring her here?" Her gaze flicked to the Meer leader.

Her reluctance was understandable. Bringing Mya to the Meer leader was like showing the Holy Grail to King Arthur. But Camelot had fallen. The Meer leader had given up his quest. He was clutching his daughter to his chest so tightly it was a wonder the poor creature could breathe. Her safety was all that mattered to him. "Because Mya can heal the female's injury."

"I thought the teens had already healed her."

"They set the bone and repaired a lot of the tissue damage, which is remarkable." Aurora shot a look of gratitude at the teens. "But it will always be a point of weakness. Mya can heal it completely, as though the trauma never occurred. After all the Meer have been through, I don't want to end things like this."

Celia's voice softened. "It's a peace offering."

"Yes."

"You do realize we'll be breaking just about every Council law by doing this?"

Aurora sighed. "We started on that path a long time ago. I'm not about to stop now." And the Council had based their decision to quarantine the planet on the belief that the Meer would return to their previous way of life. Obviously, that was a false premise. The Meer culture had been changed by their experience with the Setarips. They needed tools that would help them deal with their new reality.

"However, we can't do anything without the leader's permission. I need you to explain it to him."

"Happy to."

Watching Celia talk with the Meer leader was like watching Michelangelo carve marble. She conveyed complex concepts with body motions and facial expressions that he understood almost immediately. And he was much more receptive than he'd been when they'd arrived. When he realized they were offering to have his daughter fully healed by someone with more skill than Aurora and the teens, he looked ready to prostrate himself at Aurora's feet.

Her comband pinged with an incoming call from Mya. "How's Byrnes?"

"He's going to be fine. He had a concussion and the beginnings of an internal hemorrhage that was putting pressure on his brain. I've repaired the damage and he's resting comfortably."

So she'd been right. "That's good news." She flashed Reynolds and Gonzo a thumbs up. Then she gave Mya a quick rundown on the situation and asked how quickly she could return with the shuttle.

"Tam's in with Byrnes, so I can leave now."

"Bring medical supplies. Nothing that requires power but basic first aid tools that we can leave with the Meer. And diagrams that show how to use them."

"You're going to provide them with medical supplies?" Surprise and concern made Mya's voice rise. "You'll be violating Council law. And leaving evidence we were here."

"I realize that. And it will be on my shoulders if anyone finds out. But we need to do this. We can't leave a healer behind, but we can certainly teach them how to heal themselves."

Thirty-Six

The stars twinkled like glitter spilled from a bottle and a cool breeze blew across the canyon as Cade exited the *Nightingale*. He'd just left Justin, Raaveen, Paaw, and Sparw sleeping peacefully in the med bay, surrounded by the loving energy of the Suulh. The kaleidoscope of color dancing around the room looked like something out of a dream.

Odds were good it was the first real rest any of them had gotten since the attack. He'd spoken with Mya briefly about the healing work the teens had done while they were with the Meer. She'd confirmed it had taken a heavy toll on them. But being back with the rest of the Suulh and under Mya's watchful care would set them to rights in no time. Justin was on the mend, too. And Cade had thanked her profusely for that. From what Tam had told him, her help had been instrumental in Justin's recovery.

Clarek was healing, too, although he'd chosen to remain in a separate part of the bay. His four clan members were with him, which might have explained why none of the Suulh had approached. The Kraed were an intimidating sight. Mya was with Clarek now, tending his wounds and keeping up a soothing flow of conversation.

Much as he hated to admit it, Cade was impressed by Clarek's actions tonight to save the Meer female. Reynolds had filled him in on the details. Anticipating the danger and placing himself directly in the line of fire took guts, and an altruistic streak that Cade could respect.

Tipping his head back, he breathed in the night air

and focused on releasing some of the tension that had been his continual companion for the past few days. The fire in front of the ship had been banked for the night, leaving the canyon in relative darkness. However, as he continued forward he spotted a lone figure seated with her back against one of the boulders, her face tilted up toward the stars.

"Mind if I join you?"

Aurora's gaze flicked briefly in his direction. "Go ahead."

Not the heartiest of welcomes, but he'd take it. After the adrenaline rush of the rescue and the race back here to save Justin, he was too restless to sleep. She might be in the same fix.

Settling in next to her and resting his elbows on his knees, he studied her out of the corner of his eye. Her face was in shadow, the soft glow from the coals and the starlight providing the only illumination. He drank in the sight of her, such as it was. After all, this might very well be the last time he'd have the chance.

"What's on your mind, Cade?"

He gave a little start. She was so damn observant. He should have known she'd catch him watching her. "I haven't had a chance to talk to you since you returned. Did everything go okay with the Meer?"

She continued to stare at the stars. "We left the medical supplies and the instructions on how to use them. The guards were very receptive. Several of the female tribe members ventured into the fire circle to watch Mya and Celia's demonstration, too."

That was promising. "And what about the leader's daughter?"

Aurora glanced at him. "Mya healed her leg. She'll

be fine."

Her tone sounded flat. He frowned. "But?"

She sighed. "Celia talked at length with the leader. His mate was in charge of the tribe prior to the Setarip attack, but she died, along with all their other children and more than half of the adult females." Aurora's face pinched. "That's why they kept all the remaining females hidden from us. They couldn't afford to lose any more of them if they wanted the tribe to survive."

"No wonder he was desperate to save his daughter."

"They also lost their healers in the attack. No one was left who knew anything about dealing with injury and illness. They've suffered more deaths in the past few years as a result."

Cade stared at the glowing coals, searching for answers that weren't there. "The Council thought they were doing the right thing by quarantining this planet."

"I know. And I thought so, too. But it's not that simple."

"It never is."

They sat in silence for several moments, the sound of their breathing the only marker of time.

He redirected the conversation to a more pleasant topic. "Raaveen, Sparw, and Paaw are doing well."

A sad smile touched Aurora's lips. "Those kids are really something. Kelly offered to bring them back here while we worked with the Meer, but they refused. They wouldn't leave until we did."

He'd been waiting outside when Aurora and Mya had returned with the teens. Zelle and Maanee had raced toward the shuttle before the ramp was even down and had enveloped Paaw in a fierce embrace. They'd grabbed Sparw and Raaveen into the group hug as well. For a moment, it had looked like they were never going to let go.

"They really are remarkable." And he was feeling like a prize idiot for putting everyone through this mess in the first place. Aurora's good opinion of him had only recently been restored while on Gaia, but she'd probably never trust him again. And that really bothered him. "I'm sorry I screwed up the mission and endangered your people."

A frown line appeared between her brows. "Is that what you think?"

"It's a fact."

"Like hell!" She scowled. "Unless you've developed a psychic ability I don't know about, there's no way you could have anticipated what happened. Your team did everything right."

"Not everything. I should have gone with Justin instead of sending the teens. It wouldn't have taken much time."

Aurora blew out a breath. "Problems always seem obvious in hindsight. But that's not how life works. We make decisions based on the information at hand." She gazed into his eyes. "Cut yourself some slack, Cade. You were trying to do something nice for Paaw and Zelle."

So she didn't blame him? The knots in his chest loosened a bit.

"I don't blame you."

His eyebrows lifted. Was she reading his mind?

"And no, I'm not reading your mind. Guilt produces a very distinct emotional vibration. You've been coated in it ever since I arrived. But it just started to dissipate."

He stared at her. Her ability to read him, to understand him, even better than he understood himself, triggered something elemental deep inside.

She leaned against the boulder. "Will you be

reporting to the Admiral after we leave?"

His stomach clenched. He'd been avoiding all thoughts of tomorrow. "I guess so."

Her eyes narrowed. "You don't sound excited."

How to respond to that? His emotions were a bit of a tangle right now, but excited wasn't one of them. "I'm not."

"Why not? I thought you loved your job."

How to answer that without giving too much away? "I do love my job. But my unit has spent the past two months living in close quarters with the Suulh."

Aurora frowned. "Suulh?"

He'd forgotten she didn't know. "That's what the Lumians call themselves. Justin found out while he was creating the translation."

"Oh." Her brows drew down as she processed that information. Hearing the official name of her race was probably a little unsettling. Like finding out the name everyone's been calling you all your life isn't the one listed on your birth certificate.

"I know it's the right thing to do, sending them to the new homeworld. They'll be safe there. But putting them on your ship tomorrow and having them disappear forever just feels...wrong."

The frown lines disappeared as understanding softened her expression. "You're going to miss them."

And you. "Yeah...well, yeah." He stared up at the sky. "I just want to know they're okay. Settled. Happy." He glanced at her. "They've been through so much." *As have you.*

She let out a sigh that seemed to come from the depths of her soul. "I know." Her gaze drifted back to the stars. "Life isn't fair," she murmured, more to herself than to him. "How about this? You take the Suulh to the new homeworld and I'll go report to Admiral Schreiber for assignment."

He thought she was joking, except she wasn't smiling. In fact, as he studied her, he could see lines of tension in her jaw and shoulders. "Aren't you looking forward to getting them to their homeworld?"

Her tone was as hard as the rock she was leaning against. "Nope."

That was unexpected. And so unlike her. "Why not?"

She squeezed her eyes shut and drew in several slow breaths as her face contorted like she was in pain.

He wanted to reach out to her, to comfort her, but he didn't dare. Instead, he caressed her with his voice. "Aurora? Talk to me."

She puffed out her cheeks and then forced the air from her lungs in a rush. "Why the hell does everyone think they have the right to control them?" she snapped. "Huh? Can you tell me that?" She turned to face him, her eyes glowing with a fire from within.

The change in attitude was so abrupt he pulled back, startled. "I'm not trying to control them."

She waved a hand in the air, dismissing the comment. "I'm not talking about you. You're fine. I'm talking about everyone else." Her voice vibrated with anger. "The Setarips kept them in cages and forced them to destroy. The Meer locked them in a room and forced them to heal. And somewhere out there," she said, gesturing at the stars, "the power-hungry lunatics who orchestrated the attack on Gaia are waiting to snatch them from us and turn them back into Necri."

The venom in her voice was impressive, as was the way she bared her teeth at the sky. "Why can't everyone just leave them alone? How can I possibly keep them safe if the entire universe is out to get us?"

Us. Not *them.* Us. He didn't think she realized the slip, but it told him exactly how cornered she felt by her current circumstances.

"I should just let someone else take over the job. They'd be better off without me."

Whoa. Back up the wagons. That was not the woman he knew. Not by a long shot. He reached for her hand and she jumped, like she'd momentarily forgotten he was there. But she didn't pull away as he threaded his fingers through hers and began lightly stroking his thumb across the smooth skin on the back of her hand. "You *have* kept them safe. I'm the one who put them in danger this time."

She shook her head, her expression adamant. "Doesn't matter. Don't you get it? There's *nowhere* that's safe. There's no way to protect them when everyone they encounter thinks they're tools to be manipulated. No one sees them for who they really are."

"You do."

She blinked, as if the idea had never occurred to her.

"Your crew does. And my team does."

She stared at him as if hypnotized. Or lost. Really, really lost. The Aurora he knew didn't spew anger like scattershot from a shotgun. She also didn't turn her back on those who needed her. He wasn't about to let her do it now.

"I know you're feeling overwhelmed. And it's not surprising. You didn't sign up for any of this." He continued the gentle motion of his thumb as he gazed into the beautiful green depths of her eyes. "But no matter how you feel right now, I promise you it will pass." He used his free hand to brush a lock of hair back from her face, trailing his fingers along her cheek. "You'll make it through this. You're the strongest person I know. You always have been. And your people need you. Your strength will help them to find their own."

She remained perfectly still, like she'd turned to stone at his touch, although her gaze searched his. Perhaps seeking the truth in his words.

He started to withdraw his hand but she captured it with both of hers, holding it against her cheek as her eyes drifted closed. She took several slow breaths, her fingers gripping his like she was afraid he'd pull away.

Hardly. He'd happily stay like this until the Burrow sun rose and turned them both into sweaty, blistering wrecks. He'd do anything to keep this connection with her.

When she finally lifted her lids, he caught a hint of the light from within that was uniquely Aurora. And it sparked an answering glow from him.

Releasing his hand, she shifted to face him. "Do you want to go with us to the new homeworld?"

His brain stalled. She hadn't really just suggested that, had she? "But the Admiral wanted the location to be a secret."

Her expression became more animated. "It will be. Instead of transferring the Suulh here, you could follow us to Drakar and leave the freighter with the Clarek clan. Then your team could hitch a ride with us."

He was stunned. And more than a little concerned. "The Admiral didn't want us to go to Drakar."

She frowned. "Why not?"

"Because that's the first place he'd look for us."

She pursed her lips. "Okay. So maybe we don't go to Drakar." She gazed at the box canyon. "It's probably unwise to leave the *Nightingale* here, but we could pick a neutral location, maybe somewhere in Kraed space, where we could dock the ships together and make the transfer. I assume the *Nightingale* has an autopilot?"

"It's not high-tech, but it's functional."

"Good. Then you could set it to maintain a standard orbit around whichever planet we used for our rendezvous. After we deliver the Suulh to the homeworld, my crew can bring you back. What do you think?" For the first time since they'd parted on Gaia, she looked excited.

He savored the emerging warmth in her eyes. "I think you're amazing."

A hint of a smile touched her lips. "Flattery will get you nowhere, Ellis."

"I know." He lifted her hand to his lips and brushed a gentle kiss across her skin. He grinned at her startled expression. "But I can always try."

She shook her head, but her smile grew. "So you like the plan?"

"I love the plan."

She squeezed his hand. "Just remember that there are about forty members of Jonarel's clan working on the settlement. You'll need to be on your best behavior. Okay?"

He should have been offended, but it was a fair question. "I'll be a perfect guest."

Her eyes narrowed, but she was smiling. "Umm-hmm."

He raised his right hand, palm out. "You have my word."

One eyebrow lifted. "I'll hold you to that."

He couldn't resist an opening like that. "Lady, you can hold me to anything you like."

Thirty-Seven

In the light from the hanging lanterns, Justin worked side by side with Gonzo in the cool night air, dismantling the greenhouse. But his thoughts kept returning to Captain Hawke's announcement.

When she'd visited him in the med bay that afternoon, she'd informed him that she'd invited his entire team to accompany her to the new homeworld. The news had created quite a stir, since they'd all assumed the Suulh would be leaving on the *Starhawke*. He hadn't been the only one who was thrilled with the opportunity to see them in their new home.

Dr. Forrest had checked on him as well, and after confirming his healing was nearly complete, she'd asked him to describe his experiences with the teens while they were with the Meer. In particular, she'd wanted to know what they'd done to heal the female's broken leg.

He'd told her everything he could remember, including Paaw's healing of his injuries from the initial attack. She'd asked detailed questions about what he'd felt during the session, and how it had affected him. The direction of her inquiries indicated she might be considering taking Paaw on as an apprentice. He hoped she did. With some training, Paaw would make an excellent doctor.

"You got that thing loose, Byrnsie?" Gonzo braced his hands against the beam in question, preparing to pull. "Or do you need a break?"

Gonzo had objected when Justin had volunteered his

services for this job, but Justin had overruled him. The manual labor was exactly what he needed after the days of confinement. He'd assured Gonzo he had Dr. Forrest's clearance to work, which helped. Still, his friend was treating him with kid gloves. "Just a sec." He refocused his attention on his job and removed the last two connectors. "Okay, good to go."

Wrapping his hands around the beam, he lifted while Gonzo pulled. They hoisted the beam so it cleared the surrounding materials before lowering it to the ground.

"Four down, twenty more to go," Gonzo said with a grin.

Cade and Reynolds were in charge of loading the materials back onto the *Nightingale*, and they were keeping up a steady pace to match the deconstruction. Bella and Tam were helping Captain Hawke and Dr. Forrest sort the plants. Some would be transferred to the *Starhawke* for the doctor's personal medicinal collection, while others were being harvested by the Suulh to provide food for the first part of the journey. The remaining plants were being taken to the *Starhawke* shuttle. The following evening they'd be returned to the locations where they'd been originally obtained.

That left the rest of the *Starhawke* crew with the task of dismantling the well and irrigation system and restoring the area to its original condition.

By the time Justin and Gonzo finished dismantling the greenhouse framework, a pale peach glow from the rising sun bathed the surrounding boulders in soft light.

Justin wiped the sweat from his brow with his sleeve. "Can't say I'll miss this dry heat."

Gonzo chuckled. "You haven't experienced dry heat until you've spent a summer in my hometown, amigo."

"Yeah, yeah. I know. You're part lizard."

"Desert rat," Gonzo corrected him. "And proud of it."

Justin accepted the canteen of water Gonzo handed him. He had a whole new appreciation for the joys of drinking from a closed container rather than an open bowl, and he savored every drop.

"Justin?"

He turned at the sound of Raaveen's voice. She, Paaw and Sparw stood in a semi-circle next to the last remnants of the greenhouse. He was pleased to see that the dark smudges were gone from under their eyes and their faces had lost the haggard look they'd developed while they were with the Meer.

"Hey, Raaveen. What's up?"

She stepped forward. "We thank you."

He frowned. "Thank me? For what?"

"For guard us. For watch out for us with Meer." Her accent made the name come out sounding like Meeeer.

He winced. "Actually, I did a pretty terrible job of that."

All three shook their heads. "You care for us," Paaw said. "You make us safe."

Well, she was right about the caring part. He couldn't seem to help it. "You cared for me, too," he reminded her. "I should be thanking you."

Her smile was a beautiful thing, especially since he hadn't seen it in a while. "Heal you is easy. You is like us."

Like us. Except he wasn't. Not really. And that was part of the problem. He wasn't part of their world, and soon, he wouldn't be part of their lives, either. The upcoming trip was simply delaying the inevitable. And that knowledge was breaking his heart.

The teens, however, had no way of knowing they

were torturing him with their gratitude. So he treasured every word for the jewels they were. "Yeah, I like you, too," he said with a smile.

They all laughed, as he'd intended. God, it felt good to hear their laughter again. And if his heart was cracking in two, well, that was life.

Thirty-Eight

Aurora settled into the captain's chair with a happy sigh. No doubt about it. There was nowhere else she'd rather be.

Her ship, however, was short one crewmember and four guests. Mya had decided to stay on the *Nightingale*, as had Jonarel's kin. The Suulh had overcome their shyness and had expressed an interest in using the journey to learn more about the Kraed, since they would be encountering many more of them when they arrived at the homeworld. The Clarek clan members had been delighted to comply.

Kire looked up from the communications console. "Byrnes just reported in. They've left the canyon and are on their way to rendezvous with us."

"Good." She turned to Kelly at navigation. "Are we all set for the interstellar jump?"

Kelly pushed her auburn hair behind her shoulders. "Aye."

"Captain?"

She glanced at Celia, who was frowning at the security console. Something in her expression pulled Aurora to her feet. "What is it?"

"I'm not sure. I'm getting odd energy readings that seem to be emanating from the nearby moon, or reflecting off the moon's surface." Celia indicated several data points. "At first I thought they might be an echo of our ship, but I checked the scan logs and the signals began appearing before we brought our engines on full."

"That moon has an atmosphere. Could it be a

naturally occurring phenomenon, maybe a reaction to a solar flare?"

Celia shrugged. "Possibly. We haven't been tracking solar activity, so there's no way to know for sure unless it fades out."

Aurora wasn't about to take any chances. "Raise the shields. And keep an eye out for any changes to the readings." She moved up the incline to Kire's station. "Do a sweep of the area and see if you can pick up comm signals of any kind."

"On it."

She dropped back into the captain's chair and opened a direct channel to Cade. "We may have a problem."

"What kind of problem?"

"We're picking up energy readings from the moon that don't have a clear cause. Where are you?"

"We've exited the atmosphere and are en route to your location. Do you want us to wait while you check it out?"

She didn't relish the idea of leaving the *Nightingale* unprotected. It didn't have the defensive capabilities of the *Starhawke*. "No. But I'd feel better if we changed our exit trajectory. The original path was going to take us close to that moon. Can you locate a jump window in the opposite direction that would take us to a rendezvous point closer to this system?" *In case we need to make a quick getaway.*

His tone indicated he understood the unspoken part of her message. "Give me a couple minutes to make the calculations and I'll send the data to Kelly."

"We'll move to intercept you."

"Understood."

Aurora closed the channel. "Kelly, get us into position as quickly as you can."

"Aye, Captain."

Kire pivoted to face Aurora. "The moon's atmosphere is causing problems with all the readings. I can't detect any obvious communication patterns, but a ship could certainly hide on the far side of the moon. There's no way to know for sure."

Not what she'd been hoping for. "Star, you've been monitoring the system while we've been in orbit. Have you seen anything unusual?"

The Nirunoc's ghostly image appeared at the console to Aurora's left. "I have not. But the debris field that surrounds the inner planets of this system scatters sensor readings. If a ship approached with a specific trajectory from the outer edges of the system and proceeded slowly, it would be possible to use the debris as a sensor shield."

"Then they'd have just as much trouble getting readings on us, right?"

"That is correct."

If a ship *had* snuck into the area, odds were good their intentions were hostile. That meant Setarips...or worse. Time for a second opinion. She opened a visual channel to Cade's ship. The image showed Cade in the captain's chair on the small bridge, with Drew at the helm, Gonzo at tactical, and Byrnes at the comm.

Cade's brows lifted. "You must not like what you're seeing out there."

Aurora shook her head. "I don't. The debris field and the moon are messing with our readings. It might be nothing. But it could also be a ship."

"Are you thinking Setarips?"

"Maybe, but I doubt it. Burrow was a target while the research team was here, but now it would be of little use to Setarips except as a watering hole. I'm more concerned that it's someone else."

Cade's expression darkened. "You mean power-hungry lunatics?" he asked, echoing their conversation by the campfire.

"Yep."

Cade held her gaze. "How do you want to handle this?"

Aurora tapped her fingers against the arms of her chair. "I'd love to find out who was behind the attack on Gaia, but not at the expense of endangering the Suulh." If only she knew for a fact that someone was out there. And whether they posed a threat. "Let's begin our departure, and see if the readings indicate we're dealing with an atmospheric phenomenon."

"And if it turns out to be a ship?"

Aurora pressed her lips together. "We'll run like hell to the jump window."

Cade glanced at his team, who all nodded in agreement. "All right. Do you want to lead or follow?"

"Follow. I want the *Starhawke* between you and anything that might put in an appearance." Aurora turned to Celia. "Arm all weapons and notify me immediately of any changes to the sensor readings. Kelly, position us between the freighter and that moon and keep us there."

"Aye, Captain."

Aurora opened a channel to engineering. "Hawke to Clarek."

"Clarek here."

"Jonarel, we may need to make a rapid exit."

His voice changed to a low growl. "What is wrong?"

"We're getting readings from the Burrow moon that indicate a ship might be hiding behind it."

A brief pause let her know he was digesting that

information. and realizing all the implications. "I will work on boosting power to the engines and shields."

"Thank you."

Cade's voice drew her attention back to the bridgescreen.

"We're ready when you are. I've sent the new data to Kelly."

"We'll follow you out. If you see any indication something's approaching from around that moon. don't wait for us. Just go."

Thirty-Nine

As Drew adjusted their trajectory, Cade moved next to Gonzo's chair, his back to the bridgescreen. "If this turns ugly, what are our best options?"

Gonzo stroked his fingers over his goatee. "The ship's fast, since its primary function was transporting emergency medical personnel and supplies. That's probably why the Admiral chose it for this mission—we can get away in a hurry. We have decent offensive weapons, at least for a ship this size, and the hull and shields are solid as a rock. We can take a hit."

Not so bad. Cade wasn't in the habit of running from a confrontation, but that's *exactly* what he'd do if it kept his team and the Suulh out of harm's way.

"Cade?"

He glanced over his shoulder.

"So far nothing seems to be changing," Aurora said. "If we see any—" She cut off abruptly as a shout from Cardiff came over the line.

The cry was echoed by Gonzo.

Cade looked down at the tactical console. Three warships the size of the *Starhawke* had appeared from behind the Burrow moon. And judging by the weapons readings on the display, they definitely weren't friendly.

He met Aurora's gaze.

Her fierce expression reminding him of a mother bear preparing to defend her cubs. "Run."

Forty

Aurora's hands gripped the arms of her chair.

The ships fanned out in attack mode as they barreled toward the *Starhawke*. Though not as elegant and free-flowing as her ship, they had clearly been crafted by skilled technicians, not Setarips. And sensors indicated they were armed to the teeth.

The enemy ships fired, proving the weapons were not just for show. The blasts impacted the *Starhawke*'s shields, though not as violently as Aurora had anticipated.

"Celia, activate the hull camouflage." The advanced Kraed hull design would make the *Starhawke* virtually invisible to the attacking ships. It would also block the view of the *Nightingale* as long as the *Starhawke* stayed between them. "Kelly, keep us as close to Cade's ship as you can. Don't move no matter what comes at us. We need to help them disappear."

The *Nightingale* accelerated, and Kelly stuck with them.

The warships sent a volley of blasts, searching for their prey in what would now look like empty space.

The majority of the shots fell short, but a few of the long-range weapons found their mark. The Kraed hull couldn't hide the resulting explosions, and their pursuers altered course.

"They're following us, but they're not precisely on target," Celia said. "They're still trying to figure out exactly where we are."

"Can we outrun them?"

"*We* can. But the *Nightingale* is hauling three hundred passengers worth of extra mass. I doubt it can reach anywhere close to its top speed. The enemy ships are closing." Another series of blasts punctuated that statement.

"Then we'll need to outmaneuver them." She glanced at the bridgescreen. "Cade? Go vertical and see if we can shake them loose."

"Understood."

The medical freighter changed course, its path curving until it was running perpendicular to its previous trajectory. Kelly kept the *Starhawke* on its tail, adjusting position so the ship's bulk stayed in the line of sight between the approaching ships and the *Nightingale.*

"Did they follow us?"

Celia didn't take her gaze off her monitor. "Not yet, but they've altered their flight path. They're firing in a spray pattern to locate us." A flash lit up the bridgescreen. "Which they just did."

Dammit. Frustration welled in her chest as the enemy ships began closing again. Time to change the game. If they wanted a target, she'd give them one.

"Cade, we're going to hold them off. Continue to the jump window. We'll meet you at the rendezvous point."

He had the good grace not to argue, though the look in his eyes spoke volumes. "Be careful."

She nodded. "You too."

The bridgescreen changed to the exterior view as Cade closed the channel. She watched as his ship accelerated toward the debris field and the jump window that waited on the other side. Charging through the field at full throttle would add another layer of danger to the situation, but it was the lesser of two evils at this point.

A grim smile touched her lips. "Kelly, bring us around. Celia, deactivate the camouflage. Let's show these uninvited guests why no one messes with a Kraed ship."

Forty-One

Cade's gaze remained locked on the aft image projected on the bridgescreen as the *Starhawke* shimmered into view and swung around to engage the fighters. The warships fired first, lighting up the *Starhawke*'s shields, but this time the *Starhawke* sent a barrage of answering blasts that made contact with the enemy ships. Several small explosions flared on the hull of the closest ship.

He changed the image to the debris field ahead. A vibration coming up from the deck told him Drew was pushing the ship to its limits, sprinting to reach the coordinates for the jump window and the safety it offered. "Gonzo, how's the *Starhawke* doing?"

"Holding their own. One of the fighters tried to follow us but they cut them off with a couple torpedoes."

"Drew, how long until we reach the debris field?"

"Two minutes, fifty-four seconds."

And didn't that feel like an eternity. He said a silent prayer for Aurora. She had the most incredible ship he'd ever seen and a talented crew. If anyone could handle the three fighters and get away safely, it would be her.

Weaving through the debris field at their current velocity wouldn't be a piece of cake, but they'd make it. He'd take over for Drew at the helm as soon as they got closer. Thankfully this section of the field had been swept clean of smaller objects by the gravitational pull of the much larger asteroids.

A flash of red on Gonzo's monitor caught his

attention.

Gonzo snapped forward, his hands gripping the edge of the console. "Energy readings in the debris field!" His normally implacable countenance showed a touch of fear, a fear that slipped under Cade's skin when one of the objects that he'd mistaken for a massive asteroid tumbling through space resolved into the largest ship he'd ever seen. And it was directly in their path.

Forty-Two

"There's another ship out there!" Kire's voice indicated his disbelief.

Aurora swung around to face him. "Where?"

"In the debris field. They've cut off the freighter's retreat."

A magnified image appeared on the screen, showing a behemoth of a vessel that made the *Nightingale* look like a matchstick. Nothing in Aurora's experience came close. Even the *Argo*, the largest Fleet ship, would be dwarfed.

As she watched, a series of warships detached from the main ship, heading toward the freighter.

Aurora swore. "Kelly, get us over there. Now!" She smacked the comm panel. "Jonarel, I need all the speed you can give us."

"Working on it."

The image on the bridgescreen shifted as they streaked toward the *Nightingale*. The barrage from the three warships intensified. Clearly they didn't want the *Starhawke* racing to the rescue. Too damn bad.

"Celia, if you can make a couple of those warships disappear, I'd be grateful." A heavy barrage of weapons and a brief flare of light from an exploding ship was her answer.

They were closing the distance to the debris field, but not fast enough to intercept the warships. She opened an audio channel to Cade. "What's your plan?" Guaranteed he'd have one by now.

But he didn't answer her. She frowned at the

console. "Cade? Come in."

Static was the only response.

His ship, however, had changed course and was racing along the leading edge of the debris field, staying close to the asteroids to make the ship a harder target to hit.

"Kire, why isn't he answering?"

Kire hunched over his station. "The message is being sent, but they're not receiving it. Their communications are jammed."

"Jammed?" Aurora shook her head in disbelief. "I thought that was impossible on a Fleet vessel."

Kire's hazel eyes were grim. "Apparently someone found a way."

Forty-Three

"They're jamming us?" Cade stared at Justin. He must have misunderstood. "That isn't possible."

Justin looked helpless, which wasn't an expression Cade usually saw on his friend's face.

"Apparently, it is."

They'd had a head start in the beginning, but there was no way they could make it through the debris field and to the jump window before the warships caught up. Their only hope was to use the asteroids as cover while they waited for the *Starhawke* to reach them. Although even Aurora's ship was no match for a dozen warships and a carrier that was doing an excellent impersonation of a miniature moon.

"So we can't talk to the *Starhawke*," he muttered. Without communications, it would be impossible to make a coordinated defense. Too bad Aurora couldn't actually read minds. Then he'd have a way to talk to her.

Two warships closed on them and fired. "Hard to port!" he cried. One blast hit a nearby asteroid but the second struck the ship, sending a shockwave through the hull. "Fire torpedoes!"

"Firing." The ship rumbled as the torpedoes launched, and a few moments later a couple flares appeared briefly on the bridgescreen. "Minimal damage to targets." Gonzo said. "The *Starhawke* is heading in our direction. Four warships breaking off pursuit to engage her."

Which left five still tracking his ship. He didn't like

those odds one bit. "Head back toward the *Starhawke* and stay as close to those asteroids as you can." Fleeing wasn't an option, but at least they could bring the fight back to the *Starhawke.*

The warships followed them and continued to fire, but the freighter's shields held, giving off brief flashes of light whenever they impacted with debris from the field.

They swept past the nearest asteroid, giving Cade his first glimpse of the *Starhawke* in the distance, taking heavy fire but giving as good as she got. Two of the warships were now in pieces and a third was spinning end over end toward the debris field.

"Warship, coming right at us," Gonzo said a moment before blasts peppered the front of the ship.

"Drop us under it and return fire."

The *Nightingale* vibrated under the strain. The poor old girl had been designed to maneuver in air, not space, and she was struggling.

As they made a slow dive under the oncoming ship, two more warships appeared on their flanks.

"Power surge coming from both ships!" Gonzo cried.

"Divert all energy to shields!"

Cade braced for impact. Instead, he caught sight of a streak of movement in his peripheral vision, first from the right, then the left, right before the ship gave a horrible lurch that flung him out of his chair.

"Status report," he croaked as he pushed onto his hands and knees. His lungs protested the abrupt evacuation of air that had followed the hard landing on the floor.

Drew clung to the navigation console like a lifeline, while Gonzo hung onto his chair with one hand and shoved himself upright with the other.

Cade hauled his body into his chair and snapped his

harness in place. But when his gaze returned to the bridgescreen, the image looked like he was viewing it through some kind of filter. The engines sounded wrong, too.

The ship gave another jolt, but Cade stayed put this time. "Status report!" He glared at Gonzo, unaccustomed to having to ask twice.

Gonzo stared at the screen, his expression bewildered. "It's a net."

"A net?"

Gonzo nodded, his head moving in slow motion. "They just caught us like a piece of space trash."

Forty-Four

Aurora stared at the screen. Surely she wasn't seeing what she thought she was seeing.

Two of the warships had fired enormous nets at the *Nightingale*, wrapping it as neatly as a spider catching flies. Now they were towing it slowly but steadily toward the carrier.

Destroying the freighter would have been far simpler. She could think of only one possible explanation for such an elaborate assault. Their attackers wanted the occupants of the *Nightingale* alive.

Chills raced along Aurora's spine as the realization sank in.

"Power surge coming from warships port and starboard!" Celia shouted.

Aurora's brain processed the data in a millisecond and she launched herself from her chair. "Target the—" She didn't get a chance to finish the sentence. Two explosions detonated, one to port, one to starboard.

"Net deployment systems destroyed." Celia said.

Thank goodness for Celia's quick reflexes. "Well done."

"Wasn't me."

Aurora frowned. "Then who—"

"I did."

It took Aurora a moment to realize who had spoken. The tone of the words was so unfamiliar that only the appearance of Star's image at her side brought it home.

"You did that?"

Star's gaze held a feral look that revealed her Drakarian origins. "Yes."

Aurora had never imagined Star firing the ship's weapons without orders. Her decision had far-reaching implications, but Aurora would deal with that issue later. Assuming there was a later. Right now they needed to focus on getting the *Nightingale* free.

And she had a plan.

Forty-Five

"Full reverse!" Cade dug his fingers into the arms of his chair like he could break the ship loose through force of will. Every object on the bridge rattled as Drew pushed the engines to their limits.

"We're in danger of overheating," she warned. "No measurable effect on the net."

Cade glared at the screen as the warships continued to tow the *Nightingale* like a child's toy on a string. "Shut it down."

The rattling and whining stopped.

"Gonzo, can we fire weapons?"

Gonzo looked apologetic. "Not unless we want to blow ourselves up."

Which they just might. A quick death would be preferable to whatever their would-be captors had in mind for them on that carrier.

"I want options. We need a way out of this."

Drew abandoned navigation to join Gonzo at tactical.

Cade hated feeling so helpless. He couldn't even reach out to Aurora for help.

His comband chimed. "Forrest to Ellis."

Mya was contacting him? Why? He'd expect her to have her hands full with the Suulh. "Go ahead."

"If I tell you what Aurora's planning to do, will you follow my instructions?"

He snapped to attention. "Were you able to establish

communications with her?"

A brief silence greeted his question. "Not exactly."

"Then how do you know what she's planning to do?"

"Because I'm seeing images from her in my head."

Cade blinked. Aurora wasn't telepathic...was she? He braced his forearms on his knees. "What's the plan?"

"On her command, she wants us to go hard to starboard. She'll use the hull camouflage to slip past the other ships, then get underneath us and blast the connection to the port side."

Cade saw where this was going. "Leaving a weak point in the net and a fighting chance against the other warship." Assuming the net gave way before the *Starhawke* plowed into them. He'd take that chance. "Will you be able to give me a warning before she fires?"

"Yes. The Suulh are helping focus the connection. The images I'm receiving are appearing almost instantaneously."

Incredible. If they got out of this, he'd have a laundry list of questions for Aurora.

"Tell her we're awaiting her signal."

Forty-Six

"Activate the camouflage!" Aurora shouted over the clamor of battle. "Take us down!"

Two torpedoes sailed just past the *Starhawke*'s flank as Kelly brought them into a steep descent. The four warships were caught off guard, and several of the weapons they'd unleashed against the *Starhawke* impacted on the hulls of their own instead.

"Another warship disabled," Celia called out.

The three remaining warships fanned out, firing in a search pattern, but this time Kelly could evade to keep the *Starhawke* hidden.

Aurora closed her eyes and tuned into her connection with Mya. The form of communication they were using wasn't complex, or even something that was specific to the Suulh. Animal communicators had been "talking" to all kinds of species for hundreds of years this way. But most humans still considered it the stuff of fantasy. Aurora certainly had never imagined that one day more than three hundred lives would depend on her ability to send mental images to Mya.

"Time to target?"

"Forty-nine seconds."

Aurora placed the image of that number in her mind and then began a mental countdown sequence that Mya could follow. Forty-four, forty-three, forty-two—

Her thoughts ground to an abrupt halt as a wave of pain tore through her system like wildfire. She sensed her body tipping forward as her vision dimmed, but she couldn't focus enough to make her muscles obey a simple command.

As she slumped to the floor like a rag doll, the one thought that broke through the blanket of agony was the realization that she'd lost her connection with Mya.

Forty-Seven

"Dr. Forrest is down!"

Reynolds's alarmed cry over the communication system pulled Cade's focus from the bridgescreen, where the countdown Mya had given them ticked toward zero.

"What's wrong?"

"No idea. She just collapsed."

The words were horribly familiar. Memories of a moonlit orchard and a desperate race through the trees filled his brain before he shoved them out of the way. "What about the Suulh?"

"They seem a little disoriented. I'm not sure...wait, Paaw and Zelle are making their way to help Williams with Dr. Forrest."

Cade checked the timer. Ten seconds before the *Starhawke* was due to blast the holy hell out of the net. He sent a silent prayer that Aurora was still in command of her ship.

Forty-Eight

Shield. She needed to shield. Find. Protect. Shield. Shield!

A series of explosions lit up the bridgescreen, yanking Aurora out of the black hole into which her consciousness had slipped. Her energy shield flared to life to protect her from the perceived threat.

Pain continued to radiate through her body like coals, but she fought against it, recognizing it for what it was. Not her pain. Theirs.

"The *Nightingale.*" Her voice escaped on a whisper. Had something horrible happened to the Suulh? To Mya?

As Kire helped her into a seated position, her gaze searched the bridgescreen, desperate for an image of the *Nightingale.*

"The portside net has been destroyed." Celia said. "And the warship along with it," she added, a distinct note of satisfaction in her voice. "The *Nightingale's* motion has pulled the other warship off line from the carrier, but they're still tethered together. The remaining ships are closing in."

"The *Nightingale's* okay." The air in her lungs evacuated in a rush. She waved Kire back to the communications station as she hauled her protesting body into the captain's chair. "Get us over there. Keep the camouflage activated and hit those warships with everything we have."

A new wave of pain pulled a moan from her lips. Her head fell against the back of the chair. She knew this feeling. She'd experienced it on Gaia. The intensity threatened to rob her of the ability to breathe, let alone maintain rational thought. Every fiber of her being was screaming at her to help and protect, to find the source of the pain.

But without Mya by her side, the attack on her senses was crippling her.

An image of Mya popped into her mind, followed rapidly by images of Raaveen, Paaw, Maanee, Zelle, and Sparw. More familiar Suulh faces appeared, each one a balm to her battered soul. Their soothing touches grounded her, reassuring her that they were all right, calming her whirling emotions.

Celia's voice pulled her back to her physical reality. "The *Nightingale* is heading into the debris field."

Aurora forced her neck to pivot so she could meet Celia's gaze.

"They're dragging the warship with them."

Forty-Nine

"I can't get control!" Drew cried as the image on the bridgescreen swayed and jerked with the motion of the ship.

"Give me the helm!" Cade shoved out of the captain's chair and staggered toward the navigation console, averting his gaze from the image on the bridgescreen so that he could keep his balance.

Drew passed him, heading for the captain's chair.

He slid into the seat behind navigation. "I've had enough of this tagalong," he muttered as the warship's bulk passed in front of them. Its engines flared as it, too, struggled to stabilize the tumbling tug of war that had them both in its clutches. They barely avoided a medium-sized asteroid that flew past, setting off the proximity alarms.

Time to take control of the situation.

He had years of experience Drew didn't. His brain analyzed the *Nightingale*'s trajectory and motion, feeding him the answers he needed. The warship might be faster, but the Nightingale had more mass and, judging by how the controls were responding, more power.

He focused on the debris field ahead, his gaze coming to rest on two large asteroids tumbling close to each other. Switching auxiliary power to the rear shields and thrusters, he pushed the engines to their limits, aiming for the narrowing gap between the enormous boulders.

The warship objected strenuously, firing at the *Nightingale*, but without landing a single blast.

Cade brought them in close to the first asteroid, skimming near the surface. The *Nightingale's* profile was slim compared to the bulky warship. It fit easily, but if the other ship didn't release its hold on the net, it would get crushed between the two rocks. Cade was fine with either option as long as it freed the *Nightingale*.

Apparently the crew was so focused on the task of holding onto the *Nightingale* that they didn't comprehend the danger. The tension on the net abruptly released as the warship got caught between the two immovable objects and exploded in a shower of debris.

The *Nightingale* shot forward, pressing Cade into his chair. The net, however, remained stubbornly wrapped around the hull. Cade swore. Loudly. "Drew, can we make an interstellar jump with this net attached?"

"The net's not the problem. It's the remnant of the ship we're dragging."

He checked the display and saw what she meant. A funnel-shaped chunk of metal about three meters long and two meters wide drifted behind them like a club, waiting to smash into them the minute they slowed down.

Fifty

Aurora stared at the images on the bridgescreen.

Celia had taken out another warship, but that still left six against two.

"Shield status?"

"Down to forty percent."

She contacted Jonarel. "Can you boost the shields?"

"Only by diverting power from other systems. Auxiliary power is depleted." He sounded as frustrated as she felt.

Aurora chewed on her lip. If the warships succeeded in netting the *Nightingale* a second time, it would be game over. They had to get out of here now.

Closing her eyes, she sent a series of images to Mya, visualizing the *Nightingale* passing through the debris field and launching through the jump window.

"The *Nightingale* has changed course," Celia said a moment later. "They're heading toward the jump window. The remaining warships are moving to engage."

"Get in front of–" Her words cut off as an image popped into her head. The picture looked like an enormous red ship's anchor hooked onto a fishing net. Another image followed, this time of a sinking ship.

Aurora frowned. "Kire, magnify the visual on the *Nightingale*."

The freighter was already in the debris field, the asteroids acting as shields to their line of sight as Kelly worked to overtake the warships. But a few moments later an image of the *Nightingale* appeared on the bridgescreen.

Aurora's heart stuttered when she figured out what she was seeing. A large chunk of metal trailed the freighter like an anchor. A potentially lethal anchor.

"We'll need to get them free from that net before they can jump." She looked over at Star. "Can you take care of that?" After seeing how efficiently the Nirunoc had taken out the warships' net launchers, she was the logical choice. And if Star focused on eliminating the net, Celia would be free to defend against the warships.

Star's eyes glittered. "It would be my pleasure."

Fifty-One

Cade double-checked the readings on his console. But they didn't change. Six enemy warships closing fast. And the *Starhawke* was nowhere to be seen.

"Are you sure they're with us?" Justin asked.

Cade nodded without turning his head. "I trust Mya." She'd told him Aurora had a plan. He believed her. He had to.

Blasts from the approaching warships streaked toward them. He evaded as best he could, but a few still rocked the craft. "Status on the shields."

"Holding at thirty-four percent," Gonzo said. "But the energy to sustain them is slowing us down. The warships are gaining." And they were still dragging a huge piece of metal.

A proximity alarm blared and an image of the *Starhawke* filled the aft view, blocking out the warships.

"We've cleared the debris field," Justin said.

"Drop the shields!" Mya's voice called out over the comm.

Gonzo reacted in an instant. "Shields down."

A series of blasts streaked toward the *Nightingale* from the *Starhawke*, and Cade flinched. But rather than ripping the ship to pieces, the assault shredded the netting with the precision of a surgeon's knife. It drifted away, along with the metal flotsam that was attached to it.

The *Starhawke* tipped laterally as the pieces sailed past. The debris impacted on one of the unsuspecting warships, tearing a hole in its hull.

"Clear to our launch point." Gonzo called out.

"Shifting all power to the engines." Cade urged the ship forward.

The *Starhawke* stayed right on their tail.

"Incoming torpedoes!" Gonzo shouted. "Raise shields?"

But the *Starhawke* had already returned fire, positioning themselves between the *Nightingale* and the warships. Any torpedoes they didn't destroy hit their shields.

"Are they okay?" Cade asked through clenched teeth.

"I think so," Gonzo said. "Still keeping pace with us."

"Six seconds to jump." Cade muttered. "Five, four, three, two..."

Come on. Come on. The chant repeated itself in his head like a mantra. And then the interstellar drive engaged and they launched into the void.

Fifty-Two

When the starfield winked out on the *Starhawke's* screen, Aurora slumped against the headrest and closed her eyes.

"We've followed the *Nightingale* through the jump window," Kelly confirmed.

They'd made it. Impossibly, inconceivably, they'd made it.

Aurora's muscles went lax, but her mind started to churn like a generator, processing everything that had occurred during the battle.

The pieces of the puzzle that hadn't made sense on Gaia—the mysterious attacks, the enslavement of the Suulh, the destruction of the Setarip ship—now fit together perfectly.

If the attack on Gaia had been the prelude to a bid for galactic domination, which now seemed likely, then the Suulh would be a precious resource. As weapons for biological destruction or healers of the wounded, they were unmatched. With a smart strategy and a large enough force, they could make an enemy virtually invulnerable. Especially if that enemy had warships that rivaled the strength of the Galactic Fleet.

And that blast of pain she'd experienced when she'd collapsed during the battle? She knew what it meant. She hadn't been sensing the Suulh on the *Nightingale*. She'd been sensing the Necri on the carrier. How many crippled, contorted souls were currently locked away in tiny cages on that ship? Hundreds? Thousands?

She shivered. Right now, there was absolutely nothing she could do about it. Her job was to get the Suulh to the homeworld. And that's what she'd do.

"Roe?"

Aurora came out of her musings with a start. She opened her eyes and found Kire kneeling beside her, his face tight with concern.

"You okay?"

Was she okay? Such a simple question. And the answer was just as simple. *No!* In fact, she wasn't sure she'd ever feel okay again. But there was no point in acknowledging that. Her crew needed her.

She pushed herself upright. "I'm fine."

"I doubt that."

Smart man.

Kire peered at her. "You looked like you'd fainted again."

Fainted? Oh, right. Kire had been the one to pick her up off the floor after she'd taken a header out of the captain's chair. "Just coming off an adrenaline rush."

"Do you need to go to the med bay?"

She shook her head. "No." Besides, no one was there to help her. Mya and the rest of the Suulh were on the *Nightingale.* So was Dr. Williams, for that matter. She glanced around the bridge. Celia and Kelly were watching her as well, and Star was hovering just to her left. "Sorry if I worried everyone."

Kire tapped his comband. "She's okay, Jon."

Jonarel's deep baritone came over the speakers. "Are you sure?"

Apparently Jonarel and Kire had been in communication while she'd been lost in her own thoughts. "I'm fine, Jonarel." Although she didn't expect him to believe her, either.

A grumbled "hmm" confirmed her suspicions.

Enough of this. Time to focus on the task at hand. "What's our engine status?"

"The energy drain on the system and the damage to the shields will take two hours to correct. I will need to shut down the interstellar drive during that time. We will need to wait before making our next jump." He sounded apologetic, which was rare for him.

"You got us safely through the battle. Thank you for that. Keep me posted." She turned to Kelly. "How long until we reach the rendezvous point?"

Kelly glanced at her console. "About twenty minutes."

"Star, assist Jonarel in engineering. Run diagnostics to see if anything else needs to be attended to before our next jump. Celia, I want a weapons check and status report." She pivoted to Kire, who was still kneeling beside her. "Prepare a message for Signal letting him know our situation and the change of plan. Send it as soon as we come out of the jump."

She sincerely hoped the *Nightingale* would be waiting for them when they arrived.

Fifty-Three

When the *Starhawke* appeared at the rendezvous point, Cade let out a sigh of relief. Until that moment he hadn't been absolutely certain that they'd made it out safely. And he desperately needed them to be okay. For more reasons than he could count.

The comm pinged with an incoming video feed. He'd never been so grateful to see Aurora's face, even with her forehead lined with tension.

Relief showed in her eyes. "Good to see you, Cade."

"You too. Glad you're in one piece."

"We're a little banged up but functional. How about you?"

"We're running on backup systems. Main power was completely drained by the jump. We're essentially dead in the water."

Aurora frowned. "We can't stay here long." She stood, her stance indicating she'd shifted into problem solving mode. "We can transfer everyone to the *Starhawke*, but what about the *Nightingale*? I know we'd talked about leaving her in orbit somewhere, but that won't work now. We can't come back here."

Guaranteed the enemy would be waiting for them if they did. Cade's throat tightened as he gazed around the small bridge. It was crazy, but he'd grown attached to the old girl over the past two months. He'd expected to pilot her back to Earth when their mission was completed. Maybe even talk the Admiral into making her part of a museum exhibit. She'd earned it.

But without power, that was no longer an option. The same conclusion showed on the faces of his team. "We'll transfer everything of value and then set her on an intercept course with the star. She has enough juice left in her for that."

He appreciated the look of understanding in Aurora's eyes. "Then let's get to work."

Fifty-Four

Three hours later, Justin stood at the wide windows of the *Starhawke*'s observation lounge and watched as the brilliance of the nearby star's corona swallowed the *Nightingale*'s silhouette. A haunting melody played over the ship's speakers, the theme somewhere between a lullaby and a lament.

He sighed. "She was a good ship."

Cade nodded. "That she was."

The mood in the room was quite different from the last time he and Cade had been here. It was hard to believe only three months had passed. If felt like a lifetime.

He shifted his gaze to Raaveen, Sparw, Maanee and Zelle, who stood to his right. Three months ago, he hadn't even known they existed. How quickly everything had changed.

He and Cade were the only ones from their unit in the lounge with the Suulh. Gonzo and Reynolds had joined Cardiff, Emoto and Kelly on the bridge, keeping watch for incoming ships until they received the all clear for the interstellar jump. Bella was with Clarek and his kin in engineering, finishing up the repairs.

The Suulh who had sustained injuries during the battle were down in the med bay with Williams, Paaw, and Dr. Forrest, while the rest of the refugees huddled around Captain Hawke at the center of the observation lounge.

The battle had taken a heavy emotional toll on everyone. Many of the Suulh had reverted to the timid behavior they'd exhibited on Gaia, rather than the more outgoing, relaxed attitude they'd had on Burrow. Even Raaveen, Paaw and Sparw had lost some of their spark. It pained him to see the worry lines back on their faces.

Raaveen turned from the window and met his gaze. Concern shadowed her dark eyes, but hope shone, too. She might be down, but she wasn't out. Not by a long shot. She gave his arm a gentle squeeze before she and the others joined the group on the floor.

He couldn't see the swirl of energy surrounding them, but after watching Raaveen, Paaw and Sparw with the Meer, he recognized the signs. He hoped it was producing the calming and healing effect they needed. Having Captain Hawke in their midst certainly seemed to help.

Justin glanced at Cade, whose gaze was also focused on the *Starhawke*'s captain. In fact, he seemed oblivious to everyone else in the room. No small feat considering the number of bodies surrounding her.

He and Cade had been friends for eight years, and in all that time, he'd never seen him react to a woman the way he did with Aurora Hawke. Not that he blamed him. She was compassionate, intelligent, and a damned good leader. And while Justin preferred brunettes, Cade definitely had a thing for blondes. Come to think of it, most of the women Cade had hooked up with over the years had resembled Captain Hawke in coloring and build.

Now Justin understood why. The flame had never died. Cade's expression revealed more than he probably realized.

He couldn't do anything to help the Suulh at the moment, but maybe he could help his friend. "The captain's a pretty amazing woman," he murmured.

Cade glanced at him. "Yes, she is."

He kept his voice low. "And you're in love with her."

That got Cade's attention. He frowned, his lips forming a denial. But he didn't say it. Instead, he motioned for Justin to follow him as he headed for the multi-colored doors that led to the corridor beyond.

The doors closed silently behind them. "You know, sometimes you're too damn perceptive for your own good."

Justin smiled. "Oh, come on. It's one of my best traits."

"Not right now, it isn't."

Cade's defensiveness made Justin's point. "Someone needed to say it. Face facts. You're in love with her."

"How do you—"

He lifted a hand to keep Cade from interrupting. "And there's a good chance she's in love with you, too."

Cade folded his arms over his chest. The irritation in his expression had been replaced with something that looked like hope. "Oh?"

"Sure. She acts differently around you. I think she really understands what's happening in your head. And that's no easy task."

Cade grunted.

Justin mirrored his pose. "So what's the problem? Why aren't you doing anything about it?"

"You mean aside from the fact that once this mission is over I'll have no excuse to see her again?"

"Maybe you should consider a career change."

"Yeah, right."

"I'm serious."

Cade's eyes narrowed. "Are you after my job?"

"Nope."

Cade lifted his eyebrows.

Justin held his hands up, palms out. "Oh, I'd take it in a heartbeat if there was an opening, but that's not the point.

Have you given any thought to the future? As long as you're a part of the Elite Unit, your options are limited."

"So are yours."

"Sure. But I'm not the one with a tantalizing alternative. Think about it. She has her own ship." He ticked the items off on his fingers. "She's smart and nice to look at, and she's about to become the de facto ruler of an entire planet. She could use a man of your talents by her side."

Cade glanced at the closed doors. "Even if she wanted that, which I seriously doubt, there's still a problem."

"Which is?"

"Clarek hates my guts."

Ah. Justin had forgotten about the *Starhawke's* chief engineer.

"So what did you do to piss him off?" Every conflict had a point of origin. Maybe this one just needed to be brought out into the open.

"Nothing directly."

Justin had trouble believing that, especially after observing the two men on Gaia. They were like flint and tinder. His expression must have conveyed his skepticism.

"It's true." Cade insisted. "He hates me because he wants Aurora for himself."

Ouch. That would be a tough problem to overcome. "And how does she feel about that?"

Cade sighed. "I don't know. While we were on Gaia, I thought they might be together." His gaze strayed to the doors again. "But now I'm not so sure. On Burrow she seemed uncomfortable around him, almost like she was avoiding him. I can't believe they have anything going on. At least not right now."

"And if she made it clear she wanted to be with you, would Clarek accept that and back off?"

"He didn't ten years ago. I don't see any reason to believe anything has changed."

And the Kraed would make a formidable adversary. "Then I guess you'll have to decide if a relationship with Captain Hawke is worth fighting for."

The look in Cade's eyes indicated he thought it might be. For his friend's sake, he hoped Aurora Hawke felt the same way.

Fifty-Five

The hour of healing time with the Suulh should have helped Aurora feel better. Instead, it had tapped the depth of her fears and left her quaking from the effort of keeping everything together. Her body vibrated like a tightly wound spring, one that could snap at any moment, taking out everything in its path. She needed to find an outlet before that happened.

An intense workout might help, allowing her to let off steam in a controlled environment. And now that they'd made their interstellar jump, she could ask Celia to join her in the training center.

As she exited the observation lounge, she nearly ran into Cade, who stood just outside the door. Had he been waiting for her?

His gaze swept over her, reading her like a book. "I'm not going to ask if you're okay."

She made a face. "That obvious, huh?" She tried to sound casual and failed.

He studied her. "Let's just say you look like you could use some exercise."

An astute observation. "You know me well."

He smiled softly. "I know how I'd feel in your position." He cocked an eyebrow. "Want a sparring partner?"

Her body responded with an enthusiastic *yes*, but she gave herself a moment to consider. After all, she hadn't sparred with Cade since the Academy. And that had been an excuse to get their hands on each other, not a real match.

But to be honest, it would probably be a lot more fun than facing off with Celia, who was all business on the mat. And she could certainly use a little fun right now. "Let's go."

They took the cargo lift down two decks and then continued on to the double doors that led into the training center.

As the doors closed silently behind them, Aurora stopped at the edge of the mat and slipped off her boots. "How do you want to do this?"

Cade grinned as he pulled off his boots. "Any way you want."

She rolled her eyes, but the beginnings of a smile tugged on her lips. "Just remember I'm not a novice anymore. I spar with Celia on a regular basis. I might knock you on your butt."

He winked at her. "Fine with me."

Oh, yeah. This was *exactly* what she needed.

Her tunic and pant combination was a little more restrictive than the sleeveless top and leggings she usually wore for this kind of thing, but Cade was in the same boat. His clothes were meant for space travel, not wrestling. He'd slipped off his jacket, revealing the dark green tunic he wore underneath. It shifted deliciously over his muscles and she drank in the sight of him, an oasis in the desert. When she lifted her gaze to his eyes, she saw laughter there.

"Like what you see?"

Busted. "Just looking for weak points." She backed onto the mat and he followed her.

"Good luck with that." His gaze traveled over her body with a laziness that had nothing to do with finding weaknesses.

Her core temperature began to rise. "Like what you see?" she bantered back.

"Always have."

The comment surprised her, as did the attack he followed it up with. Before she could blink, she found herself on the mat, pinned beneath his bulk.

"Focus, Hawke," he teased, kissing the tip of her nose before bouncing nimbly to his feet.

She narrowed her eyes. So that's how it was going to be. She popped back up, then dropped into a crouch, keeping her gaze on his. "Try that again, Ellis," she taunted.

The corners of his mouth lifted. "Oh, don't worry. I will."

This time she saw the attack coming, and sidestepped before he could get her off balance. She countered with a kick that connected solidly with his torso. It was like hitting a brick wall, but he staggered, his mouth open in an "O" of surprise.

"You kicked me!"

She snorted. "And?"

A grin spread across his face, which turned into a belly laugh. His eyes sparkled as he gazed at her. "Oh, you are so going to pay for that."

"Promises. Promises." She followed the words with an attack of her own, but his reflexes were much quicker than she'd imagined. He was able to catch hold of her arm and pull it behind her, bringing her back flush with his body. The tantalizing warmth of his skin surrounded her, especially where his hands gripped her arm and wrapped around her torso.

His breath brushed the curve of her ear as he bent his head. "Sweetheart, with you, that is very much a promise."

Every nerve ending went on red alert at the huskiness in his tone, and she swallowed. The need for the sparring match evaporated as her body got completely on board with shifting to a less adversarial encounter. But her brain clamored for a modicum of self-preservation. Would she regret it? More to the point, did she care?

Turning her head, she brought their faces millimeters apart. She gazed into the green eyes that had haunted her dreams for ten years. Fire burned there, searing her. If her arms had been free, she would have fanned herself.

A voice from across the room broke the spell. "Watch your back."

Aurora's head whipped around. Celia stood just inside the doorway, her expression neutral but her gaze analyzing the situation and coming to the obvious conclusion.

Cade released Aurora immediately, stepping back. "Aurora was helping me test out a new grip."

Aurora cleared her throat. "Yes. It's...uh...very effective." She had a terrible feeling she was blushing, something Cade's crooked smile confirmed.

"So I saw." Celia moved to the edge of the mat. "Star told me you were down here. She didn't mention you had company," she added, her gaze flicking to Cade.

Aurora shifted into command mode. "Is there a problem?"

"No. I just thought you might be in the mood for a challenge." She leveled a look at Cade. "Seems I was right."

Aurora caught the double meaning. Judging from his reaction, so did Cade. He quirked a brow in her direction.

There was no way she could focus on sparring with Celia when her body was hot for Cade. And now that she wasn't in full contact with his very desirable self, she really needed to think about what she was doing. Maybe Celia had unwittingly done her a favor.

"I'm really not up to sparring with you right now. But Cade would probably enjoy it."

Cade glanced at her, a question in his eyes.

She didn't know how to respond, but apparently she didn't have to. As he held her gaze and the heat reignited, a small smile touched his lips.

Celia wasn't smiling. She looked like she was on the hunt. "How about it, Ellis? You want to show me what they teach the members of the Elite Unit?"

His cocky grin brimmed with confidence. "I'm game."

Fifty-Six

Cade wasn't about to pass up an opportunity to show off the depth of his skills in front of Aurora. Besides, watching him spar with Cardiff might nurture those flares of heat they'd been generating on the mat.

"Just so you know," Aurora said as he faced Cardiff, "you might be out of your league. Celia went toe to toe with Jonarel's father and won."

Really? He looked at Cardiff with new respect.

She stepped back to give him room but the movement wasn't as casual as it seemed. She was already assessing him, looking for any signs that would indicate a weakness of strength, flexibility, or balance. He knew that because he was doing the same thing. He sure as hell hoped her conclusion was as tough to face as his—he might have finally met his match.

They circled the mat several times, each watching for an opening and not seeing it. He was beginning to wonder if this would go on indefinitely when she dropped into a crouch so quickly his eyes barely tracked the movement. But his body felt the result as her left leg swung in a low arc that connected with his knees, knocking him off balance.

He rolled forward, ducking under the follow-up kick that would have connected with his sternum if he'd tried to stay on his feet. He took the opportunity to grab her leg in both hands, but before he could pull her off balance she lunged forward, creating a bend to her knee that allowed her to kick out again. This time she made contact with his chest, and he grunted as he absorbed the blow. She snapped her leg out of his hands and was back in position before he drew his next breath. Man, she was fast. And stronger than he would have imagined. The first point was hers.

The next round brought them in closer and he managed to land a blow that knocked Cardiff to the mat. Now they were even. But she leaped back to her feet and executed a flip and roll maneuver worthy of an Olympic gymnast. It ended with him on the ground with his left arm pinned behind his back. He used his legs to disengage her grip and regain his footing.

The back and forth continued, each scoring a blow only to have the other follow it up with an effective counterattack. Sweat rolled like tears down his forehead but he didn't dare try to swipe it away. She'd be on him in a heartbeat. Her own face was fairly dry, no doubt because her acrobatics flung most of her sweat onto the mat. Their combined exertions had made the surface slick in spots.

The sound of their breathing filled the air between them as they circled each other. She made a movement to her left and he started to counter but paused when he saw her wince slightly and pull up just a bit. It was incredibly subtle, something most people wouldn't notice, but he was trained to notice. She had a weakness in her left leg. If he exploited it, he could get the upper hand.

He anticipated her attack from her right side and was in perfect position to counter it, bringing his body in alignment so that he could deliver a powerful blow to her left leg. To his surprise, she didn't collapse as he'd expected her to. Instead, she tucked and rolled before kicking out with the supposedly weak left leg. She sent him sprawling to the mat.

As he regained his feet, he stared at her in shock.

Her tight smile indicated he'd been had. "Don't believe everything you see, Ellis."

She'd set him up, and he'd fallen for it. She'd bruised his professional pride, but she'd also reinforced his resolve to win the match. "I'll remember that."

The intensity of the battle kicked up a notch, and Cade's focus narrowed to one thought...bringing Cardiff down.

He held that focus as the relentless back and forth continued, right up until the moment Cardiff crossed directly in front of Aurora. His brain registered the expression on Aurora's face, drawing him out of his tunnel vision. The last time he'd seen her looking at him that way, they'd both been naked.

His body reacted to the heat in her gaze at the exact moment a blow struck his midsection, knocking the wind from his lungs and driving him onto the mat. Cardiff pounced, holding him completely immobile. Tension and little stabs of pain pushed against his shoulder socket, alerting him that Cardiff could dislocate his shoulder if she chose to. But it was what she whispered in his ear that really caught his attention.

"Watch yourself, Ellis." Her tone was cooler than a glacier. "If you break her heart, I'll silence yours."

His heart didn't care for that threat. It banged against his ribcage as she briefly tightened her hold before releasing him. If he'd had any doubt as to the sincerity of her words, the lethal steel he saw in her brown eyes erased it.

He held her gaze as he rose off the mat and rolled his shoulders. He'd always considered Clarek the deadliest member of Aurora's crew. He wasn't so sure anymore.

"You two should give a master class at the Academy

someday," Aurora said as they walked off the mat. "That was incredible."

A quick glance into her eyes revealed the fire still burned, though he saw concern, too.

"I've never faced a more skilled opponent." Cade accepted the defeat as graciously as his pride would allow. And he meant it. He wasn't one hundred percent convinced he would have won even without the distraction had Aurora presented.

The coolness had left Cardiff's expression. With her warning delivered, she appeared to have returned to her normal demeanor. "Neither have I." She held his gaze. "Sparring with you on a regular basis would take my skills to a whole new level."

"And would pretty much ruin any chance I have of beating either of you." Aurora studied them, her expression puzzled. She must have picked up on Cardiff's emotional shift during the match, which was at odds with the behavior they were both exhibiting now. "Though after what I just saw, a win for me might never have been on the table to begin with."

Cardiff smiled. "Maybe not. But the challenge with you is that you never give up. You can accomplish a lot with that kind of attitude. Even defeat a more skilled opponent."

"Always dangling the branch of hope," Aurora said with a small smile.

Cade caught Cardiff's gaze. "I'd like a second chance sometime."

A subtle smirk told him she understood the double meaning behind his words. Her past behavior indicated she respected him, and might even approve of a relationship between him and Aurora. After all, she hadn't warned him off like Clarek would have. She'd just made it clear that, when it came to Aurora's wellbeing, a misstep on his part would not be tolerated.

"Looking forward to it." She grabbed a towel from the rack near the door. "See you two later," she called out as she exited the room.

A small frown creased Aurora's forehead as she glanced at the closed door. But her expression changed as her gaze met his. "That was impressive."

Heat flickered in her emerald eyes, and his breath caught. "Glad you enjoyed it."

"Unless you're ready to call it a night, I have a few things I'd like to discuss with you." The intensity in her gaze went up a notch. "In a more private setting. Would you mind joining me in the conference room for a little while?"

He'd never wanted to yell *hallelujah* so badly in his life. But somehow he managed to keep his tone casual, like they were discussing the weather. "Of course."

Fifty-Seven

Watching Cade spar with Celia had flipped all of Aurora's switches, turning her into a walking searchlight. She'd always enjoyed watching his skill and agility against an opponent, and his talents had grown considerably since the Academy. She'd been tantalized by the strength and beauty of his body in motion. The way he and Celia had battled had been as much about their mental prowess as their physical abilities, and his focused intensity had been hypnotic.

The lift doors parted on the command deck, the textured walls giving the impression of stepping into the forest that surrounded the Clarek compound. The planked pathways added to the illusion, winding in curving lines that led to Kire's cabin to the right and the double doors of the conference room to the left. Her cabin wasn't visible from the lift, but the pathway followed the curve of the corridor to the right and ended at her door.

Rather than heading for her cabin, she followed the curve to the left. The conference room doors swung open as she approached.

"We're really going to the conference room?" Cade's voice indicated his surprise, and more than a little disappointment.

She glanced over her shoulder. "I have a few things I want to clarify before things get...out of hand." Although one look into his sea-green eyes raised her temperature to the boiling point.

The doors closed silently, sealing them in together.

She'd never considered the conference room, with its massive circular table and carved wood chairs, as an intimate space. But as Cade moved closer, it suddenly felt as confining as a broom closet.

"What did you want to clarify?" His voice made her whole body tingle.

She cleared her throat. "I don't want any misunderstandings. Our situation lately has been...complicated."

"Agreed."

"And it's not likely to get any easier."

"Also true."

Talking wasn't easy right now, either. The intensity of his gaze felt like a caress. She had an overwhelming urge to grab hold of him, sink her fingers into the silky softness of his hair and taste the fullness of his lips. But finishing this discussion was important. "I can't make any promises."

A touch of wariness shadowed his eyes. "Okay."

"And I don't want you to make any, either."

Frown lines bracketed his mouth and he shifted away from her, creating physical and emotional distance. "Are you saying you're looking for meaningless recreation?"

The idea obviously bothered him. Good. It bothered her, too. Their relationship had never been the kind that would allow for a casual fling. The attraction was too strong, the emotions they generated together too powerful. That's why she wanted all the cards on the table.

She laid her hand on his forearm. "No. If we do this, it's going to mean something to me. Maybe more than I realize. And I want it to mean something to you, too."

His muscles flexed beneath her fingers and the heat returned to his gaze. "It will."

Her heart thumped in response. At least they were clear on that. "But we both have a lot of responsibilities right now. And a lot of uncertainty."

"True."

"I don't want to make promises I can't keep." She stroked her thumbnail across the fabric of his sleeve and his breathing changed. "But I also want to be open to all...possibilities."

Fifty-Eight

That was exactly what he wanted to hear.

Aurora's fumbling words had sprung the latch on his emotional lockbox. When combined with the temptation of her parted lips and the sultry look in her eyes, he was a goner.

His lips touched down on hers, brushing softly as electrical currents raced through his body, warming him in a way only she could. He shifted the angle and delved deeper, settled in for what was quickly becoming a truly excellent kiss.

She twined her arms around his neck, pulling him closer. But it was the touch of her energy field that drove him insane. It created instant full-body contact, more intimate and intense than anything he'd experienced with other women. This was one of Aurora's gifts, and it belonged to her alone.

The soothing warmth caressed his skin while her lips and tongue set him on fire. He'd been dreaming about this during the long weeks on Burrow, craving it like water in the desert. But he'd never imagined his fantasy would unfold while standing in the *Starhawke's* conference room.

She nipped at his bottom lip, setting off fireworks as she eased back and looked deeply into his eyes.

"Tell me what you want from me," she murmured.

Something flickered in her gaze, and she tensed slightly. He paused, alerted by the subtle change. She wasn't asking an idle question. He didn't dare give a flippant answer.

He took several slow breaths to clear his passion-soaked brain as much as possible with her energy field continuing to caress him. He needed to consider his answer. His future might depend on it.

And that's when he realized he already knew the answer.

Cradling her face in his hands, he gazed into her eyes. "I want whatever you're willing to give me, Rory."

Her breath hitched and her eyes widened. Apparently he'd surprised her.

"Rory. You haven't called me that since..." She swallowed. "Since the last time we..." Once again she trailed off, but her gaze grew hotter than a volcano.

Fifty-Nine

No one had ever called her Rory except Cade. Hearing that name evoked a very specific reaction from her on an emotional, mental and physical level. Her body craved him with the heat of an O class star, and her heart was willing to make a leap of faith, at least for the short term.

Rational thought fled. It was time to move to a more appropriate setting. She clasped Cade's hand. "Come with me." She led him out of the room and down the pathway to her door.

"I'll follow you anywhere."

The comment made her tremble. His husky tone promised a night of pleasure, but her empathic senses picked up on the underlying emotions. There was more than just lust behind his words. How much more, she couldn't say.

The door to her cabin was a masterpiece of woodcarving that had been crafted by one of Jonarel's uncles. It depicted a family of hawks soaring on the wind, their wings spread wide. Normally she took a moment to admire the carving when she entered her cabin, but tonight she ignored it completely. As soon as the door swung wide, she hauled Cade inside and turned into his arms.

"What is it about you?" She pulled his head down and made contact with his lips. *Finally.*

His intensity matched hers. He eliminated the space between them as his arms locked around her. He broke the kiss and began nipping his way down her throat. "You tell me."

His hands stroked along her back to the band holding her braid. As he slipped it free, he used his fingers to comb through the interlocking strands so they framed her face. She shuddered. He was treating her like a present, one he was taking great pleasure in unwrapping. Much more of this and they wouldn't make it to her sleeping nook. She'd drag him down onto the floor.

"You drive me insane."

His chuckle was full of manly pride. "Is that a bad thing?"

"Not right now."

She allowed her hands to explore, becoming re-acquainted with the texture of his sculpted physique. At twenty-one, he'd had a nice body, but her memories paled in comparison to the tactile pleasure of running her hands over the well-developed muscles crafted by his ten years with the Elite Unit. Apparently he enjoyed the sensations as well, because a groan escaped his lips.

Then he put those gorgeous muscles to good use as he scooped her up in his arms and carried her to where her bed nook awaited.

"How do you seem to know what I want before I do?" she whispered as he lowered her to the mattress.

His smile was sexy as hell. "Maybe because I pay attention."

Oh, did he ever.

Sixty

Someone was calling his name.

Cade squeezed his eyes shut. He didn't want to wake up. He'd had the most incredible dream featuring Aurora, and he wasn't ready to let it go. In fact, as the voice grew more insistent, he even made it sound like Aurora. How pathetic was that?

Sighing, he flipped to his back and opened his eyes. His brain registered two things immediately. Unless he was still dreaming, the person calling him *was* Aurora. And he was in her bed. Naked.

She stood beside the nook, dressed in what he considered her captain's uniform—long tunic and pants, her pale skin and blonde hair standing out in bright relief against the browns and greens of her clothing. She resembled a wood nymph, and in his current mental state, he almost expected her to sprout wings and fly away.

"Good morning," she said with a bemused smile. "I was beginning to wonder if I'd have to douse you with water to get you up."

He was really here. It hadn't been a dream. His mind finally grasped that fact and hung on for dear life.

Concern flashed in her eyes. "Cade?" She stepped closer. "Are you okay? You look a little dazed."

As he focused on her kiss-swollen lips, the memories of their night together flooded him. He rolled to his side and tucked the sheet a little more firmly across his hips before running a hand down his face. "I'm fine. Just a little disoriented."

Her gaze traced his bare chest and her smile widened. "Yeah, I guess you would be."

He had no idea how long he'd been asleep. He lifted his forearm before he realized his comband wasn't there. He spotted it sitting on top of a neat pile of his clothes on the nearby table. "What time is it?"

"Still a couple of hours until the day cycle begins." She picked up the stack and placed it on the bed next to him.

"How long have you been awake?" He was amazed he hadn't noticed her moving around the cabin. Her hair was damp, so she'd even showered.

"A couple of hours. I brought you something from the kitchen." She gestured toward the archway that led into the main room. "But that's not why I woke you."

He went on alert. "Is there a problem?"

She shook her head. "Justin was looking for you."

His mind latched onto the key noun in that sentence. "You talked to Justin?"

She nodded. "He tried reaching you via comband, and when you didn't respond, he checked your cabin."

He had a vague memory of shutting off his comband so they wouldn't be disturbed. He hadn't counted on sleeping like the dead. "And when he didn't find me, he contacted you?"

"Bingo."

He watched Aurora closely, unsure how she felt about the turn of events. He'd figured they'd keep this night a secret from his team and her crew. Now that might not be possible. "What did he want?"

"To know if your unit would be on rotation with my crew. I told him we'd discuss it."

"Was he surprised that I was with you?"

The corner of her mouth quirked up. "Not as much as I expected him to be."

Yeah, well, Justin was the one who'd given him a push the day before. He made a mental note to thank him later. "And how do *you* feel about that?"

Instead of answering, she sat on the edge of the bed. Her expression was open, but cautious. "That depends on you."

"Meaning?"

"How do *you* feel about it?"

This was what they referred to as a golden opportunity. Given the amazing night they'd just shared, he wasn't about to pass it up. Reaching forward, he took her hand in his and gazed into the emerald depths of her eyes. "You're the empath," he said softly. "Can't you tell?"

Her expression softened for a moment as she tuned into her empathic senses. Then she gave a little jolt and focused on him like a laser.

He tightened his grip on her hand. "I know I've made a lot of mistakes in the past, Rory. Mistakes I regret, more than you'll ever know."

She tensed and her brows drew down, but she didn't interrupt him.

He pushed on. "But I'm tired of regrets. Last night you gave me an incredible gift." His thumb stroked the back of her hand as he searched her expression for a clue to how she was feeling. "I'm foolish enough to hope this is only the beginning."

He waited, trying to gauge her reaction. But as the seconds ticked by and she continued to stare at him without saying anything, he began to feel like an idiot.

Maybe he was a fool to think they could build a

future together. He'd allowed himself to hope, but she was probably trying to find the kindest words to turn him down. He'd deserve it, especially after all the pain he'd caused her in the past. He didn't really expect her to forgive him. Ever.

Shoving away his disappointment, he reached out and brushed his fingers along her cheek, coaxing a response. "But if that's not what you want, I understand."

That got her moving. She jumped up like he'd given her an electric shock. It would have made him laugh if he wasn't so damned scared that he was about to lose her. Again.

She gazed down at him, her breath hitching in and out, causing her chest to rise and fall in a way that was arousing despite the circumstances. "What do I want?" she whispered, more to herself than to him. "What do I want?" she echoed, shaking her head slightly.

He'd obviously thrown her a curve. Instead of bringing her back into his life, he might have just driven a permanent wedge between them. *Brilliant, Ellis.*

But then he noticed a hint of a smile on her lips.

She crossed her arms and studied him. "This situation is getting very complicated."

"You and me?"

"You and me. You and my crew. You and Jonarel. Me and Jonarel."

He flinched at that last part.

She paused, a shadow passing over her face. "Why do you hate him so much?"

Her tone wasn't accusatory. Just puzzled. But that made no sense. Was it possible she really didn't know? Surely someone had told her? Reanne at the very least. She'd had a front row seat during the argument, and she'd never missed an opportunity to share tasty gossip, especially with Aurora.

Jonarel Clarek was the last person he wanted to talk about right now, but if that's what it took to keep the lines of communication open with Aurora, he'd do it. He swallowed. "You know about our argument, right?"

Her eyebrows lifted. "The one between you and Jonarel? Of course. I was there, remember? I was the one who stopped you from killing each other."

He shook his head. "Not the night you and I broke up. I'm talking about the argument he and I had after the Christmas holiday. The night he showed up at my dorm room and told me I wasn't good enough for you."

Her jaw literally dropped. "He said *what?*"

Clearly, this was news to her. "He ordered me to leave you alone. I told him what he could do with his opinions. Things got heated."

"Why would he do that?" She looked horrified.

Cade shrugged. "He didn't like me. Never has."

Her expression clouded as she processed that information. "You said it got heated. But I don't remember either of you ending up in the medical ward."

"We didn't. It was just an argument. No big deal." In reality, they would have come to blows that night, but Reanne had convinced Jonarel to leave with her.

The next day, Reanne had sought Cade out and begged his forgiveness for not stopping Jonarel from going to his room in the first place. Apparently she'd been keeping Jonarel company while he was waiting to meet Aurora for a study date, and he'd started ranting about Cade, saying he was a bad influence on Aurora. He'd told Reanne he was going to confront Cade. She'd been worried about his emotional state, so she'd followed him. Which had turned out to be a good thing.

Aurora's direct gaze bored into him. "Just an

argument? No big deal? Ten years of lethal hatred is what you call *no big deal?*"

Well, no. But this wasn't how he'd hoped to spend his first morning with her. He took her hands in his and tried to lighten the mood. "That's the past. Let it go. I'd much rather talk about the future."

She didn't return his smile. "Thank you for telling me." Her tone indicated she'd be talking to Clarek about this. Soon. And when the Kraed found out that Aurora had spent the night with him, his hatred would soar to new heights.

He sighed. "I'm sorry I did."

Some of the intensity faded from her eyes, replaced with concern. "Why?"

"Because our situation is already dicey. Giving Clarek more reasons to hate me isn't going to help."

She tilted her head to the side, her expression curious. "Why do you care what he thinks?"

"I don't. But he's always going to be a part of your life. He's the one who built this ship. *Your* ship. If I'm public enemy number one with him, that makes it tough for me to be with you."

She sighed. "You're right."

Sometimes he hated being right.

But instead of pulling away, she leaned forward and brushed her lips across his in a leisurely kiss. "But that doesn't mean it's impossible."

Sixty-One

Jonarel's keen sense of hearing alerted him to Aurora's arrival in the hallway outside his cabin long before the door chimed.

"Come in."

She stood in the open doorway, her blond hair pulled back in her customary braid and a small wooden box tucked under her arm. She held up the box. "I could use a distraction. How about you?"

He knew what the box contained—the portable chess set he had made for her eighteenth birthday. He barely concealed the scowl that pulled at his mouth. That box reminded him of the discussion in his father's study. The irony of Aurora's choice made him wish he had burned the wood he had used to carve it.

However, she had come to his cabin to spend time with him. For that gift, he would gladly sit in the middle of a circle of hot coals. Or sit through a game that would remind him of all the things that were wrong in his life.

He took the box from her and set it on the low table at the center of his seating area. "A distraction is welcome." And she certainly was a distraction. This was the first time she had been in his quarters since their visit to Drakar. Her nearness was having a predictable effect on his mental and emotional state. "May I offer you some tenrebac?"

Normally he would have just served her a glass. She liked sipping tenrebac while they played. But he was still feeling his way following the shift in their relationship. He did not want to make any assumptions.

She hesitated for a moment, most likely remembering what had happened after the last time he had given her that particular beverage. It was certainly front and center in his mind.

She smiled, though it looked forced. "Sure."

Something was on her mind. He could see it in her eyes. But he knew better than to ask. She would tell him when she was ready.

She began setting up the board while he poured them each a glass of the amber liquid. He placed the drinks on the table and sank down onto the cushion across from her.

She glanced up, a flash of wariness in her eyes. "Thank you." She took a token sip from the glass before returning her attention to the board. "I won the last time we played, so you have the opening move."

Tension showed in every line of her body, though she was doing her best to conceal it. This visit might have very little to do with playing chess, but if she wanted to wait to broach whatever was on her mind, he would give her all the time she needed.

He made his first move, and she countered. Play continued for a few minutes in silence. He studiously avoided moving his queen, even when it would have put him at an advantage. He just could not bring himself to pick up that particular piece.

Aurora had claimed three of his pawns and one bishop before she spoke. "I owe you an apology."

He glanced up and found her watching him. "Why do you owe me an apology?" Although he had a theory about what was motivating her statement.

"I reacted terribly after the incident on Drakar."

Incident? That was hardly the way he would describe their passionate embrace.

"And ever since then I've shown the maturity of a toddler. That hasn't been fair to you." She gave him a small smile. "I'm sorry. You deserve better than that."

He appreciated the sentiment, but the confrontation was not her fault. "I forced that kiss on you. I am the one who should be apologizing."

She shook her head. "I asked you a direct question and you gave me a direct answer. It wasn't your fault that it wasn't the response I expected."

He should have been relieved. She was absolving him. But for some reason he felt worse, not better.

"I also want to thank you for being honest with me," she continued. "It helps, knowing where I stand. And I want to be honest with you, too."

He had a terrible premonition that he would hate where she was going with this.

"Changes have been coming at me pretty fast these past few months." She rested her elbows on her knees. "You've been wonderfully supportive, especially with the Suulh, and I appreciate that more than I can say."

Now he was positive he would hate where this was going. Her tone was wrong, like she wanted to soften the impact of the blow she was about to deliver. He tensed.

"But one of those changes affects you, and we need to talk about it."

The sinking feeling in the pit of his stomach increased.

"Cade and I spent the night together."

His heart stopped beating. That was the only logical explanation for the chill that swept through every cell in his body.

He stared at her, refusing to believe he had heard correctly. Hoping that any moment he would wake from the nightmare she had just tossed him into. *Say something!*

Worry lines formed at the edges of her eyes. He could count each one, see them with perfect clarity, along with the golden flecks sprinkled in the deep green of her irises. Cade Ellis had probably noticed those golden flecks, too. He growled.

"Jonarel?" She leaned toward him. "Are you okay?"

When she reached forward and clasped his hand in hers, he came apart. "No!" he roared, stumbling as he shoved his body backward, breaking the contact like she had touched him with a live wire. He was on his feet and across the room in a heartbeat. His hands clamped down on the edges of his drafting table, squeezing the protesting wood as he fought for control.

"Jonarel, I'm sorry."

He forced air into his lungs, beating down the rage that was blacking out his vision. His mind tortured him with image after image of Aurora and Ellis together, the fury building with each new variation.

"Jonarel?"

Her voice scraped his senses. He slowly tilted his head so that he could see her out of the corner of his eye. But he kept his grip on the table. He feared what he might do if he let go.

She looked horrified. And heartbreakingly sad. Her hand splayed across her throat like she wished she could take the words back.

"I'm so, so sorry," she whispered, her eyes beginning to glisten with unshed tears.

His   brain   whirled   with   thoughts,   questions,

condemnations. But only one really mattered. He grated it out. "*Why?*"

Her lips parted in surprise. She took a tentative step forward but halted immediately when he gave a sharp shake of his head. He was hanging on by a thread. If she came any closer, he would not be able to stop himself from doing something really, really stupid.

She was trembling. He hated himself for causing that reaction, but he hated her, too. She had just driven a dagger into his heart, and it was killing him.

"*Why?*" he growled again, proving he was a masochist of the worst kind. But he had to know.

She swallowed. "After the battle...after realizing what we're facing...I was overwhelmed. I needed some way to release the pressure." The look in her eyes pleaded for understanding. "Cade helped me do that."

His teeth ground together, the sound louder than a rock tumbler. "I could have helped you." In fact, he would have been thrilled to assist her with that particular problem. But she had not asked him. Instead, she had gone to Ellis. He wanted to rip the man's throat out.

Her look of helplessness only added fuel to the fire.

Releasing the table edge, he stalked toward her. "*Why him, Aurora?*"

Her eyes widened and she backed up.

He kept coming. "Have you forgotten what he did to you? How he treated you? Because I remember it every day."

She ran out of room as her back met the bulkhead. She halted. He did not. Spreading his arms, he caged her in, his face so close to hers he could feel the warmth of her breath on his lips. "He rejected you. Tossed you aside like garbage because he thought you were unworthy of him."

Pain flashed in her eyes, but he pressed on.

"He believes your mixed heritage makes you less than human. A freak. But I do not. I believe it makes you the most extraordinary being in the galaxy." He needed her to understand. No, he was begging her to understand. "I would never hurt you like that."

She stared up at him—his brave, strong, amazing Aurora. "I know," she whispered.

He could not read the look in her eyes. Could not tell what she was thinking. Unable to resist the pull of her nearness, he brought his lips a hair's breadth from hers and hovered there. "I love you."

"I love you, too." And then she did the most amazing thing. She kissed him.

His brain cells scattered as her hands cupped his face and her lips moved over his. He had thought he had kissed her before. But what he had experienced on Drakar was a pale imitation. This time Aurora had initiated the kiss, and she was showing him without words how much he meant to her.

Unfortunately, even as her touch sent shivers of delight through his body, his mind registered that the kiss lacked one key ingredient.

Passion.

And it ended far too quickly.

He would not let her go. As she pulled back, he stroked his fingers down the side of her face. "Let me love you, Aurora," he murmured. He laced his fingers through hers. "I want to be with you. Always."

She stared at their joined hands, but remained silent.

His heart pounded like a drum, counting the seconds. "Aurora?"

When she looked up, something in her eyes set his

senses on alert. "You've never told me why you disliked Cade. From the very beginning, you've hated him, even before he hurt me. Was it because you wanted me back then, too?"

He had not anticipated the question, and he stumbled over his answer. "Yes. No." He frowned. "Yes, I wanted you back then. But that is not why I hate him. At least, that is not the main reason."

"Then what is the reason?"

"Because he is not worthy of you. He never has been. What can he possibly offer you? You have your own ship. You are the leader of an entire race. Who is he? No one."

Her eyes narrowed. "But I didn't have a ship when we were at the Academy. And you didn't know about my connection to the Suulh until recently."

He cursed himself for the slip. "I have always known you were special. And I also knew that one day I would build this ship for you."

She pulled her hands from his grip, moving to stand next to the abandoned chessboard. "So the ship *was* a ploy to draw me in. To bind me to you."

"No." At least, not entirely. More like a tangible affirmation of what he wanted. "The ship has been, and always shall be, a gift. The *Starhawke* is yours, now and always. Whether we are together or not."

She did not believe him. He could see it in her eyes. And the more time she spent standing next to that cursed board, the more he heard his father's words echoing in his head. *She is the queen. The most powerful piece in the game.*

Had he built the *Starhawke* so that he could gain a measure of control over that power?

"You always assumed we would be together." She

was not asking.

He sighed. "Yes. I did."

She nodded, her lips forming a line that was a far cry from the tender sweetness he had experienced just minutes before.

"Thank you for telling me the truth." She stepped toward the doorway. "If you'll excuse me, I have work to do." And then she was gone.

Jonarel's gaze slowly returned to the chessboard she had left behind. And to the queen that stood proud and strong at the center, mocking him. He had failed completely. His clan. His father. Himself. And possibly driven her into Ellis's arms in the process.

He glared at the board. Maybe he would burn it after all.

Sixty-Two

When the ship came out of the interstellar jump, Justin was back in the observation lounge, as curious as the Suulh to see the new homeworld.

To accommodate all the people who wanted a good view, the *Starhawke* had shown her versatility once again. The expanse of windows that normally looked out to the stern of the ship now projected the forward facing image that the bridge crew was seeing, enabling everyone to see the planet as they approached without cramming three hundred bodies onto the bridge.

The tables had all disappeared into hidden compartments beneath the floor, and everyone was seated like picnickers gathered for a fireworks show. He'd wondered if the Suulh would be overwhelmed, but they all seemed to be doing fine, their fear replaced with eagerness.

Captain Hawke's voice came over the speakers, first in Galish, then in the Suulh language, thanks to the translation he'd loaded into the *Starhawke's* database. "We'll have visual on the planet in a few moments."

One of the children let out an excited squeal as the curving surface of the planet glided into view, growing rapidly even as the ship decelerated for the final approach. As one, the Suulh gave a collective sigh. The sound was filled with such longing and joy that tears burned behind Justin's eyes. And that was before Raaveen met his gaze.

He couldn't even begin to explain the complex emotions that showed in her expression. But he didn't have to. He was feeling a lot of the same things. She looked lit from within, her excitement palpable. But there was a little apprehension there, too. After all, her life was about to change. Forever.

The blue and white of the planet filled the expanse as the ship descended. A subtle vibration through the floor was the only indication the ship gave that it had entered the atmosphere. Impressive. He didn't know of a single Fleet vessel that could pull off such a smooth transition from the vacuum of space.

The image shifted to opaque white, obscuring what would have been a jarring image of the atmosphere attempting to burn through the ship's shields. But that eventually gave way to the vista of the lower atmosphere. The crowd hummed with excitement as the expanse of deep blue water stretched below them. The ship continued its descent, skimming close enough to the ocean that the cameras revealed the crests of individual waves.

Captain Hawke's voice came over the speakers again. "The island will be coming up on the left."

Raaveen grabbed Justin's arm and pointed at the image. "Island?"

He followed the line of sight and spotted a mountain peak rising out of the vast blue, its darker shading contrasting with the lush green that spread out in undulating hills on all sides.

It was beautiful. Exactly what he'd wish for her and the rest of the Suulh. And the place where he'd tell her goodbye.

He banished that thought as he met her excited gaze. "Welcome to your new home."

Sixty-Three

As Kelly guided the *Starhawke* along the ocean's surface, Aurora's gaze remained on the island. Or rather, the stretch of water just in front of the island. When they'd departed for Burrow, only one ship had been anchored there. Now there were two.

The *Rowkclarek* sat right where they'd left him. The much smaller ship sitting alongside was the Clarek clan's diplomatic vessel, the *Kaltclarek*.

Siginal Clarek was paying the Suulh a visit.

"We're being hailed by the *Kaltclarek*," Kire informed her.

"On screen."

Siginal's broad-shouldered visage filled the space. "Blessings on your safe return, checala."

Aurora kept her expression neutral. The words were gracious, but his tone made her feel like a teenager caught out after curfew. She tamped down a flicker of irritation. "Hello, Siginal. I didn't expect to see you here."

He tipped his head in a small bow. "Apologies for arriving uninvited. After I received Kire's message, I needed to see with my own eyes that you were safe."

Understandable. But he was acting like an overprotective father checking up on her, something she'd never actually experienced because her father had died when she was an infant.

"We're all fine. And eager to show the Suulh their new home. I assume you'll be joining us?"

"If that is acceptable to you."

"Of course." And even if it wasn't, his clan had built the place and the planet was in Kraed space. Technically, they could take charge anytime they wanted to. What an unsettling thought, especially in light of the comments Jonarel had made when she'd visited his cabin. Her skin felt tight. "I'll send Jonarel over with a shuttle to pick you up. He's going to the settlement first to make sure it's ready before we bring anyone over. I'll meet you there."

"Until then," Siginal replied. The screen went blank.

What exactly was Siginal up to? Was he really just being an overprotective parent? Was his intention simply to make sure she and Jonarel were safe? Or was something else going on?

She turned to Kire. "Report to me as soon as they're ready for the first group. I'll be in the observation lounge if anyone needs me."

She was so focused on her inner debate that she almost didn't notice Cade leaning against the bulkhead next to the lift door. He'd been sitting at the console to her left when they'd landed. Now he was standing just out of visual range of the bridgescreen. Had he purposely placed himself there to avoid being seen by Siginal?

"Mind if I join you?" His look indicated he'd picked up on her internal tension.

"By all means."

As soon as the lift doors closed, he faced her. "You don't look happy."

She gave him a half-hearted smile. "I'm fine. Just didn't count on an unexpected guest. I'm doing a little mental reshuffling."

"Hmm." He cupped her jaw in his palm. "How can I help?"

A very inappropriate image popped into her mind. She shoved it away, but not before a flare of answering heat lit his eyes.

"Save that thought," he murmured.

That brought a real smile. "You bet. In the meantime, I'm enlisting you to help me sort the Suulh into groups. It'll take a few hours to get everyone transferred. I was thinking Raaveen, Sparw, Paaw and their families should make the first run. And Byrnes. They've earned it."

"Absolutely."

When the lift stopped she stepped toward the door but a gentle tug on her wrist turned her around, right into Cade's arms. He brushed a tender kiss on her lips.

"For strength," he whispered.

At the moment, she'd take all the backup she could get.

Sixty-Four

Excited chatter from the teens filled the shuttle during the trip to the island. Cade enjoyed their enthusiasm, but his focus remained on Aurora. Her shoulders were tightening with each minute, her body winding up like a spring.

The landing platform had been crafted out of a natural promontory in the rock that overlooked the river below. The thunder of a nearby waterfall accompanied his footsteps as he walked down the ramp behind Aurora. Siginal Clarek stood with his son next to the shuttle's twin, waiting for them.

Cade had never officially met the Clarek clan leader before, though he'd seen him a few times at the Academy, where the Kraed had been the head of the astrophysics department. He was difficult to miss. Built like a bear with skin the color of evergreen needles that stretched over thick muscles, and dark brown hair that hung loose below his massive shoulders, he exuded power and authority.

After he'd greeted Aurora, his yellow gaze focused on Cade. "Commander Ellis, I presume?"

He stood up straighter. "Yes, sir."

"Your reputation precedes you."

Cade wasn't certain whether that was a good thing or not. But at least the male wasn't shooting daggers at him like his son. Jonarel looked like he wanted to roast Cade over a spit. Obviously he'd been clued in to the change in Cade's relationship with Aurora. And as Cade had predicted, his hatred had soared.

Not that he was about to let either of the Clareks intimidate him. He stepped forward and extended his hand. "It's a pleasure to meet you Professor Clarek."

"And I you, Commander Ellis," the male replied. "The Admiral speaks very highly of you."

Maybe that was the reason for the lack of hostility. Having the Admiral in his corner would carry weight with someone like Siginal Clarek. "I'm honored to be of service to him." He spotted Justin exiting the shuttle and motioned him forward. "I'd like you to meet my first officer, Justin Byrnes. He's the one who translated the Suulh language."

"Did he?" The Kraed's brows lifted as he faced Justin. "You must be a man of great talents."

Justin responded as Cade expected, neither bragging nor acknowledging the comment. "I had great teachers." He smiled at the three teens who had gathered beside him. They smiled back, though they seemed a bit unnerved by the elder Clarek's presence.

The male noticed their discomfort, and stepped back. "Please, do not let us keep you. I am certain you are eager to see your new home." He turned to Aurora. "I will join Jonarel on the *Starhawke* and help with transportation. If you have no objections," he added.

Aurora nodded, her shoulder muscles bunching as her gaze darted briefly to Jonarel. "That would be wonderful. Thank you." She gestured to the rest of the group. "Follow me."

As Cade moved to join Aurora, he resisted the urge to look back. But every fiber of his being told him what he needed to know.

He was being watched.

Sixty-Five

Jonarel wanted to burn a hole through Ellis's head. If looks could kill, Ellis would be a pile of ash. Instead, he was walking up the path with Aurora.

Jonarel spun on his heel and headed for the shuttle.

His father followed. "Cade Ellis has a more commanding presence than I expected." He sounded annoyed by the realization.

Jonarel was, too, especially now that Ellis's commanding presence was keeping close to Aurora. Jonarel's claws itched. He wanted to challenge his adversary, but he kept his body relaxed. He could not afford to give any indication that he had lost control of the situation. His father was way too observant.

He brought the shuttle's systems online as his father settled into the co-pilot's seat.

"I sense a change in you." His father studied him. "And in Aurora. Has something happened I should know about?"

Jonarel clamped down on his emotions. The tightrope of loyalty between his father and Aurora had never seemed so thin. "Aurora has a lot to think about right now."

"I would imagine so. The communications I received from your cousins upon arrival indicated the battle was intense. They also mentioned that Ellis has been spending quite a bit of time in Aurora's company during the journey here."

Jonarel's temper flared. He hated thinking about

Aurora with Cade Ellis. But he also hated the idea that his cousins had been spying on Aurora. He sincerely hoped Tehar was not part of that plot.

"As I understand it," his father continued, "Ellis is the one who allowed the children to be abducted, creating the need for a rescue in the first place."

Technically, that was false. Byrnes had been in charge of the group that had been captured. "They were ambushed. No one would have seen it coming." And his father's superior tone was beginning to grate on his nerves.

"You would have."

"They are human. They do not have our superior senses. They did their best." He realized the irony of defending Ellis's team to his father, but over the past few months he had developed a great respect for the members of the Elite Unit. They had put a lot of effort into helping the Suulh. It was obvious they cared a great deal. He did not want his father belittling them. Even Ellis. That was a shock.

"Their best ended in failure. It makes me wonder why Will thinks so highly of Ellis. Because of his ineptitude, Aurora nearly ended up in enemy hands."

Jonarel gripped the controls so tightly his claws scraped the metal. "He had nothing to do with the attack by the warships."

"Aurora was at Burrow because of him. Without his incompetence, she never would have been there in the first place."

"Yes, she would have. Eventually we would have traveled to Burrow to pick up the Suulh. And if the attack had occurred before we arrived, the Suulh would have been recaptured. Would you want them back in cages? If we had not been there, that could have happened."

"Better cages for them than one for Aurora."

"Aurora can take care of herself. She has proven that."

"It only takes one mistake, Jonarel. Only one." His father's yellow eyes glowed with banked anger. "And then she would be under the control of an enemy. If someone succeeded in turned her into a force for destruction, the results would be catastrophic."

The bottom dropped out of Jonarel's stomach. He refused to even consider that possibility. "That will not happen," he growled. "Ever."

"It might," his father growled back. "Especially if she is distracted. Cade Ellis is a living, breathing distraction. One you need to remove before he destroys us all."

Sixty-Six

This island was right up Justin's alley.

The warm tropical air reminded him of the Caribbean. Puffy white clouds tumbled through an azure sky, providing a vivid background for the kaleidoscope of greens and browns of the native vegetation. And judging from the reactions from the teens, it was everything they had hoped it would be.

Raaveen looked like a kid on her first day of school as her gaze took in the lush foliage around them. The island on Gaia where they'd stayed after the rescue had been nice, but this place had it beat by a factor of a hundred.

Her father walked beside her, her hand on his arm to guide him. His gaze was unfocused and his upper body completely still. If he'd been solid grey, he would have resembled an ancient Greek statue, like the ones Justin had seen during a class trip to an art museum during his early years at the Academy.

Captain Hawke led the way up the smooth pathway of inlaid stone. The greenery on either side was perfectly trimmed to give the feel of natural growth while not leaving a single stray frond or branch to impede those walking on the path.

They followed the gentle incline for about five minutes before it began to level off. When Captain Hawke stopped, Justin looked for a break in the foliage that would reveal the settlement. It took him a moment to realize they were already standing in the heart of the compound.

The exterior of the buildings had been texturized to

blend seamlessly with the trees and reeds. The groves lined the winding pathways that branched off in several directions from the central hub where they stood. He glanced back and discovered that what he'd mistaken for a thick copse of reeds actually formed the exterior walls for two of the outer buildings.

The main path continued forward, widening as it came to a set of steps. At the top of the steps, large double doors similar to the ones that opened onto the *Starhawke's* observation lounge, complete with colorful glasslike insets, fronted the main building.

Captain Hawke led the way forward, the doors parting as they approached.

The interior was open and airy, with ventilation points around the domed top that allowed a cross breeze to drift through. Plants flowed over arches, up walls, and down the staircase. The soothing burble of a fountain beckoned, and the plush seating at the center of the room promised relaxation.

The word that came to Justin's mind as he looked around was *nurturing*. Everything, from the shape of the building to the layout and furnishings, spoke of comfort, support, and love.

A gravelly male voice spoke. "Laanaa."

The room went deathly quiet. Raaveen turned to stare at her father—mouth open, eyes wide, hand pressed to her throat.

The word came again. "Laanaa."

This time, Justin saw Raaveen's father's lips move. *Laanaa.* The Suulh word for *home.*

Holy—

Not only was the man talking, he was looking, really *looking* at the room. But the expression on his face was that of a man who believes he's seeing a mirage in the desert.

Raaveen, on the other hand, was one stiff breeze away from toppling over. "Dawaa?" she whispered.

Her father blinked, his neck creaking down millimeter by millimeter until his gaze met hers. A frown appeared around his eyes and mouth. "Raaveen?"

The primal sound that came out of Raaveen's throat made Justin's chest constrict. She placed her hands on her father's arms tentatively, but when he didn't resist, she embraced him in a death grip.

"Raaveen?" her father murmured again, pulling his head back slightly in an attempt to see her face.

When she lifted her gaze, tears flowed freely down her cheeks. "Uia, Dawaa." *Yes, father.*

Sixty-Seven

The emotional pulse that shot through Aurora caught her completely off guard. Shock, joy, hope, fear, and confusion, all bundled together into an arrow of intensity that made her sway on her feet. Her emotional grid scrambled to sort through the sudden cacophony while her brain worked on locating the source.

It wasn't difficult.

Standing at the back of the room, wrapped in Raaveen's embrace, was a man she almost didn't recognize. And why would she? This man had animation to his features and was gazing in confusion and wonder at the daughter who held him in her arms. The feelings coming from the pair intensified the longer they gazed at each other.

The rest of the group had turned as well, and their reactions buffeted her on a second wave. She grabbed onto Cade's arm for stability. His warm hand folded over her fingers, giving her his strength.

She squeezed back before stepping forward. The group parted like the Red Sea, with Raaveen and her father on the far shore. Cade followed her, his presence a haven of calm in the sudden squall.

Raaveen's father looked up as she approached. "I know you." He spoke in the Suulh language, which the translator in her comband instantly reproduced in Galish. He frowned.

Raaveen shifted to his side but kept a firm grip around his waist, as though she was afraid if she lost contact he would disappear.

Aurora's heart ached for the young woman. Months had passed since she'd watched Raaveen's mother fall to her death, yet every detail of the moment remained burned into her mind and body like a brand. As a result, being around Raaveen was always bittersweet, more so than with any of the other Suulh.

Aurora nodded. "Yes, you do know me, though we have not been introduced."

The translator reproduced her words in his language, and he glanced at her comband in confusion. "Who are you?"

She decided explaining would be way too complicated, so she chose to show him instead. She engaged her energy field.

He sucked in a breath. "Sahzade!" Immediately he dropped to his knees in front of her, taking Raaveen down with him. He clasped Aurora's hands in both of his. "You have returned to us." His voice choked with tears. The look on his face tore at her.

His energy field lit up, a much darker shade of red than Raaveen's, nearly black. Aurora flinched at the intimate connection. She'd thought the blasts from across the room had been bad. Now she was having his tangled emotions mainlined. So much pain and sadness. So much grief and loss. So many regrets. But she couldn't move away.

"Yes, I have." She struggled to speak as her throat closed up. The depth of his need sucked her down, drawing her energy into the black hole of his suffering and eclipsing everything else.

Cade's arms encircled her body, keeping her upright, but that did nothing to relieve the pressure pushing from within. She needed to breathe, to center and ground herself, but expanding her lungs had become a real challenge. There was a good chance she was going to black out. At least Cade would keep her from hitting the ground.

But as her vision greyed around the edges, the weight suddenly lifted and her lungs expanded. She gasped, gulping in as much air as she could handle. At the same time, a gentle coolness caressed her raw emotions, soothing her. She dragged her gaze from Raaveen's father and found Paaw and Zelle standing beside her, their hands resting lightly on her shoulders as their healing blue energy joined the mix.

"Zelle?" Raaveen's father looked bewildered at he stared up at them.

Zelle's smile filled the room with light. "Uia, Ren. Veebra laanaa."

Yes, Ren. Welcome home.

Sixty-Eight

By nightfall, the Suulh had all been transported to the settlement.

Cade had joined Aurora, Mya and Clarek in the main house to discuss the warship attack at Burrow with Siginal. The rest of the crew had been given the task of sorting out the temporary sleeping arrangements in the main house and four of the outbuildings. They were habitable, though largely unfurnished, but compared to the cramped quarters the Suulh were used to, the situation was nirvana.

Siginal rested his elbows on the arms of his chair and steepled his fingers together in a gesture that perfectly mimicked Admiral Schreiber. The fact that the Kraed had picked up that particular behavior from the Admiral gave Cade insight into just how much time the two men must have spent together over the years. He had a feeling there was a depth to their relationship that he'd never imagined.

"Tell me about the ships you encountered, checala." Siginal's yellow gaze rested on Aurora.

Siginal had used that term to refer to Aurora once before, when they'd first arrived. Now Cade wished he'd asked what it meant. He didn't care for the tone in which it was spoken, like the Kraed had some parental authority over her.

"The carrier was the largest ship I've ever seen. Bigger than the entire Clarek compound." Her voice sounded flat, and her expression was carefully neutral. "And the warships were all roughly the size of the *Starhawke.*"

"How many warships?"

"We fought a dozen. But I seriously doubt that's the maximum capacity for the carrier."

"The raw materials necessary to create a ship of that size would be considerable." Signal frowned. "Was there any indication of Setarip involvement?"

Aurora shook her head. "The technology they used was advanced and very well designed. We've never encountered anything like it from Setarips."

"Do you have any theories regarding how they located you?"

Cade fielded that one. "Justin thinks it's possible they picked up on the signals from the relay beacons in that sector when Aurora and I were sending messages. Since the Fleet no longer maintains a presence in that system, repeated activity on the beacons would have been unusual."

"If that is correct, why did they not attack sooner?"

Cade picked up on the subtle challenge in the question. "It would have taken time for anyone to notice the unusual activity and pinpoint our location. And moving that carrier would take an incredible amount of energy. They wouldn't do it until they were certain they had the right target."

Aurora backed him up. "We probably arrived in the system before the carrier did. If it had already been there, our sensors would have picked up energy traces during the flight in. We didn't. But the carrier would have been able to track our signals leading into the debris field. With the field acting as a signal shield after we passed through, they were able to set their trap and move into position to intercept us without alerting us."

"They also may have been wary of making a ground assault," Cade added. "The Suulh aren't Necri anymore, but our enemy may not know that. Capturing them on a ship would be a safer course of action than confronting them face-to-face."

"They clearly wanted us alive." Aurora's lips thinned. "The warships were trying to capture us, not destroy us."

And they'd almost succeeded. "The netting system they used on the *Nightingale* worked perfectly. If they'd managed to catch both ships at the same time, we wouldn't have been able to escape. We couldn't use our weapons without blowing ourselves up." He didn't add that that's exactly what he would have done if the *Starhawke* hadn't been able to break them free.

"An effective strategy for domination." Siginal's gaze bored into him, almost like he held Cade responsible.

Cade stared back, refusing to be cowed. "The attack on Gaia was only a first foray. Testing the waters to see how the Council would respond. They responded by sending Aurora. From what the Admiral told us, that was no accident."

Aurora sighed. "Because of the Suulh. Someone knew Mya and I were connected to them. Or at least suspected." Her expression grew bleak as she and Mya exchanged a troubled glance. "They needed to bring us into contact with them to see what would happen. And apparently they learned a lot from those encounters."

Siginal's eyes narrowed. "What do you mean?"

"There were Necri on that carrier. Lots of them."

Cade's heart thumped. He'd been right. Mya had collapsed during the battle because of the presence of Necri on the carrier. Just as she'd collapsed in the orchard on Gaia. Which meant Aurora had also been affected.

The Clareks stared at Aurora in stunned silence.

"You sensed them on the ship, didn't you?" Cade

ached for her. "You felt their pain."

Aurora and Mya exchanged another look, a haunting sorrow visible in their eyes. Mya rested a hand on Aurora's arm and a flow of green energy surrounded them both.

Aurora's energy field joined Mya's, but tension still kept her shoulders rigid. "Yes. I felt them. This group." She gestured to indicate the settlement. "It's only the tip of the iceberg."

Cade swallowed. This was bad. "How many Necri are we talking about?"

"I don't know. But the impact gets weaker with distance."

Cade was good with numbers. He made the mental calculations in an instant. On Gaia when she and Mya had collapsed, they'd been in visual range of the two hundred Necri involved. This time they'd been sensing Necri on a distant spaceship. To have a similar effect, there'd have to be...

He swore softly, his body going cold. Siginal and Jonarel exchanged a look he couldn't interpret. But clearly they found the idea as unsettling as he did.

Siginal's voice rumbled like thunder. "If you are correct, the situation is more complicated than we had imagined. But you said you sensed them. How do you know you were sensing the pain of Necri and not someone else?"

"Because what I sense from the Suulh is different. I feel their pain as my own."

Cade's stomach dropped. He hadn't known. Hadn't understood. But it made perfect sense. It explained why her connection to the Suulh was so strong. And why their suffering tore her apart. Unfortunately, there was nothing he could do to help her. Except offer her his support. He threaded his fingers through hers, ignoring the glare from

Clarek.

Aurora didn't look at him, but her fingers closed in a subtle squeeze.

Mya spoke up. "What Aurora and I experience around the Suulh is a biological reaction. Our abilities work like built-in tracking devices. They let us know when our people are hurting and in need of protection, and also where to find them. The stronger the sensations we experience, the closer we are to the source."

Siginal's frown deepened. "Have you spoken to the Suulh about what you sensed?"

Mya shook her head. "Most of the adults are still too emotionally compromised to discuss the past, or the existence of other Suulh. Or Necri. It would be too traumatic. Zelle and Paaw might be able to give us some insight, but they've been through a lot recently. Asking questions will trigger painful memories. We don't want to take that step until we have a plan for how to make use of the information they may provide."

And those discussions would be as difficult for Aurora as they would be for the Suulh. Their pain was her pain. She felt what they felt. As far as Cade was concerned, they could wait. They all needed time to heal, first.

Aurora drew her shoulders back, her spine ramrod straight. "However, it's obvious that the original attack that supposedly wiped out our homeworld wasn't the genocide we'd been led to believe. Our race survived. Maybe even flourished."

"What do you know about that attack?" Jonarel asked.

"Not much. My mother refused to talk about it."

Jonarel glanced at Mya. "What about your parents?"

She shook her head. "Libra forbid them to speak of

it. They shared snippets of the Suulh culture and language with me, nothing more. I didn't even know that's what our race was called until Aurora told me. My parents never talked about their lives before they arrived on Earth."

"Even with each other?" Cade asked.

"Not that I ever heard."

"Marina and Gryphon won't go against my mother's wishes." Aurora looked as frustrated as Cade felt. "She's the Guardian of her generation. She has the final word if she and Marina disagree."

"Does the same apply to you and Mya?" Cade hadn't considered that possibility.

"No," Aurora said.

"Yes," Mya said at the same time.

Aurora shot Mya an annoyed look. "No, it doesn't. I wasn't raised in the Suulh tradition. If Mya and I disagree, we work it out."

"What about your mother?" Siginal asked. "Can you order her to tell you what we need to know?"

Aurora shook her head. "It doesn't work that way. My mother is still a Guardian. We're equals, even though technically I became the race's Guardian as soon as I reached adulthood. But that only changes my relationship to other Suulh, not to my mother."

And there was the sticking point. Cade blew out a breath. "So you'll have to convince her to talk about the attack." No small task. Libra Hawke had always struck him as a very stubborn woman.

She met his gaze. "That's right. But I don't have much hope. The last time I tried, the discussion deteriorated into a cold war that lasted for weeks."

He stroked his thumb across the back of her hand. "But you'll have backup this time. You won't be facing her alone." He'd gladly be her champion, if she'd let him.

The hint of a smile appeared at the corner of her mouth.

Siginal cleared his throat, the sound coming out more like a growl. "We have another important issue to discuss."

Aurora pulled her hand from Cade's and sat forward, her focus shifting to Siginal. Cade stifled a growl of his own. When it came to Aurora, the damn Kraed were always interfering.

"Will is missing."

Will? Who was Will? Then it clicked. Siginal was talking about the Admiral. "He's missing? How do you know?" And more to the point, why had he waited until now to alert them?

"We keep a steady communication. But my recent messages have not been received. When I inquired at the Council headquarters, I was told he was on leave."

The Admiral would never go on leave while the Elite Unit was on a mission. Especially now. "On leave? Where?"

Siginal met his gaze. "They would not clarify. They may be under orders from Will to keep the details confidential. But that would not explain why he has failed to alert me."

Cade exchanged a worried glance with Aurora. It looked like they were thinking the same thing. "We'll find him."

Sixty-Nine

A noose had settled around Aurora's neck.

She tried to shake off the sensation as she gazed at the stars, but it clung stubbornly, tethering her to her anxiety. And the knot that was constricting her throat was far worse than any rope.

The breeze whispered through the tree fronds, brushing them against the wide ledge of the upstairs balcony where she perched. The sound should have calmed her, but she barely noticed. Her brain was too busy pondering the tasks set before her. And the implications for her future.

For the past few months she'd been so focused on establishing a homeworld for the Suulh that she'd never really considered what would happen after she achieved that goal. She'd neatly compartmentalized the situation into unrelated tasks—find a homeworld, build the colony, transport the Suulh to the planet. After that, she'd mentally closed the book and considered her job done.

But the discussion tonight had pointed out the major flaw in her thinking. Her vision wasn't in line with reality. Not by a long shot. Delivering the Suulh to their new home wasn't the end. It was only the beginning.

And that left her in a tough situation. The Suulh needed a guardian, someone to lead and protect them, now more than ever. By birth, that role was hers. But she couldn't stay. She needed answers she couldn't find here.

Closing her eyes, she turned her face toward the breeze. Focusing on her breathing, she summoned her energy field, allowing it to wrap around her like a cocoon, drawing the tension away.

She sensed Mya before the patter of footsteps moved across the wood floor of the gallery. When she opened her eyes, Mya stood in the doorway, her expression untroubled but her rich green energy field swirling in much the same way as Aurora's. Apparently they both needed a little soothing.

Mya met her gaze. "You want to talk about it?"

Not really. But they probably should. After all, Mya understood what they were up against. "Better than ignoring it."

"I agree." Mya glanced around the bare space before settling onto the wide ledge beside Aurora. "We need to get some furniture out here."

Furniture. Aurora almost laughed. Wouldn't it be lovely if that were the biggest problem they had to deal with? "I'll tell Jonarel to make it a priority."

Mya smiled. "There's the sense of humor I've been missing." She nudged Aurora with her shoulder. "How're you holding up, kid?"

Aurora sighed. "Just fine, as long as I ignore the fact that there's an enormous carrier ship out there somewhere with countless Necri slaves onboard. Oh, that you and I have to abandon the Suulh on their new homeworld so we can go to Earth to extract information from our parents. And that Admiral Schreiber has disappeared without a trace. Other than those minor details, I'm great."

Mya nodded as she gazed at the stars. "That about sums it up. But at least you're not alone." She glanced at Aurora. "You do know that, right? This isn't all on you."

The pressure on her shoulders eased, indicating she hadn't really considered that fact. She conjured a semblance of a smile. "Thanks for the reminder." She stared at the shadow of the mountain in the distance. "I need to keep that in mind. Ever since Drakar, I've been a little off track."

Mya snorted. "Sahzade, you never get off track. You just try to run them all at the same time."

The observation was so spot on it stunned Aurora into silence.

Mya gazed at her. "But that's a tough way to live."

"I know." Aurora drew her knees up to her chest. "Ever since I was a kid, I've had clear goals, starting with the Academy, then becoming an officer in the Fleet, and now with the *Starhawke*. But this situation with the Suulh." She swept her hand to encompass their surroundings. "It's thrown me for a loop." She dropped her chin onto her knees. "I'm starting to feel like a passenger in my own life."

"And that frustrates you."

Aurora nodded.

"So what is it that *you* want?" Mya asked. "Honestly. If you had complete freedom to choose, how would you handle this situation?"

She chewed on her lip as she considered the question. Seeing the carrier ship at Burrow had changed everything. At first she'd been overwhelmed, thrown into a maelstrom of emotional disarray that had led to her passionate encounter with Cade, followed by her equally emotional confrontation with Jonarel.

But what had felt like pandemonium in the beginning was settling into something else. She was discovering that the core of her being was shifting, focusing, and stretching in new directions. What she was experiencing wasn't chaos. It was a part of her that had been kept in darkness coming out into the light.

She hadn't asked to be in charge of an entire race, but the Fates had stepped in and made it so. The only question was, how would she handle it going forward?

"You and I have to go to Earth," she murmured, thinking out loud. "And Cade's team has to find out what happened to the Admiral." She frowned. "But that leaves the Suulh without a leader."

"Are you sure?"

"Well, the Clarek clan could act as interim leaders, I suppose. But I don't know how long Siginal is planning to stay." Or whether she really wanted to leave him in charge.

Mya shook her head. "I wasn't referring to Siginal. I was talking about the leader the Suulh already have."

"That would be me. Or you. But we'll be on Earth."

"Not us. Think, Sahzade. Who has been the bedrock for them since the day we found them?"

Understanding finally dawned. "Raaveen."

Mya nodded. "She can't possibly replace you. But she's strong. And she's beloved and respected. You might want to make use of those skills when we can't be here."

Interesting concept. But there was one problem. "That's a lot of responsibility to dump on her shoulders. Especially with Ren just beginning to recover."

"She's not alone, either." Mya mirrored Aurora's pose, drawing her knees in. "I've been talking to Paaw and Zelle. They're talented healers. Not as powerful as my family, but they've been filling a similar role for quite a while. They can certainly help Raaveen. And who knows? Maybe before too long, Ren will be able to help her, too."

"Wouldn't that be something." Aurora still couldn't quite believe the transformation the man had undergone right before her eyes. Telling him about the death of his mate had been a challenge, but having Raaveen by his side had helped to soften the blow.

Mya studied her. "Would you be comfortable with

that solution?"

That was a big question. Because if she wasn't, she had no business leaving the planet. She couldn't spend all her time away worrying about the Suulh's safety. If she agreed, she'd need to trust Raaveen, Paaw and Zelle to take charge.

And she could do that. After all, they'd been taking care of each other long before she'd come on the scene. She needed to let go. "Yes. We'll announce it to everyone tomorrow."

Seventy

Home.

It was the first word Ren had spoken. A word with tremendous power, one that had broken a curse of darkness and isolation.

But for Cade, the concept of home had no meaning. Home for him for the past ten years had been wherever the Admiral sent the Elite Unit. Before that, it had been the Academy. Before the Academy? Well, his parents weren't exactly a cornerstone of warmth and kindness, especially after he'd made it clear he wasn't going to follow in his father's footsteps. He couldn't recall the last time he'd visited them.

But here, standing in one of the archways of the main house, he was surrounded by an image of home that resonated deep in his soul. Aurora's presence had a lot to do with it.

Following the Suulh tradition, Aurora and Mya had established living quarters on opposite sides of the main building. Raaveen and Ren had been assigned a chamber next to Aurora's. Paaw, Maanee and Zelle were staying on Mya's side, as were Sparw and his parents. Now that everyone had seen the transformation of Ren, Zelle was championing the cause to focus their collective energies on helping Sparw's parents regain mental and emotional awareness.

The remaining chambers on either side were designated for those families with the greatest need for protection and healing, which included most of the remaining teens and their parents.

By Cade's calculations, about sixty of the Suulh were currently housed in the main building. The rest were setting up collectives in the outbuildings. He'd seen a lot of teary faces as they'd moved about, deciding where they wanted to stay. But for once, the tears were all about joy, not sorrow.

Aurora had told Raaveen, Paaw, Sparw, and their families that the *Starhawke* would be leaving the next day, and that she'd designated Raaveen as the leader in absentia. Raaveen had looked poleaxed, but her father had glowed. Literally. His energy field had lit up, already looking more robustly red than it had the day before. It still startled Cade to see expressions on the man's face.

Mya had likewise appointed an interim healer—Paaw. Her family wasn't of Mya's line, but their skill set tended that way. One reason Zelle had made the speediest recovery from her Necri existence was the healing Paaw and Maanee had been able to offer to assist their mother's innate abilities.

At the moment, all the teens were helping Aurora and Mya orchestrate the preparations for a big communal meal and celebration that would be held in the main building's central gathering space that evening. The area was large for a reason—in their cultural traditions, coming together as a group was a regular activity, so they needed a comfortable space to do so.

Cade had to give the Clarek clan credit. They'd done a wonderful job of creating an environment that suited the Suulh perfectly. And Aurora moved about the space with calm assurance, every bit the leader she was meant to be.

She glanced in his direction and caught him watching her. Her smile was a welcome sight as she crossed the room. "So, what do you think?" She gestured to the busy kitchen and the smiling and laughing teens.

He slipped his arms around her waist and drew her closer. "I think you're amazing."

"So you've said before." Her green eyes sparkled. "But I'm not the one who built this place."

He tucked a stray lock of hair behind her ear. Her braid was coming undone, but she obviously hadn't taken the time to redo it. She'd been completely focused on the Suulh.

"Sure you did. You may not have put the walls up, but this entire project has been yours and Mya's from the beginning. The Suulh couldn't ask for better leaders."

"Thank you." She nestled her head against his chest and sighed. "But without you, we may never have made it off Gaia."

He stroked her back with his fingers. "And without you, we wouldn't have made it off Burrow. Give yourself some credit."

She tilted her head up. "Okay." The look in her eyes warmed the longer he held her. Slipping her hand into his, she tugged him toward the doorway that led to her chamber.

He didn't resist.

After closing the chamber door behind them, she moved back into his arms. "So, what happens now?"

That was a loaded question if he'd ever heard one. But he kept his tone light. "What do you want to happen?"

Her sexy smile spoke volumes. "I have a few ideas."

And when a thin ribbon of energy caressed his body, he had a pretty good idea, too.

"Not that we can do anything about it right now," she added. "But it will take us several days to reach Earth." Her eyes gleamed with anticipation. "We'll need to pass the time somehow."

When she talked like that, his body redlined in a millisecond. "I suppose we will." He bent his head to kiss her, but she stopped him, her smile fading.

"But then what?"

He frowned. "What do you mean?"

"Well, I'll be staying on Earth while I talk to my mother. What about your team? Will you be leaving to find the Admiral?"

He hadn't allowed himself to think that far ahead. One day at a time worked much better. But they didn't have that luxury much longer. "I suppose so. We'll need to secure transportation first. Reanne might be able to help with that." Not that he relished that conversation. Talking to Reanne was like verbal fencing. You never knew when you'd get stabbed.

Aurora flinched at the mention of her former roommate. Apparently she felt the same way. "Makes sense." Her expression closed down, shutting off the warmth like a cloud passing in front of the sun.

She started to pull away, but he locked his arms. "I can see the wheels turning. What's on your mind?"

Her gaze searched his, like she was trying to read something written behind his eyes. "I guess I hadn't really considered that reaching Earth would mean splitting up the crew." She frowned. "Which logically means leaving you."

His stomach pitched. He didn't like where this was going. "You mean, for good?"

"No. Well...I don't know." She shook her head. "You have a job to do. So do I. And they're not exactly compatible." She lifted a hand to his face, tracing the line of his jaw. "The problem is, I've kind of gotten used to having you around."

He cracked a joke so she wouldn't notice the pain digging into his heart. "Like an old shirt?"

She pinched his arm and he yelped. "No. Not like an old shirt. Like a friend. A crewmember." Her voice deepened. "A lover."

His body really liked that last part. "I've enjoyed that, too."

"Unrealistic as it is, I somehow convinced myself you would be staying on the *Starhawke*."

"As what? Your sex slave?"

She pinched him again, harder. "No. Although the idea has a certain appeal." She shook her head, a bemused smile on her lips. "What am I going to do with you?"

Love me. But he couldn't say that. "I don't know. I don't have anything to offer you that you don't already have."

"Don't you?" Her energy field enveloped him again, but this time the contact didn't feel the least bit sexual. It felt like bonding. "Are you sure about that?"

Now his heart was doing a conga. The look in her eyes had his brain on tilt. Was Justin right? Was it possible that she wanted him to be with her...because she was still in love with him, too?

He suddenly had a sense that this was one of those pivotal moments that he'd look back on for the rest of his life. And if he made the wrong move, he would regret it. Forever.

But a lot was on the line. His job. His team. And his heart. Which began thumping so hard he was certain she'd hear it. Taking a deep breath, he cupped her face in his hands. "I've made protecting people my life's work. And I'm good at it. Very good. But you're the one person in the entire universe who doesn't need my protection."

"That's not true."

Her breath caressed his face, scattering his thoughts

like autumn leaves. He tried to remain focused, but he could barely hear over the rushing sound in his ears. "It's not?"

She shook her head. "You're the only one who can protect me from losing you."

He closed his eyes as her words sunk in. "Oh, Rory." He let his forehead rest against hers. What a gift she was. An incredible, precious gift. One he didn't deserve.

He drew back. A frown line had appeared between her brows. He smoothed it out with his thumb as he gazed into her eyes. Those beautiful, amazing eyes. "You have no idea what you do to me." Although given her empathic abilities, maybe she did. "And my previous behavior not withstanding, I'm not an idiot."

He had, in fact, been an idiot ten years ago. He wouldn't make the same mistake twice. "If you're asking me to stay, the answer is yes."

Seventy-One

Justin's muscles moved with the pleasant ache of a good day's physical labor.

He'd spent the previous eight hours working alongside the rest of his team, helping the Clarek clan with the construction of the outbuildings. Four were already livable, though not completed. The remaining four still needed interior work before they were habitable. They'd called it quits at sundown, breaking for a quick cleanup and change of clothes. Now they were headed to the main building for the evening's festivities.

He should have been excited. Instead, he was restless. This was his last night with Raaveen, Paaw and Sparw. And he didn't have any idea how he was going to say goodbye.

But the sight that greeted him when he walked through the doorway to the main house brought his thoughts to a screeching halt. Apparently it surprised the rest of his team as well, because they all stood rooted to the floor like four life-size statues.

The Suulh were gathered into a semi-circle facing the door, with the children in front and the teens and adults standing behind them. The members of the Clarek clan stood to either side.

Cade, Captain Hawke and Dr. Forrest stood at the center, with Siginal and Jonarel Clarek just behind them and the rest of the *Starhawke* crew flanking them.

"Welcome." Captain Hawke motioned his team

forward. "Join us."

He got his feet moving again, and the rest of the team fell in step with him. He stopped in front of her while the Suulh and the Clarek clan shifted positions to close the circle behind them. *What was going on?*

"Tonight, we come together to honor our family, our friends, and our new home." Captain Hawke's voice filling the large space with ease. "Your efforts, sacrifices, and dedication have made this moment possible." Her gaze settled on each member of the team as she spoke, every syllable infused with appreciation for all they had been through together. "You have given of your time, resources and talents graciously. Now we would like to offer you a gift in return."

Justin flicked a glance at Cade, but his friend just gave him an enigmatic smile.

"No words could possibly express the gratitude Mya and I feel for each of you. You have overcome great challenges with courage and selflessness in order to bring our people safely here. Thanks to you, we now have a new homeworld to call our own." She motioned to Raaveen, who stepped into the center of the circle, followed by Ren, Paaw, Maanee, Zelle, and Sparw.

Raaveen spoke in the flowing Suulh language, but Captain Hawke's comband translated her words. "You have been our teachers, our guardians, our friends." Her gaze settled on Justin. "We come from different worlds, but in our hearts, you have become part of our family."

Since he'd written the translation program, he knew better than anyone that the Suulh word that the comband translated as *family* went way beyond the Galish definition. Galish simply didn't have a word that encompassed the unique connection that the Suulh experienced with each other, and of the deep emotions that bound them together.

He suddenly found it difficult to swallow.

"As a token of our gratitude and connection, we would like to share our gift with you."

Raaveen extended one hand toward him and waited until he moved forward to grasp it. She held out her other hand to Cardiff. Paaw moved to Justin's other side while Ren, Sparw, Maanee and Zelle joined hands with the other members of his team and the *Starhawke* crew to form a large circle.

Captain Hawke stood in between Cade and Clarek, and Dr. Forrest moved to the opposite side of the circle between Williams and Emoto. The Suulh and the members of the Clarek clan in the outer ring joined hands with each other.

Justin glanced at Raaveen, but her gaze was fixed on Captain Hawke. A moment later Justin felt two distinctly different sensations wash over him—a powerful warmth that flowed up from his left hand, focusing his thoughts and emotions, and a soothing coolness coming from his right that released the tension in his muscles. Both were familiar to him, as he'd experienced them on Burrow when Captain Hawke had protected him from the Meer and Dr. Forrest had healed his injuries.

The differentiation in the two energies lasted for only a millisecond, before they blended and intensified. New notes joined the symphony, including Paaw's cooling touch, which was less refined than Dr. Forrest's but had a similar feel, and Raaveen's warm strength.

As the energy flowed through him like a river, tapping into emotions he usually kept buried deep, he trembled from the strain of resisting the siren call. He didn't want to feel this. He didn't want to feel anything. Ever. And he definitely didn't want to say goodbye.

Raaveen's dark-eyed gaze met his. her energy growing stronger, pulling at him, resonating with the sadness in his own heart. She knew what he was feeling. He could see it in her eyes. Because the same pain was tearing at her.

And that's when he stopped fighting. The real tragedy wasn't leaving them, never to return. That was a pain he could learn to live with, because it was the only way to keep the teens safe. But by avoiding the agony of impending loss, he'd been blocking out the joy of unconditional love. And that was something he would regret for the rest of his life.

Tomorrow he would leave forever. But tonight, he could allow the teens to know how much he cared.

He surrendered.

Seventy-Two

As Aurora guided the energy around the circle, she tuned into the array of emotional responses it elicited.

Kire was having the most fun. The smile on his face gave visual proof of that. Drew and Gonzo were openly curious, glancing at each other like they were trying to analyze what exactly they were experiencing. Dr. Williams and Celia had their eyes closed in a near Zen state, while Reynolds and Kelly were neither accepting nor rejecting, but simply observing, acting more like spectators than active participants.

Cade and Jonarel were an interesting dichotomy. Cade's emotions were wide open in a way she had never expected to feel again. She was still adjusting to the revelation that he wanted a future with her. She had no idea what it would look like, but her heart wanted to believe they'd figure it out.

Jonarel, on the other hand, had locked down his emotions so completely it was like he wasn't even there. She knew it was an act of self-preservation, and she hated being the cause. She'd never imagined that following her own heart would mean pummeling his.

But it was the notes of intense sadness coming from Byrnes, Raaveen, Paaw, and Sparw that really surprised her. Byrnes's emotional reaction was the most startling. She'd always sensed a subtle emotional wall from him, indicative of someone who didn't make strong attachments. But that barrier had collapsed, allowing an intense combination of pain and love to flow in its place. The teens' feelings echoed his.

The emotions spoke of deep bonding, particularly between Justin and Raaveen. That wasn't surprising, actually. She'd recently lost her mother, and her father had been little more than an automaton until yesterday. Making a connection with Byrnes, who she clearly liked and admired, made sense.

But it also presented a problem. Cade had mentioned that his team wanted to see the Suulh safely delivered to their new home, and Aurora had been happy to comply. However, it hadn't occurred to her that some of them might have formed strong emotional bonds with each other. That placed her in the uncomfortable position of gatekeeper between her people, who couldn't leave, and Cade's team, who couldn't return. She'd have to give the matter some serious thought before the morning.

Returning her attention to the circle, she allowed the energy current to slowly fade. Mya followed suit, the swirling prism of color dissipating like smoke. Releasing Cade and Jonarel's hands, Aurora stepped into the center of the circle, and Mya joined her.

"Tomorrow, Mya and I will be leaving." A murmur started up but she lifted her hand for silence. "We will return, but we don't know how soon. In the meantime, we have selected a guardian and healer to stand in our stead." Aurora motioned to Raaveen and Paaw, who stepped forward.

Aurora clasped their hands, as did Mya, forming a small circle. "We place the protection and well being of our people with you," she and Mya said together in Galish. "May the love and support of family be a source of courage and strength."

"We accept this honor with gratitude and joy," Raaveen and Paaw replied in the Suulh language.

Aurora glanced at Ren and Zelle as the teens returned to them. Their faces were streaked with happy tears. The sight tugged at her heart, but in a good way.

"The Clarek clan will remain to finish work on the settlement, and to assist you with any other needs that may arise. But this planet is yours now." She drew in a slow breath, struggling to keep her composure as the Suulh reacted to her words. "Nourish it. Explore it. Make it your home."

She faltered as their emotions washed over her. Her gaze met Cade's. He didn't move, but the look in his eyes gave her an anchor, steadying her.

"From this day forward, this planet shall be known by the name you have chosen. Azaana."

The Suulh word for freedom.

Seventy-Three

Jonarel spent the entire evening watching Aurora. And he had come to one inevitable conclusion. She was in love. But not with him.

The man in question had been by her side most of the night. Not because he had inserted himself there. Because Aurora wanted him there.

Observing her with Ellis was worse than being sucked dry by a relquir. Much worse. Every time she touched Ellis, Jonarel wanted to strip the man's skin from his bones. He hated Ellis with the force of a supernova, and trusted him even less.

But that did not matter. This was about Aurora. It always had been. And he was losing her. Which placed him at the dead center of a no-win scenario.

If he sabotaged her relationship with Ellis and somehow convinced her to choose him instead, overriding her judgment, he would be manipulating her and betraying her trust. What kind of future could they hope to have together if they started that way? He would have her by his side, but to keep her there, he would have to destroy the very qualities he cherished about her—her independence, her confidence, and her empathy. He would hate himself every second of every day. And she would grow to hate him, too.

But if he did nothing, his options were far worse. He would be betraying his father and his clan, and leaving Aurora vulnerable to another rejection by Ellis. He had witnessed the devastating results of their last breakup. It had taken years for Aurora to recover. He could not stand by and watch that happen again.

And if Ellis actually stayed? That presented the greatest threat of all, one that could destroy everything. His father would not allow that scenario to proceed for long. He would step in and do whatever he deemed necessary to separate Ellis from Aurora. Permanently. But if something happened to Ellis, and Aurora discovered that Jonarel had known about the danger and had not warned her, she would never forgive him.

She was a powerful ally. He did not want to find out how powerful she could be as an enemy.

His father had stated that Aurora had no choice in the matter. Jonarel disagreed. There was only one choice that mattered. Hers. But was he prepared to stand against his father and clan, and the yearnings of his own heart, so that she would have the right to make it?

He was brooding over that quandary when the object of his contemplations approached him.

Her expression was cautious. "Hi."

"Hello."

She gestured to the doors that led to the back deck. "Care to join me?"

Always. "After you."

The warm breeze carried the sweet scent of the nearby vegetation and the faint notes of salty sea. He wished he could draw comfort from the soothing surroundings. Instead he was trapped at the center of a frozen lake.

Aurora sat on the steps that led to the pathway. He settled in next to her, but far enough away that they were not touching. He needed that distance right now.

She stared into the darkness. "I talked to Cade. He

and Justin are going to visit the Council headquarters and see what they can learn about the Admiral's disappearance while we're having a chat with my mother."

She had provided several key pieces of information in that sentence, but he pounced on the one that was most relevant to him. "*We?*"

She met his gaze. "That's right. If you're willing, I'd like you to go with me to see my mother. Mya's coming, of course, and I've asked Kire, too. But your presence will give more weight to what I have to say. It might tip the scales in our favor."

He would gladly follow her to the edge of the galaxy and back. "Of course. I will do anything you ask of me." And Ellis would not be joining them. That helped.

Her gaze searched his. "I didn't want to make any assumptions. I know you're hurting. And it's my fault. I'm sorry."

Of course she would know. She could sense everything he was feeling if he allowed it. And he was not hiding his emotions at the moment. But he did not want her to suffer, too. "It is not your fault."

She sighed. "It sort of is. And even if it's not, that doesn't make it easier." She looked away, curling in on herself. "I hate this."

He swallowed. She was torturing herself. And that was torturing him. "Aurora, stop." He slipped his hand over hers and pulled her around to face him. She kept her head down, so he tucked his finger under her chin and applied pressure until she met his gaze.

Silent tears tracked down her cheeks. "I don't want to hurt you."

He used the pads of his fingers to wipe the moisture away. "I know." He might be in Hell, but that did not mean he wanted her to join him there. "I do not want to hurt you, either."

"Can't help it. You hurt, I hurt."

He held her gaze. "I understand." He brushed a tendril of hair off her forehead. She had worn her hair loose tonight, the waves trailing like spun gold over her shoulders. "That is another reason I want you with me. As long as I am by your side, no one can hurt you."

She frowned. "Meaning Cade."

He nodded. "I do not trust him."

Her eyes got that far-away look that meant she was tuning into his emotions. "I can understand that," she said softly. "But do you trust me?"

"With my life."

Tears gathered in her eyes again. "Oh, Jonarel." She gripped his hands in hers. "I wish..." She trailed off, her expression bleak.

"I know. So do I."

She was silent for a long while as they stared at each other. Her tears fell onto the dark fabric of her tunic. But eventually she pulled on the mantle of control he knew so well. "So, you'll come with me to see my mother?"

He nodded.

"Thank you."

She leaned forward just long enough to brush her lips against his cheek before rising and heading into the house.

Jonarel remained on the steps for much longer, collecting his wayward emotions before he followed. His father tracked him down as soon as he stepped into the room.

His expression was grim. "Aurora has been crying. Is there a problem?"

Jonarel looked his father in the eye...and lied. "No. Everything is fine."

Seventy-Four

Justin's heart was an anvil in his chest.

He'd spent the last hour with Raaveen, Paaw and Sparw, sitting out on the upstairs balcony, talking about everything and nothing. But he'd said what he'd needed to say. Every painful word. He'd told them how much they meant to him, and how much he was going to miss them.

And they'd echoed it right back at him, surrounding him with gratitude and love as they'd wrapped him in their incredible energy.

His eyes were still damp. He swiped at them as he headed down the stairs. Captain Hawke had sent him a message asking him to stop by her room before he turned in. Not a problem, since there was zero chance he would sleep tonight.

The door was partially open, so he knocked softly on the doorframe.

"Come in." She looked up from her datapad as he entered.

"You wanted to see me?"

"Yes, I did. Have a seat."

He settled into the chair next to hers, the only other item of furniture in the bare room.

She set the datapad on the floor. "I spoke with Raaveen during dinner, and she told me about the stealth pod lessons. And the Galish tutoring. That was a wonderful idea. They really enjoyed learning from you."

He didn't need to be reminded. And he really didn't want to talk about the teens right now. He already felt like a human punching bag and her comment hit him like a blow. But he respected her too much to walk out. "I enjoyed teaching them. They have a lot of natural talent."

"I know. And I want to encourage that." She studied him. "You mean a lot to them."

Bam! Another punch to the gut. He had to swallow a couple times before he could respond. "They mean a lot to me, too."

"I can tell." She paused, her gaze assessing. "They're hurting right now, you know."

Oh, yeah. He knew all about hurting. "I know."

"And so are you."

He flinched. Of course she'd realize that. According to Cade she could read emotions like he'd read words in a book. Even without that talent, his appearance would give him away. His eyes were probably still red from the blubbering he'd done upstairs. He met her gaze. "Yeah." He sighed. Might as well tell the whole truth. "I love those kids. The thought of never seeing them again is ripping me apart."

Compassion shone in her eyes. "I can understand that. They're easy to love. And you've shared some intense experiences recently."

An uppercut this time. Was this torture ever going to end?

"I don't want to add to your pain. Or theirs. In fact, I'd like to help if I can. But first I need to know how committed you are to doing what's best for them."

Finally, an easy question. "I'd give my life for those three."

The corners of her mouth lifted slightly. "I believe you. And I think they'd say the same thing about you." She folded her hands in her lap. "Things are a little shaky right now, especially after encountering that carrier."

No argument there.

"We have a lot to accomplish, and I'm going to need help to keep things moving forward. After we leave, one item that will be critical is keeping in close contact with Raaveen. However, depending on what I learn from my mother and where that takes me, communication may not always be easy." She held his gaze. "I have a proposal for you."

Justin's heart thumped in his chest.

"I want you to establish and maintain a communication link with Raaveen. If anyone can set up a secure system that won't compromise the secrecy we need to maintain, it's you."

The air suddenly got thin, and he had to concentrate very hard on breathing in and out. Had he heard her correctly? "You want me to keep in contact with Raaveen? On a regular basis?"

She nodded. "That's right. And if any issues arise, it will be your job to alert me. Immediately."

"What about Emoto?" He felt like kicking himself the moment he asked the question, but it was a valid point. She already had a communications specialist on her crew. A good one.

"Kire's going to have plenty to keep him busy without worrying about what's happening here. But if you don't think you can—"

He cut her off. "I'll do it. Absolutely." He'd agree to anything if it allowed him to maintain a connection with the kids. Doing something that was in his wheelhouse was an unexpected gift.

She smiled. "Good."

He hesitated to push his luck, but he couldn't ignore the question that was banging around in his brain. "Will I ever be able to see them again?"

Her brows drew down. "I don't know. I wish I could say I have all the answers, but I don't. I'm winging it." She held his gaze. "What I can promise is that if I see an opportunity to get you back here, I will."

His throat tightened, but the emotion coursing through him wasn't pain. She'd just offered him the moon. "Thank you, Captain."

"You're welcome. And one other thing."

"Yes?"

"As far as I'm concerned, you're a part of my crew, regardless of whether you're on the ship. From now on, call me Aurora."

Seventy-Five

Aurora's fingers tapped out a syncopated rhythm on the arm of the captain's chair. Snippets from her conversations with Cade, Jonarel and Justin collided with visions of the impending confrontation with her mother, creating a vortex that left her unsettled.

Returning to the *Starhawke* hadn't provided the sense of peace she'd expected, either. Without the distraction of the Suulh to keep her mind occupied, she was on edge. It wasn't a sensation she enjoyed.

She was glad she'd talked to Justin, though. The emotional cloud that had hovered over him and the three teens yesterday had evaporated. Unfortunately, she couldn't say the same for Jonarel.

"Clarek to Hawke."

She jumped, revealing just how high-strung she'd become, especially around her chief engineer. She touched the comm panel. "Go ahead."

"Final engine checks are completed. All systems ready on your command." Jonarel almost sounded normal. Almost.

"Acknowledged." Her voice sounded odd, too. She didn't anticipate the situation improving over the next few days, either. Might as well get this show on the road. "Kire, notify Signal and Raaveen that we're departing. Kelly, take us out."

"Aye, Captain."

The image on the screen shifted as the *Starhawke* taxied out of the bay and accelerated toward open water.

Aurora usually loved this moment, but as they soared upwards, breaking the grip of the planet's gravity and hurtling into space, the dominant emotion flowing through her body was apprehension, not joy.

Confronting her mother about the past rated the top spot on her list of least favorite things, partly because she'd failed every time she'd tried. Her mother took stubbornness to a whole new level. And it didn't take much to set her off.

Aurora's one hope was that having Jonarel and Kire there would tip the scales in her favor. They would give weight to her request. And that was important. Her mother needed to understand that this wasn't just about her anymore. Many other lives depended on the information she was withholding.

The lift doors parted and Cade stepped onto the bridge, heading in her direction. As he slid into the chair to her left, his eyes narrowed. "You look tense."

She didn't even try to deflect the comment. "That's because I am." She didn't need to explain why, either. She could see the understanding in his eyes.

"Have you decided when you're going to contact your mother?"

"I'm not."

His brows lifted. "You're planning to just show up on her doorstep?"

"Mya will alert Marina as soon as we reach Earth. She can pick us up at the transit station. But I don't want to give my mother time to think." She knew better than anyone how her mother could stonewall if she worked up a head of steam. Catching her off guard was the best strategy.

"Are you sure you don't want me to go with you?"

She appreciated the offer, but he had his own task

to accomplish. She shook her head. "You need to focus on locating the Admiral. I'll be fine."

"Will you?"

She held his gaze. "Yes. It's time to go home."

A gentle smile touched the corners of his mouth. "Okay. But I'll be waiting for you at HQ when you get back."

She was already looking forward to that moment. "Good to know."

She shifted her gaze to the glitter of starlight as the ship approached the jump window. She had no idea what revelations awaited her when they reached the other side, but she wouldn't be facing them alone.

And that made all the difference.

Continue the adventure in

THE HONOR OF
DECEIT

Starhawke Rising Book Three

Her past is a myth, her present is a ruse,
And her future...well, her future is still
up for grabs.

Captain's Log

The Soundtrack

I write to music. It's a ritual. If I don't have music playing, the silence is deafening. But it can't be just any music. Each story has its own soundtrack that sets the tone, draws me in, and keeps the words flowing.

The problem with having a particular soundtrack for each story is that after I've associated a piece of music with a book, I can't use it again. I tried. It was an epic failure.

After I completed *The Dark of Light*, I loved the soundtrack I'd chosen so much that I put it on when I started this book. It didn't work. I kept thinking about the story I'd just finished, not the one I was beginning. After a couple days of struggling, I changed the music to something else and presto! The story found its groove.

If you'd like to experience this story the way I did, listen to the soundtrack for *Captain America: The First Avenger* while you read.

Justin and the teens

I never intended for Justin to be a major character in this series. When he was first introduced, I cast him as Cade's best friend, somebody who was going to be his first officer. Justin filled that role well. But he wasn't critical. Certainly not somebody who would have a point of view.

But Justin had other ideas. From the moment he showed up on the page, he couldn't be ignored, not because he was pushy or flashy, but because something about him got to me. I found myself wanting to know more about who he was and what his relationship was to the other characters in the story.

I had little tendrils of that in *The Dark of Light*, but when I got to this book, Justin really wouldn't get out of my head. No matter which direction I went, he was there. He wanted to be heard. He had an important story to tell.

This ended up being a turning point because I hadn't pictured the three teens becoming important characters, either. In book one, much like Justin, they were placeholders. I didn't know much about them. But very quickly in the writing of this book, it became clear that they had a lot to say, too. And they were bonding with Justin.

So I ended up with these four amazing characters, none of whom I'd anticipated being part of the larger narrative, but who demanded that they be given their story and their time. They had grown to be so much more than I had ever imagined, which is one of the great delights for an author—to have your characters stand up and say, "You will pay attention to me."

I love when that happens. And I can assure you this will not be the last you will see of any of them. They have much more to share.

I hope that you will fall in love with them as much as I have.

The Meer

Of all the elements in this story, the Meer proved to be the most challenging to lock down. During my first draft, they were very human, to the point that they were having conversations with Aurora and Justin. And it felt wrong. Very wrong. Justin's the one who let me know that communicating with the Meer would be a challenge, something he and the teens would have to deal with as part of their captivity.

I knew the Meer would be smaller than humans, but it wasn't until I began asking questions about how they lived that they came into focus. I pictured a desert environment, with brush and rocks and very little water, at least on the surface. A little research online told me that the images in my mind were closest to the deserts in Africa. And the most humanoid species that burrows in the ground there were the meerkats.

Suddenly, the Meer came to life. Their mannerisms, attitudes, social structure, everything, took shape with clarity. As did the tragedy they'd endured when the Setarips attacked.

The Meer leader and his daughter were part of the story from the beginning. Their relationship dominated the action, and provided a wonderful parallel for Justin's developing connection with the three teens. While the leader took actions that caused harm, he did it for all the right reasons.

And that made him a character whose story I wanted to tell.

Audrey Sharpe grew up believing in the Force and dreaming of becoming captain of the Enterprise. She's still working out the logistics of moving objects with her mind, but writing science fiction provides a pretty good alternative. When she's not off exploring the galaxy with Aurora and her crew, she lives in the Sonoran Desert, where she has an excellent view of the stars.

For more information about Audrey and the Starhawke universe, visit her website and join the crew!

AudreySharpe.com

CPSIA information can be obtained
at www.ICGtesting.com
Printed in the USA
BVHW03s2246280318
511827BV00007B/774/P